THORN KISSED and SILVER CHAINS

SHANNON MAYER
KELLY ST CLARE

Copyright © 2022 by Shannon Mayer, Kelly St Clare

All rights reserved.

Published by Hijinks Ink Publishing

www.shannonmayer.com

All rights reserved. Without limiting the rights under copyright reserve above, no part of this publication may be reproduced, store in or introduced into a database and retrieval system or transmitted in any for or any means (electronic, mechanical, photocopying or otherwise) without the prior written permission of both the owner of the copyright and the above publishers.

Please do not participate in or encourage the piracy of copyrighted materials in violation of the author's rights. Purchase only authorized editions.

Here's to working with great authors, editors, and cover artists. This is a team effort and we are eternally grateful for all those who take part and help in the process of turning random words into a living, breathing novel.

PROLOGUE

I crouched next to the base of the cloud tree. Birds barely bigger than insects flitted from bloom to bloom. I smiled and held my hand out. Three of the birds landed across my chubby hand.

"Little one."

I looked up at Lilivani. "Liliwani," I struggled with her name still. She scooped me up into her arms. Something she hadn't done for some time. I giggled and buried my face against her neck. She smelled like flowers and sunshine.

"I must leave you," Her voice hitched as she smoothed my hair down my back. "You are too young, but Underhill has declared it is time for me to leave."

"Momma stays with me?" I blinked up at her. Momma Underhill was everything. Beauty. Food. Warmth. But also...fear. She scared me with her hard face and her hard words.

Lilivani had tears on her cheeks. "You must be good, little one. You must work hard to make Underhill pleased with your progress."

I frowned. I didn't understand. At four years old, my life had been simple so far. Lilivani looked after me, and I loved her fiercely as only a child could. She was the closest thing to a mother I had.

"Do you remember how to use your magic? How to recognize other magic?" Lilivani walked with me still held in her arms. "You know that you must show Underhill how capable you are? Strong. Smart."

"Kind." I whispered.

She squeezed me tightly. "You are kind. But...I do not know...Be brave. Strong."

I shrugged as I lifted my head to stare into the clouds that formed the tops of the trees. There was a whoosh of wings.

The flying horses were here, somewhere. I liked them, but I wasn't allowed to come and see them on my own.

"Tell me about the magic, little one." She whispered against my ear.

I sighed.

"Balance in all things. My magic is silver. Yours is blue. Underhill's is gold. Dark colors, mean danger. Be careful!" I yelled the last two words. Lilivani nodded.

"Yes, be careful." She set me down now that we were at the edge of the forest. And that was where I saw Underhill waiting.

I looked up at Lilivani. "Love you. See you later?"

Her eyes closed, and tears streamed down her face. "Go, little one. You must go."

I took her hand. "You come too."

"No more earth speak," Underhill said. "Use words sparingly. As creatures of Underhill would."

The command made me swallow hard. "Yes, Momma Underhill."

"Mother is name." Her voice was not unkind, but I still found myself struggling to make eye contact.

She motioned for me to follow her, and I did. Because she was Underhill.

"No more soft, daughter. Each day, accomplish something."

I blinked up at her as I reached for her hand. She smoothly folded her arms so I couldn't reach her.

Uncertainty rolled through my little body. I bit the inside of my lip. "Like puzzle?"

"Defeat a creature. Survive new places. Discover. Push limits."

I looked over my shoulder for Lilivani. She was still there, watching me walk away. I turned and ran, straight back to her. I didn't understand what was happening, but I wanted the comfort of the woman who sang to me at night. The woman who fed and bathed me.

A bright light opened behind her, and she stepped backward, her eyes never leaving mine.

"Goodbye, little one. Be kind, when you can."

Alone.

I was alone and I began to shake. I'd never been alone, Lilivani had always been with me. *Always.*

Underhill crouched beside me. I turned to throw myself into her arms as my tears fell.

She reared away. "No. Stand alone. Fierce. Strong. Brave."

I sniffed. "I try."

"Good. Good daughter."

Her magic swirled around me, gold and warm, washing away... Who was I looking for? I glanced over my shoulder and frowned. I couldn't remember who had been there before.

"Come. Must learning." Underhill beckoned again, and I hurried after her. Something in my heart hurt, but I didn't know what or why.

I had to be brave now. I had to be fierce.

I practiced making a face that would scare a monster away, then looked up at Underhill as we walked from the cloud forest. I would make her proud, I'd show her I was the bravest, fiercest and best of all her children.

ONE

Sand erupted in my wake as I sprinted across the Naga Plains, the scorching heat underfoot barely registering with my blurring speed. A furious roar filled the sky, making the granules leap as though in fright.

I bared my teeth in a smirk.

Drawing red energy from the ground to fuel my silver power, I blasted a bolt into each leg. My power catapulted me through air and across the plains.

Far enough to get me to my planned station.

Another roar, closer this time.

Perfect. If the dragon had popped his head above the forest before I'd gotten here, then the gig would've been up.

I crouched in the divot of two dunes and threw tendrils of power out in front of me like a blanket. Drawing the texture, smell, and appearance of the sand into my power, I then drew the blanket back to cover me. A little masking trick I'd learned last year during a tangle with a tarbeast.

Rhythmic blasts of wind swept across the plain. No one who knew anything could mistake *these* gusts as being from my mother–she preferred to send hurricanes and the like.

I peered through the curtain of my dirty silver hair, squinting against the grit whipping through the air. My lips curved again.

Ah, there he was.

The dragon.

Convincing him to leave his damn bed had been a job in itself. The old bastard hated flying. You'd think mother would take his wings away as punishment, but nope. This dragon had the biggest wings in Underhill, and aside from a few times a year, they were just for show.

But they sure were something to behold. And hear. The beat of his wings as he flew above the trees toward the plains was akin to a giant beating on an enormous drum.

Slow. Final.

Boom.

Boom.

Boom.

The rhythm of my heart slipped into tandem with it. Another trick I'd picked up. The old bastard had excellent hearing, especially when it came to hearts.

"Keep going," I muttered quietly, shifting in my crouched position.

The dragon bellowed, swinging his great head from left to right in search of me. I caught the flaring of his nostrils and grinned again. I'd rolled in naga droppings already to conceal my smell. Had he thought I'd make this easy?

A disturbance beneath the ground caught my focus. Without moving, I watched as six naga heads popped out of the sand fifty spear-lengths in front of me. There was a good reason I'd leapt over that particular section. The naga were so damned attuned to any shift in the plains around their treasure trove. I'd snuck around their trove, of course, but even I could never hope to achieve the stealth required to get *inside* the trove without detection.

Lucky for me, I didn't intend to. At least not today. I just needed their help.

Because if there was one thing the dragon hated?

It was the nagas that liked to encroach on his territory from time to time.

Whoosh.

The dragon banked right and skimmed along the plains, nearly silent now that he was gliding. The expanse of the plains gave him good visibility. He'd prefer to seek me out here rather than fleece the trees.

Everything was going according to plan. He just needed to get close enough to the trove.

Without staring directly at the naga, I checked for the presence of their treasure. Gold coins poked out through the sand in every direction. With naga, there were two rules. Don't mess with their young, and don't mess with their gold.

I never messed with a creature's young, no matter what the game.

But the other rule seemed like it was meant to be broken.

Half my attention on the roaring approach of the dragon, I focused my power on a single gold coin without looking directly at it. I eased the coin out of the sand with my silver tendrils but kept it in contact with the top layer of granules. They'd notice if I didn't.

I peered left at the incoming dragon.

This had to be timed just right.

I filled the coin with my silver tendrils, waiting . . .*waiting*.

Screeching, the dragon flattened and homed in on the naga herd.

Yes!

I whipped the coin toward me, careful not to let the gold touch my skin, and the six nagas erupted from their sandy sentry points as if connected to the treasure with strings. They all peered at me.

The top halves of the naga were serpentine in appearance, they otherwise had two legs with skin like mine. I'd always considered them beautiful in an exotic kind of way, something my best friend emphatically disagreed with. Belts of gold coins hung low on their hips and also criss-crossed over the females' chests and around their large, heart-shaped snake heads in circlets. What *wasn't* beautiful was getting sprayed with naga venom or, worse, getting bitten.

The dragon reared his head in surprise. In his usual little territory game with them, the naga didn't fight back because they didn't have anything on him.

Too late to change his flight path, the dragon lowered his great head again, fierce gaze on the small herd.

I shot the gold coin outward.

Like a missile, it hurtled toward the dragon's snout. Six sets of naga eyes tracked the coin through the air. Slowing the coin's path, I placed it gently on the old bastard's nose.

Now, he just had to make one mistake . . .

The dragon fixed his eyes on the gold coin.

Gotcha.

His furious eyes glazed over, and I burst upward from my hiding spot. If I directly looked at or touched the treasure, it would be game over—the naga power infused in it would hold me in an endless trance, but the dragon would shake it off in no time. Something the naga knew all too well. Streams of venom shot from their fangs, and they launched forward to seize their advantage on their predator.

As I seized mine.

This was it.

The end of the game.

Fast though I was, I couldn't easily beat a dragon. Drawing more energy inward, I threw off my magical camouflage. A tremor rippled through the dragon's scaly body.

Running out of time!

Shoving every iota of power I had into my legs, I exploded from my hiding place toward where the unfreezing dragon was being attacked by nagas. They looked tiny next to him–all fae did. They wouldn't win.

But *I* would.

At full speed, I threw my body under the dragon's soft belly, sliding beneath him. A deeper tremor ran through him. He knew I was here. As any predator would know there was a threat close to their most vulnerable body part.

It all happened in a matter of seconds—

I blinked into my magical vision and saw it.

There.

The jewel, right at his center.

The space tightened as the dragon lowered to crush me. But he'd noticed my presence too late. Ripping the jewel from the soft flesh of his stomach on my way past, I continued in my blurring slide.

I just had to make it to his wing. I gritted my teeth as he continued to lower his belly, the space narrowing.

He was going to crush me.

New plan. Drawing power from my legs, I shoved the tendrils of power underground instead, burrowing into the sand and dropping into the cavity it created. The dragon's belly sealed the top, and laughter burst from me after a few seconds proved I was safely sealed away.

This was a new one. How to get out?

I shifted, and my gaze widened at the tell-tale high-pitched ring of gold.

I peered down at the buried pile of coins I'd burrowed into.

Oh...shit.

The sand shifted, and I didn't stick around to confirm that the entire naga herd now had a different target. I shot through the sand, blindly aiming for an exit past where the dragon's left wing should be. Pain erupted in my left calf, and I yelled as fangs ripped through my flesh, only to choke on a mouthful of sand. But *out* of the sand I shot, prized jewel in hand.

Spluttering and spitting out sand, I didn't dare stop.

The dragon had other plans.

My feet were ripped from under me, and the breath slammed from my lungs as the dragon's tail hit me from behind. I flew, limp in the air from the whomping force of the blow.

I was catapulted away from the plains. Back the way I'd come.

This was going to hurt.

I struck the ground like a pebble skimmed across a lake. One, two, three impacts. I rolled in a tangle over thorny shrubs and jagged rocks until I rolled to a halt.

"Hurt," I wheezed.

My body unlocked enough to drag in a weak, hitching breath. Even when the wind gusted around me in the rhythmic way that alerted me to the dragon's approach, I couldn't move.

He landed, and the ground shook.

Groaning, I sat and hugged my legs into my chest until my breathing returned to normal. Cuts and rapidly growing bruises marred every part of my body.

Lifting my head, I held the jewel high and glared at the huge creature.

His body shook.

With laughter.

"Victory. Late moves belong in no game," I hissed at him. Bastard had swiped me after I'd secured the jewel! That was cheating.

He lowered his great head, and hot air washed over me. "Turn back," he hissed. "Or be turned."

I rolled my eyes. Always trying to teach me a lesson. Though perhaps I shouldn't have lowered my guard when the naga herd attacked. I tossed the jewel aside. Convincing him to let me go for it had taken years. Typical dragon, he'd only agreed after I made it into a deadly game. Old Bastard never complained, but it must have caused him pain.

Mother would be impressed, I was sure of it.

The dragon inclined his head and naga venom dipped off his snout. I didn't offer to wipe it off, just as he wouldn't offer to heal *my* naga bite.

He walked away, back to his nest. Staggering to my feet, I limped off in the opposite direction, the pain in my calf rising with each step. I scoured the ground for *Laziye*. Even with the ground cover's help, I'd be laid up for a few days.

Dizziness hit me harder than the dragon's tail, and I slammed to my knees, blinking to clear my vision. I waited for the ground to stop moving.

Then peered closer. The rocks were actually shaking.

No wind. No boom of a walking dragon.

Voices.

My heart quickened. Voices from fae like me!

The urge to run and see them, to touch skin to skin had me bowing my head. How long had it been since Mother had so much as touched her hand to my shoulder? Years, at least.

I was shaking, my skin dancing as if I were a fly stung horse. The craving for a gentle touch was strongest at times like these, when I was face to face with the fact that I was always alone.

That there was no one like me here.

I'd seen fae come into Underhill before, but Mother had always driven me away from them. She must have been too busy to notice that they were on a collision course with me.

No. No, I did not need to get close to them. I shook my head and backed off. Getting close to them was a path to pain. To tears. I pushed the urge to go to them, away. I would watch and observe. If they were dangerous, I would kill them before they hurt me.

I lifted my head and spotted them immediately. A scoff left me. The fools were fanned out a dragon's length away, walking high on the sparsely shrubbed plain. Did they have any idea Old

Bastard was over the rise? What about the barbed-beaked giant falcons currently nesting in the forest? *Imbeciles.*

A male fae in the middle with brown hair covering his chin paused, and the others stilled in response. He sniffed the air, then wrinkled his nose.

Naga droppings. Perfect to hide me in a naga trove. Not so great right now.

His gaze met mine. Without blinking–in case he took it for submission–I closed my fingers around the first rock I could find.

"There she is," he called.

The others, two males and two females, peered in my direction. The gaze of the shortest woman found me next. "Her hair isn't silver."

"It is," the first male said. "Just like the Oracle said. She's filthy, but the color is right."

What were they talking about?

Two-legged fae came to replenish themselves in Underhill from time to time, and they came in and out for their semblance of 'training', too, but they'd never come for *me*. They'd said that the Oracle sent them.

My heart beat faster, my instincts flaring.

Escape.

I wouldn't last long on foot. The faster I ran, the quicker the naga venom would spread through my system. That limited my options.

The bearded male looked away, and only then did I take another glance at my surroundings. Plenty of rocks, but not the kind I generally liked to stab things with. These were the flaky kind. I grimaced at the rock in my grip. Unlike the other rocks, this one was black. I dropped it and eyed the grimy, black residue it had left behind on my hand.

The least of my problems.

The youngest man, perhaps a few years older than me and bearing a sunbeam on his tunic, spoke. "We aren't going to hurt you, but we *do* need to speak with you."

"If she's responsible, then I beg to differ, Aaden," the other woman said. "I will certainly hurt her." She cracked her knuckles for good measure.

I threw a rocky camouflage over myself and jumped to the right. White fire licked up my leg, but when I landed, I forced myself to leap again.

Yelling and the clamor of armor and weapons rang at my back. I tracked their magic behind me.

Damn it all. One of them was fast. The youngest male—Aaden, was it? Injured as I was, he was gaining on me.

Another leap.

I caught sight of my goal. The river.

Every resident of Underhill knew the river was as likely to kill you as help you—it operated entirely on mother's calculations of balance. If you weren't needed for balance, then you would die. If you were, you would live. Guess I was about to find out which category I fell into because I'd learned long ago that having Underhill for a mother didn't mean shit.

A final leap.

Nearly there.

Arms closed around my waist. I growled, clawing at the muscled forearm, but the man didn't relent.

Not for the first time that day, air whooshed from my lungs as we landed in a heap.

I didn't need air in my lungs to bite.

Yanking the male fae's arm to my mouth, I tore into his flesh. He shouted, but his lips settled into a grim line as he threw his body on top of mine.

The flowing river sat just behind the reeds. So close. I glared up at the man. Aaden, the fast one.

"You have answers we need," he said from between gritted teeth. "You know what happened to them. You're coming with us."

I relaxed suddenly, and he nodded, sitting back.

His head whipped back as the heel of my bare foot connected with the underside of his chin.

Ha! "Turn back. Or be turned," I roared at him. See if he liked a dragon's warning.

I launched into a scrambling crawl for the reeds and river beyond. The water was in sight. The pounding footsteps of the other two-leggers were far enough away that I could make it.

I could—

Strong hands gripped my legs, fingers digging brutally into the naga bite on my left calf. The venom surged hot through me, stilling my muscles. Black, much like the grime covering my hands, coated my vision. *Naga venom. Bad.*

My head lolled as I was thudded onto my back.

Five hostile faces stared down at me, their details lost to the increasing black spots in my vision.

"Tie her up," the bearded one spat. "She's a damned animal. Stinks like one too."

"Will we take her to the courts in Unimak, sir? To the Oracle?" Aaden asked.

"To Alaska? No, lad. These are our people. We're away to Ireland. The Ríchashaoir will decide her fate."

Two

Ireland. The word floated toward me, and I could almost pinpoint the deep rumble of the voice and what it meant. The last thing I truly remembered was the naga bite and the venom rushing through my veins. Hallucinations and memory loss weren't uncommon side effects.

My left ear throbbed as though I'd been punched in the side of the head, and an ache between my shoulder blades made me twitch and bite back a moan. I rolled to change position, only I didn't roll so much as I *flopped*, my head thudding against solid ground a beat later.

Why was everything non-magical dark? Either my eyes were covered or I'd been blinded by the naga venom. Either way, I could only feel and see magic. My legs were tied tightly together. An attempt to straighten them caused my back to arch, so whatever was binding my legs was attached to my hands, also bound. I was in the shape of a pain-filled crescent moon. The aching shoulders made a hell of a lot of sense now.

Had I been caught up in a bush of tangle vines? They were nearly as poisonous as the naga and certainly sentient enough to creep over immobile prey.

I blinked in the darkness, and something soft brushed against my eye lashes. Fabric? Covered then, not blind. That, at least, was in my favor.

Except...who'd covered my eyes?

I fought the instinct to thrash. If I truly were caught in tangle vines, thrashing would only tighten their hold on me. I had to think this through.

Where am I?

Footsteps above me. *Thump.* I risked lifting my feet slightly and bringing them down. *Thump.* My bindings didn't tighten with the movement. Not tangle vines then, and there were wooden boards above and below me. The presence of green energy there confirmed it.

I inhaled through my nose and licked my lips. Salt.

Fae.

The last memory from before I blacked out came rushing back over me like the brush of the dragon's wings.

Earth Fae kidnapped me. With the naga venom coursing through my sluggish veins, they'd taken me down. Tied me up and kidnapped me. I used my magical sight to peer through the wooden ceiling and count the bundles of power that denoted fae.

Nothing came between me and Underhill. They'd screwed up.

My lips curved.

I reached to use my magic and ... nothing. I flicked my fingers, then clicked, trying to spark even a tiny bit of magic. Nothing. What in two realms? *True* panic reared its head. I'd never been separated from my magic. I could see it everywhere but couldn't do a thing to access my reserves or draw from any of the surrounding living materials.

My breath came fast.

"Ya won't be finding nothing to help yous out of dis situation, missy, not even yous magic."

I threw myself bodily around at the gruff voice to my left. My bindings dug in, but I focused on the threat, baring my teeth and snapping them at the speaker, a bundle of gold and gray power. Old. Powerful.

"Get. Get away from me!" I accompanied each word with a click of my teeth. No one could misunderstand the challenge. I watched the old man with my magical sight.

"Och, missy, you don't be knowing, so I'll fill you in." The man stepped closer. I tried to rear back and only succeeded in bashing my head against something hard. The pitching of the floor beneath me didn't help matters, though it connected the obvious clues that my foggy brain had missed. Water, I was on water. In a box of some sort. Had to be an ocean, judging by the salt smell. There was only one ocean in Underhill, so at least I knew where they'd taken me.

"Go on, fly, run, go!" I growled. I'd sent tarbeasts running with my warning display—a calf perhaps, but still. I could channel menace when I needed to.

The gruff fae drew close. Too close. I bit down with all I had on what felt like a finger.

His scream was music to my ears as I crunched through bone and flesh.

I smiled as he reeled back. *Thump, thump, thump.* There was a different thump as he leaned on a wall. The room wasn't large, then, which explained why his voice seemed so loud.

I listened to his ragged breaths.

"Bitching child, you bit me . . ." He grumbled. Three steps, and a boot landed square in my middle. The air rushed from my lungs, and I jerked against the bindings to lunge at the person. But I could neither breathe nor reach my magic. I could barely move.

These invaders were going to kill me.

I acknowledged that fact coldly. Without fear. Fear was good for one thing only—warning me that I was in danger. Once it had done its job, I pushed it away.

A hand grabbed my jaw, and my blindfold was yanked off. White light blared around us, attacking me with its sudden brilliancy. I blinked through watering eyes at the slowly spinning lantern hanging just behind the stranger.

The gnarled man in front of me was hunched, his back knobbed and ridged as though his spine had been deliberately twisted. Other than that, he was oddly nondescript. Aside from his unusual gold-gray combination of magic. The light seemed unable to illuminate his features. Or my eyes couldn't focus on them. I blinked a few times to no effect.

"I am trying to help you, brat. And you go and try to bite my fingy off! I was told to help you, so I am doing it. But I don't be liking it!"

He showed me his finger. Nearly healed already. What was he whining about?

I let out a low growl to let him know I wouldn't go easy and watched as he paced two steps, turned, and then paced two back.

"The fae on deck don't know I'm down here wit' you," he muttered, "I snucks aboard. Easy to recognize a child of Underhill. Yous all come out feral, beasties in your own right."

He thought me feral? A small burst of pride spread through my chest. But why was he complimenting me prior to killing me? On second thought, his tone had seemed to imply that being feral wasn't a compliment. Who knew? These people were backwards. "In Underhill care. In Underhill give," I tested. If he knew of my mother, then maybe he'd give me back to her.

"Bah, I can't fight all of them." His back was to the lantern, his features still a mystery to me. "But I can give you something to help. A guide to light the path. You tell your mother I helped you, don't be forgetting! I still honor her. I'll always honor her. I've learned."

Despite his words, the imbecile clearly didn't understand my mother. If he did, he'd know that me passing on a message was unnecessary. She was watching everything unfold. Tallying. Deciding whether this moment would destroy or preserve the balance before she chose to intervene.

Or not.

The faceless old man reached up to his neck and yanked. "This be a gift from Underhill, a precious gift, and now I be giving it to her daughter."

The object fluttered down to me. In the most literal of senses. Tiny leather wings spread as the bat circled down to land on my right shoulder.

He was giving me a bat before he killed me? I was starting to think the fool had lost his mind. If I played this right, I might be able to get him to sever my bindings.

I twisted my head to look at the bat.

"Hallo," she whispered, her voice so high-pitched that I wouldn't have heard her had I not been staring her in the face. Her fur and leather wings were a soft gold, her eyes a brilliant sea green. Her tongue darted in and out. Nervously. "I love your hair. What I wouldn't give for hair like that. Your teeth are bared. Scary. Please don't hurt me."

"Fight and find," I grumbled. The tiny bat didn't stir my fighting instincts at all. Though I'd been laid on my ass by smaller fae in my time.

She smiled. "Excellent. I don't plan to find a fight with you ever."

Using the claws at the tips of her gold wings, she scooted across my upper body and paused at my neck.

"Bite and the full moons will devour," I hissed.

"I would never bite you; I bite fruit. Mostly mango, but I'll eat any fruit you will give me. Almost. I hate banana." She wrapped her wings around my neck, locking herself onto me. "This is better. You're quite warm. You stink though. What is that, camel shit?"

"Naga." I twisted my head to look at the one who'd brought this strange gift to me and inhaled sharply.

He was gone, but he'd left the spinning lantern.

"What is your name?" the bat asked.

"You?" I countered, feeling my hackles rise despite her distinct lack of threat.

"Orlaith, but you can call me Orla, or Orry works." She tucked her head behind my right ear, and when she spoke, her whisper was plenty loud enough. "Can I do your hair? I could braid it and style it. Goddess, what fun I would have."

My shoulders eased as she moved on from her question about my name.

I ignored her as she rattled on about nonsense. *Can I do your makeup, can I pick your outfit, can I find you pretty lingerie?*

Makeup and lingerie were curious words, but I was more curious about how to escape.

Did it matter that I had a bat attached to me or that I had no idea why an old man had just given her to me? Nope. Not a day went by when mother didn't throw something strange at me. A gold bat didn't even register as unusual. Orry wouldn't be the first animal I'd cared for.

Still bound, I wormed around on the wooden floor, making my way to a pile of implements in the far corner. I could spot several sharp objects. What kind of fools were these fae? I rolled so my back was to the weapons, then wiggled my fingers to find the edge of a serrated blade.

"Imbeciles crossed," I whispered. "Imbeciles think mercy is easy."

"Who's stupid?" Orry whispered in my ear. "Well, please don't kill the hot guy up on deck. He's easy on the eyes. Hmm, damn, an ass like that could crawl into my bed any day. He would light any woman up."

I paused at her words, a slight sadness twinging under my ribs. She was speaking just like my bestie would. Though . . .

"Fire-found fae?" I asked her. I worked my hands against the blade with small movements, barely the breadth of a bee's wing–the only movements I could manage while bound like this.

Orlaith laughed. "The hot guy? No, that's not what I meant—"

Footsteps rumbled above us, more thumping. I stared at the ceiling as dust trickled down. What was I in? We were floating.

That much I could tell, but otherwise, this numbered high on the list of unusual occurrences in my life–which was saying something.

"Belly of wooden dragon?" I felt the first strands of the rope let go.

Thump. Thump. I followed the footsteps as they grew louder. Closer.

"Um. Hopefully not. We're on a ship. My father brought me with him in the hopes that... well, I can't say. But when he heard Lord Aaden was coming along and needed a tracker, he offered his help. You were really hard to find, did you know? They searched for nearly three weeks, which was far longer on this side of Underhill, in the Earth realm, rather, but even so they looked, and looked—"

Thump.

"Hush." I worked faster, and three more strands broke before the footsteps paused across the room on the other side of a door.

I wasn't quite free, but it would have to be enough.

I went limp and closed my eyes.

Creak. More footsteps. This person was lighter on their feet than Crowbait had been. A shadow fell over me.

"Who took her feckin' blindfold off?" the man yelled.

I cracked an eyelid open just enough to confirm the boots in front of me were turned away.

Yanking my arms as hard as I could, I snapped the last of the strands, freeing myself. I grabbed at his ankle and jerked him toward me, biting into the back of his leg. He bellowed and kicked out with his other leg, but I was already scrambling away, leaping to my feet and lunging toward the person who'd come in response to his call. The woman's face was the color of a storm cloud, ashen gray. She fumbled for something at her side.

A weapon? What about her magic?

I reached for my magic again, to no success. *Don't panic.*

Instead, I grabbed her throat and threw her across the room, then clawed my hands in preparation, ready to tear, rip, or bite my way out of this so-called ship. They would not hold me, they would not keep me captive. Now I knew fae were after me, I'd be much harder to locate in Underhill.

"Out, Orlaith, where?" I said quickly.

"There, toward the stairs." The little bat tapped the left side of my neck, and I turned. No idea what stairs were, but there were cuts in the wood similar to those leading up the side of Dragonsmount. I raced up and out into bright sunshines, thankful to Crowbait's strange lantern for allowing my eyes to adjust in the darkness.

I took in the cliffs in front of me and frowned, trying to pinpoint exactly where we were. My vision skimmed to the water. *Blue* water? Dark blue. More importantly, *not* purple. The cliffs were black, and the beach was rocky and dark, no golden sand. I spun in a circle on the wood floor, my mouth ajar. Then I glanced directly up.

At one sun.

One shine.

Not sunshines at all.

This place wasn't Underhill! I backed up until I hit a wooden protrusion at the edge of the ship. Where was I?

"Stop her!"

The cry was taken up as I bolted across the strange deck. Cloth hung in all directions, along with what appeared like coiled vines. More wood. A tingle at the base of my skull warned me of danger nearly too late. I dropped to the wooden slats, flat on my belly, as a blast of magic shot straight through where I'd stood.

Power surged around me, none of it mine. The water wasn't the shade it was supposed to be, but this was not the time to stay and fight. I was about to find out what blue water meant.

A man with hair covering his chin blocked my path to the ship's edge. He was familiar for some reason, but I couldn't place him.

"You're coming with us," he said flatly.

"Doubtful, face of dead grass," I threw back, eyes darting as I took stock of the others' positions. Four in sight. Three to my left. Fanned out. My magical eyes picked out another five who were fanning to surround me too.

He frowned.

I turned and sprinted for the blue water. Ducking under a swinging arm, I dove. Nearly there.

Something struck my leg. Pain shot through me, the sharp sensation not unlike the teeth of the naga. I looked down at the iron spear tip that had been shot through my lower leg. Barbed and pointed on one side, with a wooden shaft on the other. The wooden part was wielded by a man who had a round face, ears so big they flopped, and spittle dripping from his mouth. He looked part pig.

He jerked the wooden spear hard, knocking me to the ground and holding my leg up like a prize. "There, we got her now. See her escape this? I think not." He laughed, hoisting my injured leg a little higher.

Refusing to scream, I sat up and shot a fist out at the wooden shaft, relishing in the *crack* as it snapped in half. I grabbed the spear tip and hissed at the burn of iron against my fingertips as I yanked it out of my flesh.

I lurched up and drove the iron tip into the man's flabby belly, meeting his shocked gaze.

He shrieked and fell backward into the water, flailing and screaming at the top of his lungs.

"Piggy squeals." I snorted before facing the others.

The one with the hair on his face stared at me. I lifted my chin in defiance and didn't bother to jump. I just leaned back and fell.

Orlaith squeaked and her hold around my neck tightened. A creature of the fae, she was at no greater risk of drowning than me.

Of course, that didn't mean we couldn't be killed should my captors decide to throw more spears my way.

I hit the water hard, flat on my back. For a moment, I was suspended on the surface and then I sank into the icy cold, turbulent waters.

Twisting about, I swam down to hug the edge of the ship, tiny sharp pieces of rock jabbing my body and palms. My legs ached—one from the remaining naga venom, the other from the spear.

The ship leaned to one side, and the distant sound of shouting tugged at my ears even under water. I pushed off in the opposite direction and swam toward the sandy shore I'd spotted.

Orry had warned me, but I hadn't registered her earlier words.

... this side of Underhill, in the Earth realm ...

They'd taken me from my home. Everything I knew and understood. They didn't even speak properly here.

A dark shape slid in front of me, and I pulled up short at its fins, tail, and snout. Its head turned, and a pair of large dark eyes found me.

The sparkle in them screamed of magic, and I knew what she was at once, because these creatures were also found in Underhill.

Selkie.

I closed my ears against the lure that would drag me to the ocean's bottom and swam harder, unwilling to give up even if my injuries ensured she'd outswim me.

I swam on, my surprise mounting with each passing second when her claws didn't hook into my legs and drag me down. The water was getting shallower. I could see the bottom of the ocean now.

So close.

Breaking the surface, I took a breath and spotted the shoreline not far off. The selkie bobbed in front of me, blocking my path, her dark eyes swirling with color. She preferred not to fight me then. She wished to use her lure.

I splashed water at her, breaking the spell.

"You. Fins become trophies. I will," I screamed.

The selkie dropped just below the surface, bubbles rising from her mouth, and flashed the wicked sharp teeth she'd kept hidden behind a gentle smile. "You think you can escape my waters? Then more fool you, sweet one."

I searched again for my magic and let out a shriek of sheer frustration when I couldn't find it *again*. Throwing my head back, I howled to the sky, uncaring that the sound would carry. The magic trapped within me bucked and shrieked, too, fighting to get to the surface past whatever had blocked the connection.

At the peak of my scream, as the air in my chest dwindled to nothing, a burst of pain erupted in my left ear. The one that had been throbbing when I'd first awoken. A golden loop plopped into the water; its shine only disrupted by a sheen of blood. Flashing and dancing, the loop disappeared beneath the dark waters.

The selkie lifted her head in tandem with me, her beautiful eyes huge.

Magic crashed into me, and I drew a deep, vibrating breath. "Orlaith?"

The shaking presence on my neck squeaked, "Yeah?"

"Hungry?"

"Sure, I could eat. What ya cooking?"

I tilted my head, already pinning the creature in place with my power. "Selkie Stew."

Three

I listened to the faint underwater scream of the Selkie as she disappeared far faster than she'd appeared. I blew out a breath as my stomach rumbled. "Flesh gone."

Orlaith chuckled. "She actually believed you'd eat her."

Glancing back at the ship in the distance, I started picking my way over the pebbled beach feeling the pain from the burn in my ear ebb with every step now I'd blasted through the block on my magic. The naga bite would heal slower—a few hours—and the wound from the iron spear would take a day or two to fully heal.

"You didn't really mean that . . .did you?"

"Waste bad, balance good," I replied. I wasn't about to leave perfectly good fish lying about. Not that I'd eat the top half of a selkie, unless I was in a real pinch, but the bottom half was fair game.

I took in my surroundings as the pebbles underfoot changed to brown dirt dotted with gray stones and larger boulders. The thorny, wiry shrubs were almost familiar, but the colors were off. Where were the purples and golds, the silvers and reds and blues?

In Underhill, my garments helped me to blend in. Here, my golden leather vest and the purple ties that laced together the front and back panels did nothing to camouflage my body. The red and-silver hood and shoulder piece I'd fashioned to protect against the sunshines was akin to waving a flag to announce my position to the enemy. Even with the hood soaked and heavy, I wouldn't get rid of them. These clothes were quality and hard to come by, and I didn't plan to stay in this realm long.

Dizziness assaulted me as I peered at the one sun again.

"You got hit pretty bad," Orry whispered. "Why don't you sit for a while? Catch your breath, as the humans say."

Humans. Interesting.

I'd never seen a human. My bestie said they had skin like mine but were filled with shit that you couldn't smell from the outside. I wouldn't mind seeing one before I returned home, but I didn't break stride until I reached the trees, where I paused and pulled blue energy from a large boulder to funnel into my power. I inhaled deeply, then cocked my head toward the ocean before scanning the horizon.

No trace of my attackers.

I took stock, first on my left leg, then my right. Not ideal shape for maintaining a lead. They'd search for me. If they'd kept up the search for three weeks in Underhill, then there was no way they'd give up now.

I needed to get back to my home turf. To my mother. And with my magic, I had a chance.

Drawing on the red energy next, I pushed more of my silver through my body. Naga bite and iron wound aside, the aches disappeared from my muscles and joints, and my head cleared of fatigue and any remaining pain from the gold drop in my left ear.

What in the heck had that been?

I shivered. Tie me up and beat me raw, but take my magic? That was the worst fate imaginable.

"What's the plan, Stan?" Orry whispered.

I cocked a brow. "Stan is me?"

"Just a saying. But you can be Stan if you like?"

I considered that. "Perhaps."

She left her perch on the side of my neck, clawing gently around to tangle her way through my hair and peer out from behind it. "They're gonna come for you, sweets."

Agreed. I pushed my power out in every direction through the ground, pouring silver through my palms and into the soil. The energy here was so ... *weak* compared to what Mother had at her disposal. I hardly ever felt drained in Underhill—only when I was badly injured. But here . . .

How did fae live here? My steps were heavier—granted, I was injured—but I felt the weight of being here in my soul. Like the branches within me were limp, my leaves shriveled.

"Mmm," Orlaith said. "You're so warm. You're humming, did you know? Your power."

I tuned out her voice and her gentle clawing movements as she combed through my hair and started separating pieces out. I pressed both palms to the ground, looking at the hundreds of tendrils visible in every color. They intertwined in places and overlaid in others, but the energy had ample space to stretch out. Not what I was looking for. At a gateway to Underhill, there would be hundreds of thousands of tendrils in a tangle so thick that making sense of it would be impossible. But these tendrils were a start. I just had to figure out what direction they amassed in.

Uh-huh. "Found." I gazed to the far right as I stood.

"What's found, hun?" the bat murmured. She'd pulled my hair back from my face, and it felt like she was braiding it like I would vines.

"Mother."

She dropped the strands of my hair. "Your *mother*? Oh gosh, I'm a mess. What will she think?" The bat worked around until she was in front of my face, gripping me by the cheeks.

I stared at the bat. "Energy of mother. Gateway." That seemed like the best response. What had her so worked up?

Orlaith sagged and slid down my nose and over my chin until she was clinging to my neck again. "Don't scare me like that. Meeting parents is a big deal."

Was it? I shook my head and started off in a jog toward where the energy was thicker. I'd had to send my power out a fair distance, and there wasn't near enough of it in what I'd discovered to be the actual location of a gateway, but it was a start.

The one sun disappeared as I jogged on and off, replenishing my body with magic in a way that was unsustainable. Light shone through a gap in the trees, and I squinted up.

One moon too.

This place was strange.

The trees were all the same. The most ferocious animal I'd come across was a red, bush-tailed critter bounding across a tree limb to stuff food in its hiding place. Where was the danger? Was this why fae had built their courts here and why the queen of all fae resided on Earth? Did the safety make up for the drained feeling?

Orlaith snored softly from where she'd hooked into my hair and hung upside down. She didn't seem to mind the swinging as I kept my steady pace, jogging along.

The magical energies had steadily thickened over the night, stretching toward the gateway—a weak point between the two realms. Reds, greens, blues, purples. Every possible hue twisted over the drab, non-magical colors like warring tree roots in a bid to reach the gate.

Moonlight poured down on me, and I crouched at the edge of the forest that had covered me until now. Unlike the beach I'd landed on, the place before me was . . .barren. Grass and boulders. Not dead—the energy was more vibrant here—but either life here was harsh or a predator reigned. I couldn't be sure what had caused the emptiness.

Keeping low, I reached the peak of a hill and scrambled down the slope beyond it, scurrying over impediments and stopping behind a uniform collection of rocks that acted as a barricade. "Put here," I said grimly. *Dammit.* This was fae or human made. I vaulted over the other side, and my eyes widened. My vision moved from my feet to the stretch of land in front of me and then over my shoulder.

It was a gray pathway, hard and smooth as ice, only not slippery. White bars had been painted onto it. It . . .*what?*

My jaw dropped as I traced the wide path, which extended as far as my eyes could see. How had they done this? *Why* had they done it? I crouched and put a hand to it. It was not smooth but rough under my fingers. Like crushed stone packed incredibly hard.

Lights flared in the distance, like the eyes of a great beast. Maybe this was the predator that ruled this land. My heart thundered as I sprinted across the gray path and launched over the barricade on the far side.

A thundering sound louder than the fattest tarbeast careened toward me as I crouched, frozen. The lights illuminated the skies. I covered my ears, cursing myself for assuming Earth had no predators.

Just when I expected to be confronted, the noise began to lessen–the lights too. I blinked a few times, then cautiously poked my head above the rocks. Moonlight glinted off the shell of the beast as it rolled over the hill and away.

Orry patted my head. "Just a car, sweets. Nothing to worry about."

A car. Nothing to worry about. Was she crazy? I had no choice but to believe her, as I had no time or energy to spare hunting down the car to see if it was indeed harmless.

Focus. I breathed in and recovered my stillness, waiting until my heart stopped pounding. I should have realized that life here would congregate around the gateways, just as it did in Underhill. Other fae, creatures and humans would likely be near.

Keeping my pace to a limping walk, I left the strange path and continued across the rocky, barren plains. The roar and crash of water far away registered. I'd crossed an island. As the one sun peeked over the horizon, I took in the deadly cliff-faces and the crashing water clamoring at their base.

A gateway was near.

But my instinct for danger rose along with the sun. I threw my power over the terrain and copied its textures and colors before drawing the camouflage over myself.

An echoing ring cut through the calm of dawn, and I whirled as four figures were revealed.

It was the bearded man. "She was just here," he growled.

"She's still here," the younger man, Aaden said, staring at me.

Fuck. Could he see through my camouflage?

"Where?" A woman said. "I can't sense her magic anymore."

"You can't?" he asked, frowning slightly.

Voices from behind. "Where is she?"

I turned my head to find five fae had snuck up on my flanks and rear. Apparently, I wasn't the only one who could camouflage myself. Though they hadn't taken on their surroundings, it was like they'd erased themselves entirely. Along with their magic and any traces of their movement. I searched their ranks for the hunched old man who'd gifted me Orlaith, but he was nowhere to be seen.

More importantly, I was still in bad shape. Magically and physically. My senses weren't as sharp as they'd usually be.

Aaden crouched and peered directly at me again. He *could* see me.

"Killing is good, maiming is good," I warned him.

He tensed, shuffling back a spear length.

The bearded man grunted. "Why does she speak that way?"

"Raised by animals," another woman threw my way.

Aaden lifted his hands and crouched a few paces from me. His eyes were a clear green, but otherwise he wasn't much to look at. His mane was clipped short, though it curled in an interesting way across his shoulders. His haunches were strong in appearance, but he was oversized. Better to be low to the ground with a build like that. My memory twinged as I recalled him being faster than the others, however.

"You're warning me to stay away," he said quietly.

I bared my teeth.

He shuffled back a little, and I narrowed my gaze at him.

"We've chased you from your home," he said just as quietly. "I'm sorry we tied you up, but we were warned you are very strong and inclined to fight. Some of us have been away from the court a long time in pursuit of you. And our reason for seeking you out isn't pleasant. Will you listen to us? Talk with us?"

The more time he wasted yapping, the better for me. I dipped my head.

He spoke over his shoulder. "She'll speak with us, sir."

"Five minutes," the bearded man sighed. "If she won't walk herself, then she'll be carried." To the others, he ordered, "Keep a perimeter, but fall back."

Good.

I focused on the man in front of me, Aaden.

"What's your name?" he asked. "I'm Aaden."

My heart thumped faster at the question. Unlike Orlaith, who was somehow still snoring in my hair, he didn't move on to one hundred other questions while I stood there silently.

Finally I spoke. "No name." The two words dared him to ask why.

Names weren't a usual thing in Underhill. My bestie had a name, but he was the only person I knew, aside from Mother, who had one. I hadn't thought much of it before meeting the few fae who'd crossed my path. All of them had been given names from their parents, they'd said. My Mother had never deigned to give me a name. Not even when I'd asked for one when she came to see me last year on my twenty-first year of life.

His clear green eyes flickered with something I'd never experienced before. Something soft. "I see. That's okay. You grew up in Underhill?"

"She's feral," a male spat. "You're wasting your time trying to get anything through to her!"

No. I was wasting *theirs* while I drew energy into my body in a slow trickle.

Aaden ignored the man and drew closer. "We were sent to find you by the Oracle and the queen of all fae. Do you know of them?"

I lifted my head. I'd never heard of the Oracle, but other than my mother, the queen was the fae most deserving of respect. "Why?"

A shadow darkened his gaze, and all I could think was that the change was a shame. The green eyes were his only redeeming feature, after all. "Something has taken our children."

"Like she doesn't know," someone hissed.

Aaden burst upward. "Siobhan, have you ever considered that the Oracle sent us to get her because she can *help*, and that by treating her poorly, you're only ensuring she won't want to?"

The woman's mouth snapped shut, and I snorted. She focused her vitriol on me, and I winked, then shrugged at Aaden. "Young die. Nature circles. Life is this." Balance sometimes required brutality. Not everyone could survive and attempts to extend life past its natural expiration point only created more death at a later day.

He crouched again. "But nature didn't do this. Thirty of them, stolen from their parents without a trace."

My stomach churned. That was a lot. But . . .I shrugged. "Nature. Life. Death."

"Time's up," the bearded man said.

Aaden leaned closer, eyes earnest. "One of them is special. One of them could be the next queen of all fae–"

"*Enough*," the leader snarled.

I stared at the oversized male fae whose eyes tugged at something in me, turning his words over in my mind. Words that changed everything. In balance, there was order. There was prey and predator, and life and death. Only two things reined above that: the queen and Underhill.

The next queen had been taken. There was something more ominous in that than in the random machinations of nature, which suggested the other stolen young were not part of a normal life-death cycle either. I dropped my camouflage and leaned back against the boulder behind me.

I considered the events of the last two days. A naga bite that had weakened me and allowed me to be easily caught. An old man who'd given me a bat guide. A spear through the leg that had further weakened me, making it easier for them to track me to this place.

With a mostly absent mother, I'd learned to interpret her silences. Mother wanted me *here*. It was a baffling thought, but hope stirred in my chest. Was she really trusting me with saving the next queen? Did she hold such faith in me?

I held my hope in with a steady rein, too wary of past misunderstandings to bask in what could be praise or nothing at all. Like all other fae, I could only try to interpret her wishes.

Still holding Aaden's regard, I slowly stood, then scanned the company. "Help is rare. Knowledge, rarer. Show, tell, figure. Sight may come."

A smile spread across Aaden's face. I tensed, but he didn't display teeth.

"That's all we ask," he hurried to say. "The Oracle gave us your description for a reason. We'll figure it out together."

Mentally checking that Orry was still in place, I strode to the bearded man, fighting my limp so as not to show weakness.

One of the others glanced over my head. "How the hell do you understand her, lad? She speaks nonsense. Worse than a toddler."

Aaden paused beside me and peered down. He seemed confused as he uttered, "I just do."

The bearded man scanned me up and down, and his upper lip curled. "Everyone be on high alert. We've seen what she can do. Don't be fooled. Her cooperation could be an act." He lowered his head to mine in a direct challenge. "Try it. I have no qualms in putting you in your place."

Unfortunately for him, I was raised in a place where backing down from a challenge was never wise. Winding back, I whipped my head forward with brutal force, crunching my forehead into his nose.

Blood sprayed. Yelling erupted. The surrounding fae descended on me.

Four

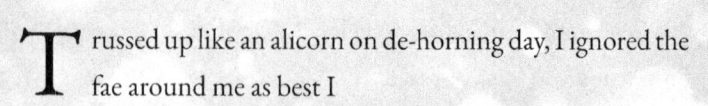

Trussed up like an alicorn on de-horning day, I ignored the fae around me as best I could. With my hands bound behind me, I fiddled with the thick gold bracelet they'd locked on my wrists. My magic had been cut off again. Apparently they used gold to do it—or maybe they infused the gold somehow.

"Owen, this is not going to help us." Aaden walked just ahead of me. I was sitting strapped to the back of a horse, my legs tied together by a rope that ran under her belly. Her golden coat shimmered under the sun, and her flaxen mane was well groomed with just a slight curl to it. My bestie would fucking love her. I wished I were half so beautiful.

"Our task was to get her back to the regent as quickly as possible. He's under orders from the queen," Owen said. His voice was thick, owing to the fact that I'd broken his nose for challenging me. To be fair, it was his fault for letting his guard down after talking shit. "And we are doing that."

Orry stirred in her hiding spot in my hair. Finally.

"Where are we now?" she muttered.

"Stolen," I said.

Aaden looked back at me. "I'm sorry."

He was ... trying to make nice with me? If nothing else, he was trying to work with me and not against me. I wasn't sure I could trust him. But of all the fae I'd encountered so far, he was the kindest. Which, according to my bestie, made him weak. Still, I liked Aaden's green orbs.

"Don't apologize to her. She can't even speak correctly. As far as I'm concerned, we treat her like a good hunting dog. Train her up, set her to her task, and if she's disobedient we beat her. Understand?"

Owen looked over at me, his face purpling from the blow I'd given him. I smiled, showing my teeth. "Pretty face colors."

He flushed more, apparently understanding *that* well enough. Aaden choked on a laugh, but I turned away from them both.

I listened to the chatter around me, trying to pick up on anything useful.

Talk of courts and fae.

Of the Oracle and whether or not they should trust her.

Discussions about meals they couldn't wait to eat.

Stupid, pointless talking.

My jaw ticked. I didn't like their constant nattering. Like the chatter finches in Underhill. Constant noise, and not even a song to orchestrate a bloody attack. Just noise.

Orry tugged on my hair. "The regent is like a king here." She stroked her tiny claws through my tresses, remaining out of sight.

Aaden didn't show any sign that he'd heard her speak. Her voice was soft, but should have been easily audible. I'd assumed that these earth fae were traveling with the hunched old man, but with the way Orlaith had remained hidden in my hair—and the old man's absence—I was having doubts on that.

"He rules Ireland and all the fae that live with us," she continued. "He has three children, all born in the last three years, and all by different women. Bit of a scandal for a ruler, but no one comments about it too loudly because he's regent, and the lack of children has been a major issue for the fae for so long. You know?"

"What's the squeaking noise?" a female asked.

Aaden was peering at me. "I think she has a critter on her."

"In her *hair*?" the woman said in horror. "A mouse?"

"No more than what I'd expect of someone like her," Owen sneered.

I closed my eyes against the bright sun. "No hearing from stupid ears your words?" I asked her.

"Other than my father, you're the first person who can hear and understand what I'm saying." Orry sighed. "It's nice to finally be heard."

I drew in a slow breath, but I wasn't surprised. I'd always been able to communicate with the animals back home. "Speak more."

Aaden slid me a glance, but when I shook my head, he just pressed his lips together.

"Where were we?" she whispered. "Oh, so the regent is a true man-whore ... you know what that is?"

"Stallion?" I offered, earning another side-long glance from Aaden.

"Um. No. But he is hung like one!" Orry let out a high-pitched giggle. "No complaints from the ladies, if you know what I mean. I mean, *I am* complaining, but that's a whole other story that I don't think we have time for right now."

I didn't know what any of that meant. "More."

"He's not a bad man, just very into himself. Selfish as men are wont to be. But one of his children is missing, too, from whatever is taking the kids. He blamed what he thought was a jealous mistress—banished her, even—but the kids kept on going missing. So many of them now." She slowed in her stroking of my hair. "I didn't hear what the Oracle said about you exactly. I only know that the gist of it was that the silver-haired girl hidden in Underhill would answer for the lost children of Ireland."

Answer for the lost children of Ireland...

No wonder most of my kidnappers were hostile.

I frowned, thinking through what my mother could want me to do besides find the children. Because if there was one thing I knew? When it came to my mother, very little was straight forward. One task would mean another, then another and another until the true goal was revealed. The faster I got to that true goal, the faster she'd let me return home.

I already felt homesick. I hated this place. The Earth was draining, and I didn't trust these fae to protect us. They weren't engaging their senses to track their surroundings at every moment. They'd let themselves grow vulnerable. Lazy. And they kept putting locks on my magic.

This was the last time I'd allow them to do that. Next person to put gold on my body without my permission would die.

"How long?" I asked.

Orlaith didn't have a chance to answer me. Aaden walked beside my mount. "How long until we're at the keep? About three hours at this rate."

That wasn't what I was asking. I wanted to know how long it had been since the children started to go missing. But Aaden's response did answer a question I'd had since being slung on this horse.

I glanced at him, mostly because I wanted to look at his green orbs more. They were so different from other orbs. I couldn't figure out why they intrigued me so much. I didn't feel any animal attraction to him ... but there was something about the earth fae.

"Who are you looking for?" Aaden asked. He reached over to rest a hand on my arm. I looked at where our skin touched. His hands were warm, and his fingers calloused.

That felt nice.

Aaden removed his hand. "Sorry."

What was he sorry for? The touch had left a strange, pleasant tingling in my body. I buried the urge to look into his eyes again.

"The regent will want to meet with you right away, but he's going to have a hard time understanding you," Aaden said, almost to himself. "And you are going to need a bath."

I raise both eyebrows. "I stink not."

Orlaith giggled, and Aaden replied, but at a staccato drumming of hoof beats in the distance—just barely there—I tilted my head and ignored them both. The sound came from very, very *big* hoof beats that I felt all the way to the marrow of my bones. I knew that sound well, and it brought me hope.

I wasn't alone on this earthside any longer.

I grinned down at Aaden, unsure why he returned my challenge with an answering smile when the rest of his posture was friendly. "I meet regent. Now. Bath no."

"Now?" He twisted in his saddle.

The hoofbeats soon had everyone's attention as the thundering noise swelled. Some mimicked Aaden, while others like Owen fully turned their mounts to face the incoming threat.

I thumped my heels against the golden mare's sides, and she leapt forward, startled into a gallop.

Orry squeaked and clung tighter, her tiny nails digging in. "Where are we going?"

"Stone hut." I leaned forward in the saddle, bumping the mare's sides with each stride until she picked up enough speed. The wind whistled through my hair and ears, but I could hear the fae chasing me yet again, ignoring the beast that was catching up to us.

I grinned and glanced back over my shoulder. "Tarbeasts shit-for-brains." That was one of my bestie's favorite lines. Speaking of . . .

The thundering hooves caught up to me and my golden mare, pulling alongside us like we weren't at full gallop. Then again, no one could keep up with my bestie but me—and I could only manage that by drawing hard on my magic.

Icicles hung from the land kelpie's mane and tail as he raced next to us. He'd been my companion and protector since before I could walk, and I could not have had a better friend. Kik easily kept pace with the golden mare, and I noted how he eyed her up. He liked her dainty stems, no doubt.

"Lugh's blistered ass! Earthside?" he bellowed. His sharp teeth clamped through each word as if he were breaking bones.

I was hardly here by choice. No need to bring the state of Lugh's ass into it.

"Mother," I shouted back. He blew out a heavy snort that sent a spray of cold fog up and around us.

"Damn it. Quiet was blanket. You ripped off. Home?" Even I could hear the doubt in his voice. If Underhill wanted me here, I wasn't going home any time soon, not even on a land kelpie.

"Regent," I grunted, knowing Kik would give me hell for continuing to 'rip off his quiet blanket'. He hated being bored anyway. So full of shit.

"Up. Meet giant turd with me." He flicked his head to his back, then winked at my mount. "Me. You. Later."

"*Flirt* later." I lifted my hands as best I could to show him the bindings and the thick bracelet. "Not easy. Trapped."

His head shot forward, and I didn't flinch as he easily bit through the bindings and bracelet. He threw them backward, and I snorted at a scream and heavy thud. "Imbeciles. Earth infested. Fucking twat waffles."

"Twat waffles!" Orry howled with laughter. "Oh, what I wouldn't give to say that to the regent's face. Maybe I will!" She added nervously, "Or maybe I'll just think it."

Kik's head snaked down to the mare's belly where my feet were tightly trussed. I twisted to the side, making the rope easier for him to snap his teeth through. A quick slice, and I was free.

The fae shouted behind us, and Aaden's voice was distinct from the rest. I didn't look back as I pushed into a crouch on the mare's back. "Thank you." I touched her neck, then leapt across the space between her and Kik, landing across his broad back on my belly. I swept my legs around and straddled his barrel shaped back. "Regent, Kik."

He wasn't paying attention. "Mmm, gold beauty." Kik growled the words, and the mare squealed and struck out at him with a front foot. "Sass! Inside her later. Long face, four legs, fair game."

"Kik," I snapped his name and thumped him with my heels. "Regent. Now!"

I was *not* going to the regent trussed up like a captive. Not on a mission from my mother. I was going to find out what she wanted, but I'd do it on my terms.

Kik grunted and turned up the speed. *Ha!* The horses behind us didn't stand a chance at keeping up. Aaden had said the castle and regent were three hours away, but I felt sure Kik would have me there in less than half that. By the time Green Orbs and Colorful Face caught up, my conversation with the regent would be done. More than done.

I pursed my lips, then gave in and sniffed my armpit. *Dammit.* Aaden had been right. "Find water close, Kik."

Maybe I did stink a *little*.

***

Kik took me to a thin waterfall that tumbled into a rocky pool at the base, just deep enough to be used for bathing. The water rushed down the sides of a hollowed-out cliff that curled around in a semi-circle, hidden from view. There was no way that Kik's hoofprints could be missed in the soft turf that had led to this area of the woods, so I knew the fae pursuing me would track us here if I dallied overlong.

I sloshed into the bitterly icy cold water and Orry flew off me. "I ain't getting in there if I don't have to. I'll braid your hair after it's clean though?"

I'd enjoyed having my hair tucked away and off my face. I nodded and dove into the water. The bracing cold made my skin tighten, contracting every muscle as I made myself stay under for long enough to grab a handful of the loose sand at the bottom. Surfacing, I scrubbed it over every inch of bare skin, face included. Double on the pits of my arms.

I stepped out, pulling on the red and green tendrils within the plants and earth around us. Weaving it through my hair and across my skin, I used it to throw off the excess water and the last of the dirt.

"Less dirt?" I asked Kik.

"Less. Never gold mare. Can't make silk purse from tarbeast's ear." He focused his attention on me for a beat, then shuddered. I rolled my eyes. Kik thought me ugly—well, except for my mane, he'd always liked that, and I often caught him nuzzling it when he thought I wouldn't notice. He said the muscles in my haunches were inadequate and my neck was fragile–the same size at the top and bottom. Those were just his *main* complaints.

Was I ugly to other fae as well?

In the past, Kik's words had never really bothered me. I mean, beauty had its perks for attracting a mate or luring prey in for the kill, but I'd never been interested in the first, and didn't need it for the second. A flash of green eyes in my mind's eye told me why the thought had suddenly come to me. With the image came a flush of heat through my body that made me squirm. What was this? Was I prepping for a breeding season?

Horror came quick on the heels of the flush of heat.

No. This could not be.

"Orlaith. Hair." I managed to choke the two words out.

"On it. I will do a lovely crown braid that waterfalls down the left side and over your shoulder. These silver strands are so lovely, so unique. They show so well with your blue eyes! The regent is going to want to bang you, so be careful with him. Okay?"

Bang me? He'd try to beat me up?

Kik stomped a foot. "There will be no banging of the girl, Bat."

My brows shot up at his very real ire.

"Girl bat. Bat Girl," Orlaith sing-songed, not realizing she was about to get severed in half. "Here, almost done. Let me grab a few of these." She swept off my shoulder and made her way through the long grass, pulling up some early spring flowers with her tiny claws. "There." She tucked them through the braid.

"Not ugly?" I asked Kik.

He tipped his head as though the angle might help him say something nice about me. "Still ugly. Clean-ugly. More impossible." The land kelpie's mane danced and tinkled, making the icicles bump against one another. "Time. Clodhopping shit-for-brains come."

They'd caught up sooner than expected. I leapt onto his back, and Orlaith swept in around my neck, hanging so her back feet bounced on my chest.

"I'll hang here like a bat necklace. This way I can talk to you and help you answer the regent," she said. "Most fae won't know I'm here."

Kik trotted back up the slight incline that had taken us to the waterfall, then out onto the main path—which I'd learned was called a road. A short while later, we rounded a curve that led us to the large gates of a stone hut. The castle, or so Orlaith informed me.

Two guards stood at the gate, their weapons in hand.

"State your business," the one on the left barked.

"Regent. Now," I barked back.

The one on the right chuckled. Through his helmet, all I could see were deep amber eyes staring at me. Like a winter wolf.

He didn't howl like a wolf though. No. His words were chillier than the water I'd just cleaned in. "Nay, Lass, you don't get to be ordering us around like that. If the Ríchashaoir agrees to see you, then you will enter his presence wearing these." He held up gold cuffs.

I arched a brow. "Try, imbecile. Die, imbecile."

"Why does she speak like that?" the first guard muttered.

"She's saying if I'm stupid enough to try, then I deserve to die," the wolf man replied.

"...how do you know?"

His amber eyes hadn't left mine. Now he flung up a hand, his magic curling out and around him, dark, nearly black, with the slightest edge of amber.

Unseelie.

Not the first I'd ever seen, but certainly the first I'd ever spoken to.

More to the point ...

I'd already decided the next person to put that gold on me would die. Time to make good on that.

I grinned at him. A fight it would be.

FIVE

Wolf man had gathered his magic in warning. That approach was fine if a creature had enough juice to put another animal off. But this Unseelie fucker didn't.

Not against *this* animal.

Riding hard to cross the bridge spanning the moat, I pulled my silver magic back like a bowstring and released, shooting the lethal weapon of concentrated power at the Unseelie.

The second guard shouted and bodily flung himself away from the gates and off the bridge.

Amber-edged darkness exploded with a *boom,* and my eyes narrowed as my dagger of silver power disintegrated on the Unseelie's magical shield. Damn. He was stronger than I'd thought.

And I was obviously stronger than *he'd* thought. My lip curled at the slight wideness to his gaze.

Kik twitched his tail with a chiming of icicles that rang across the bridge. "Hoof fucker into next moon?"

Tempting.

But this fight felt too personal to hand off to someone else. The guard hadn't broken his challenging stare—not even to track the whereabouts of the other guard. If I hadn't known better, I would have thought he'd grown up in Underhill—he obviously understood breaking eye contact conveyed weakness.

I'd never fought a personal fight. Well, maybe every fight was personal when it was for survival. I'd never fought a fight for the joy of it.

Something told me that was about to change.

Inhaling, I cast my senses wide, if only to try to make sense of the strange tension crackling between myself and the guard, who was very clearly drawing energy from his surroundings even as I did. People milled around beyond the castle gates. Hundreds. It dawned on me that the moat wasn't just a moat—there was magic in it. Probably a defense spell.

I chuckled, then patted Kik. "Mine to kill."

The Unseelie guard's eyes widened a second time.

Kik huffed. "Fun thief. Sure? Stallion has strong neck."

Strong neck or not, I didn't need help with this Unseelie. I scanned the stone walls of the castle and the heavy wooden doors. Otherwise, there wasn't much I could use to my advantage aside from the moat. "Go."

Gently prying Orlaith's claws from my neck, I held her up at eye level and placed a finger across my lips. She nodded, and I rested her on Kik's mane without telling him. He wasn't averse to eating bats.

Muttering, Kik retreated across the bridge, Orlaith in tow.

"Afraid of a little gold, silver seelie?" the Unseelie taunted across the ten feet that divided us. I could spit that far.

I widened my stance and increased my draw on the energy around me. "Name not Silver," I snarled. "Gold not shine where goes."

He snorted. "You're going to shove these cuffs where the sun doesn't shine? And I've decided Silver is the perfect name for you."

"Asshole you."

"I've been called worse. But I can't say anyone else has been stupid enough to try and kill me. So, here's what you're going to do. You're going to kneel at my feet with your hands behind your back. I'm going to put these cuffs on you. After that, I'll send someone to inquire whether the Ríchashaoir wants to see you. I can't fathom why he would want to, especially when I inform him that you attempted to kill me and seek entrance by force. Unless you'd like to apologize for that? Then I may forget to include those details."

"Kneel," I tried out the word for size, then, "Apologize."

Amber eyes glinted over a cruel smile. "At my feet, Silver. I want to watch those lush lips forming each word."

I smiled back, then launched another magic dagger at him.

The worst animals to fight were the ones who learned. The man simply shifted to one side. Amber darkness shot from his fingertips like forked lightning.

No problem. I'd expected a pointed attack like mine. Nowhere to dodge.

I threw up a shield, wincing as ten impacts or more hammered into it, one after another.

Whoosh. A scythe of dark magic swept through the air toward my neck, I dropped to a crouch to keep my head in place, then hooked my magic around the hinges of the castle doors to sever them. The onlookers had scattered long ago. Throwing out power, I dragged the heavy gate doors back to crush the Unseelie standing beneath them.

Yelling, he rose both arms, and I grunted when he proved strong enough to hold the door up. He was awfully occupied now . . .

Grinning, I sprinted across the space and put everything into the blow as I charged directly into him, shoving hard with my shoulder. The Unseelie catapulted off the bridge, and I kept rolling to avoid the reverberating crash of the castle doors hitting the cobblestones.

"Ha!" I popped to my feet, hoping he could swim in all that armor. Not.

My grin faded when no splash sounded.

Nothing.

At all.

Too quiet. Both within the castle gates and here. Where was the Unseelie fucker? And did I dare walk through the entrance with him unaccounted for?

The fae who'd stolen me from Mother had the ability to turn invisible.

Shit.

I backed up against the castle wall.

With a roar, the Unseelie burst upward from beneath the bridge, his armor gone. I took in the crescent moon on his tunic the instant before my instincts kicked in. Yanking five stone blocks from the castle wall with my magic, I flung them his way. He incinerated the blocks in a burst, gray dust exploding out, and light erupted in my eyes a second later as my head was smashed into the wall behind me. Blood filled my mouth, and I hurled myself to one side, throwing up a shield.

I pulled a wave of energy into my body, whispering it to my injuries. The light filling my eyes receded.

But I had no time to recover, because *he* was there.

I leaned back to avoid his huge fist, then kicked at his knee, followed by a jab to his groin. His breath was as audible as mine, and as we danced back for the next flurry, a wildness filled his amber gaze. A wildness I knew.

He was an animal like me.

And unfortunately, I knew how animals like me fought.

I doubled over in response to a crushing kick to the gut, then enjoyed his grunt as I tore into the flesh of his forearm.

Stomping on his instep, I clawed at his neck. His fist wove into my hair, yet his triumph was short-lived as I simply tore myself free, leaving a handful of silver strands in his grasp.

Jumping, I kicked both legs into his stomach, then pushed off the ground to launch at the Unseelie and wrap around him tight. Silver power answered my call and flooded down my arms and legs. Over my body.

I chanted rapidly.

"Not fucking happening." He punched me in the throat. The weak shield I erected wasn't able to absorb the entire force.

I dropped like a sack of shit, wheezing for air. Stretching my power, I yanked more stones from the castle wall and watched as one collided with the Unseelie's head a moment later.

It bought me enough time for me to stagger upright and realize that those within the walls were no longer quiet. *Pounding footsteps.*

They were coming.

The Unseelie rolled to his feet. Fury filled every line on his face. The eyes I'd thought were amber now resembled molten gold. Asshole was far stronger than I'd anticipated. And he really knew how to fight too. He'd proven that without drawing any of the weapons I could see sheathed on his body.

Sometimes fighting wasn't the answer.

I sighed and dropped to my knees.

His shock was evident under the dirt and blood streaking his face, but he was quick to recover his swagger. I ground my teeth against the urge to knock every one of his teeth out as he held up the gold cuffs. "Good girl, Silver. Don't you worry. These won't hurt a bit. Unless you want them to."

Keeping him in my sights, I half-turned to observe the incoming guards. A lot of them.

The Unseelie called over my head. "Seelies. Always late to the fight."

And he'd taken his eyes off that very same fight.

Smirking, I threw out silver and pulled camouflage over myself. Not waiting for the inevitable outcry, I darted away. I'd made it to the castle wall before the Unseelie cursed. The stones I'd yanked out hadn't been at random. Climbing rapidly using the formed hand and foot holds, I reached the top and peered back down at the milling fae.

Imbeciles.

I would see the regent.

I wouldn't be wearing any trace of gold.

And I certainly wouldn't go to him on my knees and apologizing.

My blood boiled just under the surface, but I tempered the rage that the Unseelie had incited to focus on my descent into the Irish court.

I dropped down the last ten feet of stone, then moved to the next wall within. I could hear the sounds of other fae. Close by. Crouching behind a door, I paused to get better bearings.

Metal keened. Wood splintered. Raw power threw me face-forward to the dirt ground and a hard surface joined the attack to hold me there. *Pinned*.

Black boots occupied my vision, and I craned my head to glare first at the door pinning me down, then at the Unseelie as he wrapped yet another fistful of my hair around his bloodied hand. With his other hand, he held a blade to my throat.

"Thought I'd borrow your idea," he murmured. I wasn't lured into a sense of safety by the casual words. Not with the pressure he was applying at my throat. "Drop your power and keep it that way. This is the only time I'll warn you. If it appears, then I'm slitting your throat."

There was no bluff in any part of his body.

Hatred filled every bruised and scraped particle of my being. I'd never wanted to slowly carve out someone's heart. Never wanted to see the acknowledgement of death in their eyes in their final moments. To me, death was impersonal. A matter of survival.

Not now. Not with him.

I called my power in.

Dagger to my neck, the guard then released my hair to dangle the cuffs before me. "You get an A for effort, Silver. I only asked you to get on your knees, not to throw yourself at my feet. You're not the first though. Won't be the last either."

My focus didn't leave the cuffs. I let an absolute promise fill my voice. Because I wouldn't hurt him now. Maybe not even within the hour. But this man would feel pain by my hand, and I hoped it was slow and full of agony. "Dare. And. Die."

The Unseelie flicked a finger. I listened as the door was drawn up and flung away. Amber eyes met mine as he snapped on one cuff, then the other. My power cut away, and I choked on the panic that rocked me to my very core. *Tears* stung my eyes, and the absence of magic within me was a physical ache.

I was dragged up, and the guard lowered his head to stare directly at me. With quiet menace, he said, "I dare." Straightening, he jerked his head. "Now move."

Six

I was yanked to my feet by the man I would gleefully strangle one day with my bare hands. He barked orders over his shoulder, and I tried not to physically react when a winged ball of gold blurred toward us before taking up residence at my neck.

"You okay?" Orlaith whispered.

I cocked a brow. Did I look okay? "Alive. Kik snap?"

"Yeah. Hey, horses don't eat bats, right?"

Calling Kik a horse to his face would be her last words. I lied, "No."

Amber Eyes shot me a quelling look, and I winked.

Orlaith squeaked, her tiny claws digging into my skin. "That's *Cormac*, the Wolf of the Green Isle. That's what they call him. Oh, gosh. We've never met. I've seen him in passing and had to fight not to drool all over myself because that ass ... damn! Best fighter we have here in Ireland, dynamite in the sack according to rumor, and basically the guy every woman dreams of when ... you know they ... *you know*."

I didn't know, and I didn't care who dreamed of him. I would fight him again, and then all the dreams of him would be replaced by those of the Unseelie begging for my mercy. Just as soon as I got these fucking gold cuffs off.

The Unseelie clasped a bare hand to the back of my neck and gripped me hard enough that his fingers dug into my flesh, making my vision fade in and out. "Move, Silver."

That wasn't my damn name. Well, it could be, but I didn't *want* it to be my name because it had originated from his mouth. I also didn't want to give him the satisfaction of acting like I cared. Because he was nothing to me. I clamped my mouth shut until my teeth and jaw ached.

"The silent treatment now? I prefer my women quiet. Good girl." He patted my cheek and steered me into and then through the castle, his hold unyielding.

First, I'd smash his baby makers to a pulp. *Then,* his face would be reordered. I couldn't wait to end him.

I would have loved to fantasize about all the different ways I could do it, but instead, I took note of the turns, the corners, and the rooms branching off each section. This castle was like the maze deep within Dragonsmount. But if I could conquer that twisted tunnel system, I could figure this place out too. Even if the building made no sense with the strange and soft mossy-like fluff under foot, and the odd shimmering cloth covered with pictures that hung from the stone walls. Weirder yet, floating, tiny, white flames hung from tangled tree vines.

I took it all in and felt my mind ache and squeeze at the newness. I'd made a mistake. I'd interpreted my mother's messages incorrectly. This surely wasn't what she'd intended for me.

If—no, *when*—I got loose, I'd make a run for it. Mother couldn't expect me to fix these earthside fae's problems, not when they treated me like tarbeast shit.

I was almost certain of it.

Three flights of stairs and numerous long halls of strangeness later, we stood before a massive open-arched doorway. Gold covered branches framed it, leaves and a round, ripe fruit weighed down nearly every branch and glistened with dew as if real. The fruit was of all sizes and shapes. Unusual. I squinted at the tree, and the branches moved, shivering.

It was *alive*.

Intriguing.

"Real?" I asked Orry, but Asshole looked at me. I snapped my teeth at him, clicking them hard in warning.

Orry adjusted herself a little. "That's the tree of souls, honey. The castle was built around it, and the tree has kind of integrated itself into the stone and mortar. It's real, yep, totally alive. And it reacts to different people differently. Some get no response. I think the tree likes you."

"Asshole?" I nodded my head at him. He glared at me with his gold-amber eyes but seemed to have adopted my silent stance.

"You mean does he make the tree react?" she replied. "I don't know. Look, you can see the trunk in the middle of the room." Orry flung a tip of her wing out, pointing. My gaze followed. The branches and fruit had so taken my attention that I'd not looked further.

A thick trunk, twenty feet around, occupied the middle of the room, spanning floor to roof. It had bark as gold as its branches and fruit, but tiny fissures of black ran through them. I knew nature. I knew without asking that black didn't belong in this beautiful soul tree. My fingers tingled with the need to check whether the black fissures ran deep.

"Welcome," a deep sonorous voice rang out, "I see that you have met our wolf. Thank you, Cormac, you can leave her here with me."

The person that went with the voice stepped out from behind the tree. Orry let out a grumbling hissing noise that made my lips curve.

My soft-hearted bat hated this person. Good to know.

"Regent?" I asked Orry.

"On your knees." Asshole put a foot to the back of my knees and dropped me hard to the tiled floor, then forced me to bend my head so I was looking down. The tile was covered in sunburst patterns, a pattern chosen for the Seelie fae and, I assumed, the Seelie regent.

"Come now, Cormac. I know you wish to protect your regent at all costs, but this is not necessary."

Asshole grunted. "It is. She is wildly unpredictable with enough power to level the castle, sir. It's only because she hasn't been formally trained and isn't mentally acute enough that I was able to take her down."

I'd show him mentally acute. Bastard.

The regent clucked his tongue. "A beauty like this has enough power to put my wolf on edge? Surely there must be some mistake ... Wait, are there *two* cuffs around her wrists?"

My jaw ticked. There was no way I could lift my head with Asshole holding the back so steady. I hated waiting. But patience, I'd learned, was as valuable a tool as any weapon. In Underhill, if I wanted to eat, I had to hunt. Hunting was ninety-five percent patience.

I slowed my breath and let tension flow from my body, relaxing my muscles and stretching my fingers. I could just feel the edges of the cuffs. The regent had seemed surprised that I was wearing two pairs. Which meant Asshole hadn't felt one pair was enough. That suggested the cuffs weren't infallible.

I closed my eyes to think about how the ring in my ear had felt. How had I blasted it off? There had to be some trick. Or maybe there had been a fault in the ring that didn't exist in these cuffs, because I surely couldn't sense any weakness in them.

Asshole's hand didn't ease off the back of my head. It was as if he knew me, as if he could sense that I was looking for a new way to bolt. *Fucker.*

"When the regent speaks to you, try to be civil." Orry whispered in a sulky tone. "He has all the power here. He could do terrible things to you if he decides you are against him."

I frowned. I thought this regent wanted my help? Or did he just want a dirty little scapegoat to take the fall for what had happened?

"Let her stand, Cormac. Let her up."

The hand slipped from my head, and I kept my eyes down, my head, too, then slowed my breathing further, slipping into a semblance of my light hunting trance.

My fingers traced the edges of the cuffs. If there was the slightest crack in them, the slightest imperfection, then I could attempt to even the odds in this meeting.

"This is a bad idea, Ian," Asshole said, his voice rumbling against my skin in a way that drew my anger tightly around me. "She's not trustworthy. She's a fucking animal."

"Like you once were, my friend? I wish to speak to you, girl. Do you have a name?"

Girl. Animal. They both saw me as lesser than.

Asshole answered for me. "Silver." The smugness in his voice was thick as mud.

"Stand up," Orry urged. "You must. Please don't get on his bad side."

Trusting my new friend, I stood, but I kept my eyes closed. Kept my fingers moving along the cuffs. Testing. Touching. Exploring the energy.

"There." A coarse finger touched my chin, tipping my face up. "Come, let me see your eyes, Silver."

I drew a breath as I found the cracks I'd been looking for. Where gold met fae magic, the fusion of the charm wasn't complete. *Weakness.* Glancing up, I had a split second to glimpse his pale-gray eyes, before I smiled. "Boom."

He tipped his head, a wrinkle forming between his brows.

I jerked on my connection to my magic through those tiny cracks in the cuffs and splintered them, sending shrapnel spraying in every direction. Asshole snarled and leaped for me.

I dropped to the ground, rolling out of his way, and was on my feet in an instant, running for the tree trunk in the middle of the room.

Gasps filled the air as I leapt toward the trunk and clawed my way to the top, where the branches spread out. I could crawl to a window from here.

I could do it.

"Peace!" The regent roared the word. "What has taken hold of all of you?" There was a clattering of feet, and the room filled with additional guards.

Hidden in a high fork of the tree, I peered down.

Aaden, from my first set of guards, was down there.

He shook his head as he looked up at me, then marched to the regent and bowed. "Sir, she's defensive because we took her roughly. It was a mistake. She doesn't trust us."

What was he apologizing for? He, at least, had been trying to help. There was no *we* about it.

"Making words like tearcat," I admonished him. Tearcats were notorious for taking the consequences for their kin's actions.

"I'm not lying," Aaden called up. I could feel his green orbs as well as Asshole's golden stare.

Too many eyes.

I adjusted my seat.

Aaden stood before the regent, who stared up at me.

I glared down.

"The regent has made some shit choices," Orry said softly.

Wanting the regent to understand me, and not wanting a fucking translator, I repeated her words. "Regent has made shit choices."

He nodded after a beat, but I saw the flash of anger in his pale eyes. "I am doing my best, Silver. We have children who are missing. We wish to beg your help to find them."

"Funny way to beg," Orry snorted.

I nodded, liking our system. "Funny fucking begging."

Orry gave a soft, "Oh, I have so got you girl. Tell him you want to know why you should help."

"Why I should help assholes?" I threw down at the regent. Beneath me, the tree warmed and shivered. Laughing? I liked to think so.

75

Maybe they didn't treat the tree of souls right. Maybe that was why black marred its gold. I could feel it breathing softly beneath me. So beautiful.

"Will you come down out of the tree and speak to me face-to-face?" the regent asked. He spread his hands, palms up in supplication.

Orry grumbled, "Forget what I said earlier. We are going to give him what he deserves."

"Nope." I said, not needing a prompt from Orry.

"Try again, dipstick," she muttered.

"Try it again, stick dick," I threw down.

Orry choked and squeaked. "Oh my goddess. I love you, Silver." She clutched me harder and pressed her tiny bat mouth to my skin.

The stare off continued for another ten seconds before the regent lowered his hands. "Fine. I can see you don't trust us, and by the sound of it, with good reason."

Aaden flinched.

Asshole smirked.

The regent continued to stare up at me. I hoped he got a solid crick in his neck.

"Our children are missing, Silver, being taken seemingly at random. Thirty-one of them. Thirty-one *innocents* who have done no wrong. There is no warring going on in our territory. There has been no war since the giant, Rubezahl, tried to seize the fae courts and was defeated, in fact. There are no factions that would consider doing such a thing. We reached out to the Oracle for help. Her only advice was to seek out the silver-haired woman who resided in Underhill. That's you. We didn't know if you were the one who took the children—"

"Garbage," I snapped.

He bobbed his head. "We were wrong to entertain the possibility. But if you are the one the Oracle sent us to find, then you are the one who can help us. Please. The children ... we don't ..." He choked and took a moment to clear his throat. "We don't know if they are alive. We hope, but every parent who has lost a child knows that death is a possibility. At the very least, we wish to bring our precious ones home for proper mourning. Will you help us? Will you help bring our children home?"

Something in his words stung my own heart, and I struggled to speak. "Suns passes."

"She needs a minute," Asshole said, and I was too choked up to care that *he* had translated for me.

I drew back from the branches and tucked in behind all the leaves that I could, feeling my heart do funny things. I closed my eyes against the tears that threatened. These children had parents who'd loved them, protected them, and were terrified that they were lost.

Their parents might not know where to look, but they hadn't let that stop them. I fought through the emotions, pushing them down and away. The events since Underhill were beginning to wear on me.

Swallowing hard, I scrubbed my face. Orry tapped me with a tiny claw. "Hey, Silver, you okay?"

I gave a quick nod. "Help agree."

"You got it. Tell him that you will help if the price is right," she said softly. "After all they've done, you can't do this without compensation. He has plenty of dough, I'll tell you that right now."

"No needs." There was nothing I needed. Possessions would only weigh me down.

"You're as capable as they come, honey, I know that. But this is about posturing. If you make demands now, they'll know you aren't a pushover, and they'll be less likely to play games later. Plus, people always value others more when they perceive their time is worth something. It's shit earthside fae politics, but trust me on this—you gotta stake a claim."

That was . . .bizarre. Yet so was the way these fae danced around what they truly wanted to say. Things were different here, and Orlaith had not led me astray yet.

Blowing out a breath, I climbed down the trunk of the soul tree, drawing a little strength from its warmth and power.

I observed the regent, noting his thin frame and mussed hair. The dark rings under his gray eyes.

"What the price of helping?" I asked.

The regent's eyebrows shot up. "You will help?"

I screwed up my face and fought to find the right words, putting my thoughts and Orry's earlier words together. "Price for the compensation must be on the right side of the scales."

Aaden stepped around the regent, disgust written on his face. "You ask for payment for saving children?"

I leveled him with a cold look as I slowly lifted my hands, the red marks from the gold cuffs still visible. I then touched the still bleeding spot on my ear before indicating where the second cuff had bound my leg. "Compensation for assholes."

Seven

"Is that all?" the regent said, his deep timbre laced with annoyance. "Three chests of exquisite gems, twenty chests of gold, food for a year, hunting clothing for ten, and fifty weapons of your choice from our stores."

I pondered that while Orlaith–who'd been whispering treasure demands in my ear for the last hour–cackled. I shook my head, then pointed at the Unseelie who'd beaten me with my own trick and snapped new cuffs on me. Cormac the wolf. I searched for words more like what they spoke on Earth. "Fight him too. In deal." Just to first blood, though I could be convinced to a death match if he pissed me off again.

Aaden choked from where he stood near the soul tree.

Cormac smirked, crossed his arms, and widened his stance.

The regent's brow lifted. "We do not deal in fights in this realm, Silver."

I didn't like that the name Silver was sticking. And I'd just fight Cormac another way. "Shame. I agree."

The regent perked up. "That's it?"

I dipped my head. "I hungry and need wash. Where?"

This whole Earth-talk thing wasn't so hard. They just put in more puff words. Kind of like what they did with everything. Time-wasters.

The regent waved his hand, and soon a person in plain clothing scurried in through the door.

I stared.

It was a *human.*

"Food and clothing for our esteemed guest," he said dismissively. "Show her to a chamber and draw a bath."

The human bowed several times in quick succession. "Yes, my liege."

Her effort went ignored, and the regent lazily surveyed the room. "Cormac, it seems we better not keep you too close to our guest. Aaden, I am assigning you as Silver's personal guard. We can never be too careful–other forces could be aware she is here and why."

Orlaith snorted. "He wants to keep an eye on you."

The regent's gaze shifted to Orry's hiding spot and away again. A few fae had peered around to find the source of squeaking, but he appeared to know exactly where she was. Did he know Orlaith was more than she seemed?

And why did she hate him so?

Aaden swung the door open for the human, then stood there watching me expectantly. Resisting the urge to press my hand to the soul tree behind me, I traipsed over, walking *very* close to Cormac on the way. I twitched my fingers, and he reared back a step.

The sound of my mocking laughter filled the chamber as I left.

Aaden shut the door after me, and we trailed behind the nervous human.

"You've been busy since you escaped us," he said.

I glanced into his green orbs, then away to the branches of the tree on the wall. I trailed them with my fingertips all the way to the corner, where they congregated in a knot which then spread out into multiple hallways. "Beautiful."

"Isn't it?" He paused beside me, and the human paused up ahead. "We tend to take it for granted, I suppose. It's always been part of the scenery."

Something like this should never be taken for granted. It should be revered and treated as the treasure it was.

Aaden rested his hand on a branch, and we both jerked back with a yelp as the tree blazed black-tinged gold.

"It stung me," the Seelie said in horror. Blood beaded on his forefinger, and I lifted mine for inspection to find the same. Sucking on my finger, I peered closer.

"Black thorn," I said. That wasn't there before.

Aaden squinted. "I've never had that happen." He stroked the branch again, more tentatively. The tree wiggled under his touch like a happy alicorn foal. "Whatever it was, she's forgiven me."

We continued winding through the labyrinth of halls, and it struck me that I'd always be able to find my way in or out based on the thickness of the branches and leaves covering the wall. At the heart of the court, they were thick. Out here, further from the center, they thinned to twigs and pointed shoots.

How long would I be here?

It looked like I was helping to find the children for now, but who knew what the next hour would bring. I only hoped that I was passing my mother's test, and I could prove that she was able to trust me. I was old enough now. Maybe she could lean on me a little more, confide in me sometimes. Visit more.

Cursing floated from a chamber to my left. I pivoted on my heel without thought and entered the open door. A ridiculous-looking bed with material hanging all over it was the centerpiece. Colored mats covered the stone floor, and still others hung on the walls. I pointed to something strange. "Hole in wall?"

Aaden's brow cleared a beat later. "That's a fireplace."

I walked farther into the room, then peered through an archway. I pointed again. "Hole in floor?"

He joined me, then smiled. "That's a bath."

Shuffling footsteps. The human appeared in the doorway. "Excuse me, ma'am, sir. This is not the esteemed guest quarters. If you'll follow me—"

I approached the woman in dyed brown clothing. She had hair like me, though limp and thinning. Her face showed the first signs of age. She wasn't as tall as me, but Kik had always said humans were the perfect height for a hoof to the face. Weak haunches. She had a weak neck like I did. "Human."

Her breathing was rapid and shallow.

I rested a hand on her arm. "No hurt. Curious."

Her shoulders relaxed slightly in response. "You've never seen a human before?"

I shook my head. "Family here?"

"No, ma'am. I moved here to work for the fae."

That's what she called running around after them? "Not good where you from?"

"It's fine, ma'am. I've always been fascinated by your kind is all."

Looking into her pale, blue eyes, I caught a tinge of awe there. "Like us better than yours?"

She glanced at Aaden, who cleared his throat. "She's asking if you like fae better than humans."

Pink tinged her cheeks. "I love my family, but something draws me here. I can't be a fae, so this is the closest I'll get to being one of you."

The reverence and adoration with which she spoke only made me want to shudder. "All like you?"

Her flush deepened, and Aaden answered. "It's been three years since Rubezahl tried to wrest control of the fae courts, and his attacks killed a lot of fae and human alike. Relations with humans have been strained ever since. He didn't hold much love for humankind, and unfortunately many humans have assumed the rest of us feel similarly."

Orlaith whispered, "Because many do."

I hummed in response. I'd seen how dismissive the regent was toward her. In his defense, this human seemed to love being treated that way.

"I stay here," I announced.

The human shot another glance at the Seelie, who gave me a dry look. "It's okay. The regent won't mind."

She curtsied low. "I shall fetch food and clothing then, sir." I watched her cross to the hole in the ground and turn a series of metal rods. To my shock, *water* started pouring from them. As she departed, I hurried to watch as the hole in the floor filled.

"What is this magic?" I demanded.

Aaden laughed, and momentarily all thoughts fled my mind at the sound. So rich and light. I blinked a few times and resumed breathing. What was *that*?

He joined me, and I held still as the sleeve of his tunic brushed against my bare arm.

"That's a human magic called plumbing, Silver."

From his mouth, that name didn't sound so bad. I shrugged off the thought as more cursing floated in through the opening to the outside. That's where it had come from, then. "Only Seelie here?"

Aaden sat on a soft-looking, raised blue seat. I circled it as he replied, "No, no, there's none of that now. Queen Hyacinth has united the Seelie and Unseelie courts. Well, Queen Kallik sacrificed herself to do that, but—"

"*Kallik*," I hissed.

He tensed. "You knew her?"

"Of her," I spat. Kik hated her. More than most, which meant she'd really done something bad to him, though he'd never specified what. He'd never said a good word about her anyhow. She was dead and gone, luckily, but if I'd gotten the chance to meet her, only one of us would've walked away from the fight.

That was not the worst of Kallik's sins though. She'd broken something in my mother. There are some sins that are unforgivable, and damaging Underhill was on that very short list.

I slowed my breathing, then asked, "Seelie and Unseelie get on?"

Aaden ran a hand through his hair. "I wouldn't say that. We've spent hundreds of years apart. Reversing that will take time and conscientious effort. But we are trying. I mean, it's only been a few years of attempting to work together."

Sounded like a no to my ears.

The human woman returned; her arms full of material in a multitude of colors. I observed as she laid them out on the bed, then she went to the bath to pour something in. My eyes widened as foam appeared. More human magic?

Aaden winked at me. "Bubbles, Silver."

Bubbles. Fascinating. So was the twinkle in his gaze when he winked...and the way his laugh had made me feel. "Stand."

His lips twitched. "You're ordering me around?"

"Yes," I jerked my chin upward.

I ignored the stream of humans bringing in trays of food, though my nose twitched at the delicious aromas. They disappeared as suddenly and silently as they'd arrived. The sounds of pouring water stopped, and the first woman followed after them, leaving the door open.

Aaden stood with his feet hip-width apart, staring straight ahead with his hands clasped behind his back. "So what now?"

My first inspection of him hadn't shown up much in his favor. Yet, unless I was wrong, what I felt in his presence was attraction. The way Kik was attracted to the golden mare. Checking him a second time would help me figure out the truth, one way or the other.

Kik had taught me what to value in a person's appearance. I liked Aaden's green orbs, that was a definite positive. Stretching up, I used fingers to push his lips back and inspect his teeth. Good pink gums. No fractured teeth. I let go, enjoying the pleasant, lingering tingle from touching him. I frowned as Aaden's shoulders started shaking. Still, as I glared at him, I noticed the smoothness and symmetry of his face. I circled around him to remind myself of his weak haunches, but I felt drawn to them instead with a distinct urge to touch them. I wanted to squirm from the shivers between my legs. Extending a hand, I grabbed a large handful of his haunches.

Aaden coughed, then took my hand, removing it from his body.

The heat in my stomach intensified from that simple touch. I surveyed him critically. "Grow your mane. Aaden look better then." Again, his appearance, though ugly, wasn't deterring me. I moved closer, gaze on his lips.

The Seelie gripped my shoulders. "Um, Silver. We need to talk."

I paused. "Why?"

He winced. "You mentioned a mane before. Can I ask ... Did your land kelpie teach you about...uh, lovers?"

Naturally. Mother and her underling hadn't been interested in those types of lessons. "Why are your cheeks red?"

Aaden released me to draw a hand over his face. I took the opportunity to assess his crotch. With my fingertips. He leaped back and grabbed my hands. "Shit, Silver. Okay, look. Fae like us don't show our attraction that way."

I shrugged a shoulder. "Not sure I attracted."

He straightened. "You aren't?" His brows drew together. "Are you sure?"

"Checking," I said in exasperation.

Aaden gestured to the soft seat, sitting down. I perched by him.

His throat worked. "The thing is, we don't touch people without asking here. Even if we're attracted to them, and even if we're checking whether we're attracted. It's considered offensive."

"You were offended?"

"More taken off guard. But that's because I'm attracted to you. If I weren't, or if I didn't want to be touched for other reasons, then your, uh, checking would be un-welcome."

My brows shot up. He was attracted to me. The thought filled me with warmth. Not low in my belly, but higher, in my chest. Stranger and stranger. "I check you?"

The redness in his cheeks deepened. "Look, I feel like an idiot for not letting a beautiful woman grope me, but it feels like I'm taking advantage of you because you're unaware of our ways."

I snorted. "Battle with us, you lose."

He leaned forward. "Is that right?"

Staring into his green orbs, I forgot what he'd asked. The feeling he inspired, aside from the heat, was unsettling. I'd have to think on it. "Bath now." My hands went to the laces at the front of my vest.

Aaden scrambled to his feet. "I'll give you some privacy. I'll be just outside the door, Silver. If you need anything, just . . ." His last word was lost as he almost ran out of the door, slamming it behind him.

Shrugging, I dropped my leather vest to the ground, then unlaced my shorts and let them fall too.

Orlaith scrambled up to my hair and began unwinding the braid. "That was like watching soft porn, sweetie. Maybe next time, I'd better leave when your body temperature starts climbing, hmm?"

"What porn?"

"I have so much to teach you, honey. But bath first. I didn't want to say anything, but … yeah, there's a stench floating around us, and it ain't from me."

She flew to the bath, but I crossed to the window first and peered down to look at the reason I'd selected this room.

The view.

Kik pranced below, snapping his teeth at horses occupying the field. The herd had nothing on the golden mare I'd ridden on the way here. And my friend was establishing dominance anyway. I leaned through the opening, enjoying the cool breeze on my bare skin. "Kik."

He swung around to peer up and trotted over. "Strong neck kicked your ass, kiddo."

I scowled at my bestie. "Not next time."

"Probably then too. He's got moves as well as great haunches."

Great haunches weren't everything. But why the hell was Kik speaking Earth? "Speak fucked."

"Earth speech isn't *fucked*. And don't swear or I'll kick you in the face."

"Is fucked." Kik had never spoken Earth in my life. Always Underhill. Of course, he was thousands of years old to my twenty-one years. "Why?"

He grumbled. "I needed to order the stable hands to arrange my feast and slipped into the tongue so they could understand. Earth is a pompous, asshole sort of language, isn't it?"

Pompous. Asshole. Kik had literally just described himself. "You like."

The land kelpie bared his teeth. "I don't *like* it. It's a necessity."

I hummed. My best friend loved to hear himself speak, and that was what Earth speak seemed to be about. All the fluff and filler words.

He glared at me, then huffed, "Ready to go back to Underhill yet?"

"Save children first." I pursed my lips.

He huffed again. "You don't order me around. I'm the oldest land kelpie in existence. I don't save children. I kick them in the face. I kick everyone in the face. I'm out of here."

"Bye."

Scoffing at my casual farewell, Kik twitched his tail, making the icicles ring. He lifted a foreleg and gazed expectantly at the air before him. A tiny hole appeared.

Then closed.

His mouth hung ajar. "What the fucking fuck? The fuck is this shit, you Underhill bitch?"

I cringed as he continued insulting my mother. He'd made the mistake of crossing her many times in my life and usually wasn't so vocal against her anymore. There was no way she'd let that slide.

Mother may not get her revenge now, but it would come.

In saying that, Kik *was* the oldest land kelpie in existence. He'd never been blocked from accessing realms. "Can't do?" I asked.

"I'm sure there's just something wrong," he muttered, cursing some more. He twitched his tail again, then lifted his foreleg. Another tiny hole appeared, and this time a little meadow cloud managed to squeeze out before the hole disappeared. The meadow cloud immediately began to water the grass, hovering at shin level, but my bestie didn't seem to care. A bellow thundered from Kik's lips. He bucked and yelled in an epic land kelpie version of a tantrum.

Guards came running. They'd be imbeciles to get too close, but I really didn't care what happened to them. I'd started to turn away when a familiar Unseelie joined the other guards. He paused at the edge of the field and looked from my tantruming bestie to that little meadow cloud. The other fae were spreading out around Kik, but Cormac drew his gaze from the cloud up to the castle. To me.

His golden amber focus slid from my face and down my naked body, where it lingered. Lifting my hand, I dragged my thumb across my throat and spun away from the opening, storming to the table laden with food to grab a platter before storming back to the bath.

Cormac's gaze had made my skin heat. With anger of course.

Orlaith was already floating on her back in the water. "What got you worked up?"

"Cormac the worm." I selected a large leg of meat. I'd say it was naga, but the skin was golden and crisp, the meat white and not pale blue.

"Great ass on that one. What I wouldn't give. Well, those days are behind me. But a bat girl can dream, right?"

I slid into the water and groaned. The water was *warm*. Why had Kik never mentioned this human magic? Devouring the leg of meat in record time, I tossed the bone away, then dunked under and scrubbed my skin with a coarse pad hanging on the bath's edge.

Orlaith circled her wings backward through the water to swim my way. "Can I wash your hair?"

Her claws felt nice against my scalp. "Sure."

I floated on my back and closed my eyes as she started working.

She sang a wordless song, then said after, "What's next, Silver?"

Good question. "Find kids."

I'd only ever hunted for food. Sometimes I played games with the creatures of Underhill—like my game with Old Bastard, the dragon—but my mother's rules made sense. Animals hunted to eat, or sometimes they attacked to establish territory or to protect their young. Their actions followed a predictable kind of logic. In this realm, it seemed people sometimes acted for emotional reasons, anger and revenge for instance. The only other person I'd known in childhood, Lilivani—my mother's most trusted underling—had never been emotional. Probably a good thing considering she'd been a lethal blood fae. "Unsure how."

Orlaith lathered in a sweet-smelling concoction. "Well, I know one thing."

"What?"

She grunted. "Those dresses the human lady brought in? We're gonna have to do something drastic with those if you're planning on fighting."

I shuddered. "Most definitely."

Then, one way or another, the hunt would begin.

Eight

"This is not going to work; there isn't anything in this pile that we can turn into useful clothes for you," Orry mumbled from under a stack of fluffy material. I crouched, naked, next to the pile of clothes on the floor. The dresses ranged from velvety soft to the lightest and most cloudlike of materials. Then there were the colors. Red. White. Yellow. Orange. Beautiful in sunsets, and the perfect camouflage in Underhill, but how was I supposed to hunt for anything on Earth wearing colors that would make me stand out like Kik in a herd of horses?

Stupid Earth fae.

"Useless." I agreed with her assessment. There was nothing of a protective nature, nothing that would work to keep teeth and claws from digging into tender flesh—so they would both reveal me and make me vulnerable. It was almost as if the fae here wanted me to get hurt. I frowned and stood. "Find other clothes. Now."

I strode for the door, bare feet slapping lightly on the smooth, white tile.

"Wait, don't go out naked!" Orry scrambled out from under the mountain of material.

Backtracking, I bent to pick her up. She sighed and crawled up my arm to settle her belly flat against my right shoulder. "You need to put something on, Silver. You can't just go out in your birthday suit. It isn't done. Not even among the most depraved of fae. Well, two-legged fae."

I shrugged. "No storm clouds to me. Move like lightning fae."

She snorted. "Yes, they will move out of your way faster if you walk out naked ... oh. Yeah, I guess if it doesn't bother you. You have a good number of scars, hun. You don't care that anyone sees you like this? I just don't want you to get hurt."

I answered her question by walking forward. I wouldn't get hurt unless I wore those clothes to hunt. And the thought of Aaden seeing me without anything covering me was ... intriguing. I was quite sure this fell under the scope of the discussion we'd had earlier. About respect and intrusiveness. My lips quirked. His face would turn bright red when he saw me being intrusive to him. I moved faster.

He'd said he'd be right outside the door.

One step out of my room and the gasps started. To be fair, my silver hair fell past my haunches, except for a small section that had been torn off in a fight with a tarbeast, so most of my torso was covered.

"Miss, you need clothes on," the human servant said, her voice timid.

I looked around. No Aaden. Disappointing. I'd looked forward to seeing his red face.

"Going find clothes." I waved at her, then paused. She might be able to help.

"Ask her where armory is," Orlaith said. "I don't know. Never been there, but Ian has one. Oh dear, this is going to be a problem."

She sounded gleeful about that.

I opened my mouth to ask the servant about the armory, but the bane of my current existence interrupted me before I could even speak.

"You think walking about naked is going to make anyone think of you as less of an animal?"

Jaw tight, I turned to glare at Cormac, headed my way. "Asshole. Where clothes?" I pointed at his chest and then pants and boots.

His focus drifted over my body in a way I wasn't sure I liked. That I wasn't sure I *didn't* like it either was far more distressing. I snapped my fingers twice and reached for my magic, then cracked him across the haunches with it. Bastard didn't even flinch. "Eyes up, Asshole."

His golden eyes took their fucking time to rise and meet mine. "You don't want a pretty dress, I suppose? To go with a pretty pair of golden cuffs?"

"He's trying to bait you. Don't take it," Orry whispered. "You need him if you want to find the proper kind of clothes."

Ha, she was right. That's exactly what Asshole was doing. I looked around for Aaden again, only to find my mousey little human friend scurrying away. No Aaden. I sighed. He was supposed to be helping me. Balor's left nut, I did *not* want to accept help from Asshole.

I also wanted to find the children so I could go home.

Time to eat my pride. "Leather. Pants. Boots. Right clothes. Now."

His laugh was dark and rumbly, and I grimaced as if he'd let off a blast from his back end. The sound chafed at my chest and slid under my skin. He really irritated me on every level.

Cormac crooked a finger. "I'll show you the way. Seeing as Aaden is shirking his duties. We can't have you wandering around on your own. Be aware that if you try so much as a single fucking thing, I'll lay you flat. Again."

Orry sighed against my skin. "He could lay me flat any day. I wouldn't fight him."

"We see who lays who flat." I growled under my breath.

His laugh said that he'd heard me. Good. I wanted him to hear my threats, every last one of them.

"Seriously—" Orry tapped my face with a tiny toe, "—how can you not want to bite that ass?"

Bite his ass? I frowned and stared at the figure ahead. He did have nice, firm haunches. Unlike some of the other fae men, he wore clothes that fit him, hugging his muscles. I knew why. He was a fighter and the loose pants the others favored could get snagged easily in a battle. The best clothes were fitted, yet gave you room to quickly run and strike. Cormac wore the kind of clothes that I wanted. Too bad we weren't of a size. Otherwise, I would've knocked his head on the wall and stolen his clothes.

The image of him lying flat on the floor, naked, while I took everything he owned had me laughing under my breath.

"What could you possibly find amusing?" Cormac looked over his shoulder. "You're the one people are staring and laughing at."

I smiled, baring my teeth, and dredged up enough fluff words to make him understand. "Dreams of stealing clothes after I bash Asshole's head to wall."

His eyebrows shot up. "That makes you laugh?"

I shrugged. "Makes heart happy."

His smile was unexpected. "Go ahead and try to take my clothes off me, Silver. We'll see who ends up against the wall."

"Oh fuck me. I can give that a different meaning," Orry breathed. "Make him say it again, just slower. I want to lock that in my memory banks for alone time."

Where I came from, bats were attracted to bats. Kelpies and alicorns and tarbeasts sometimes dabbled with one another, and all belonged to similar species. Orry clearly preferred men, though, which suggested she'd once been a two-legged fae herself. Either way, it was strange to hear such requests from a bat.

A particularly loud gasp rolled out from my left, and I turned to see a woman with a rather large bosom. Her bright blue eyes locked onto me. I found myself staring right back in sheer defiance.

She wanted to look?

"Fucking fill boots." I made a mocking sweep of my arms.

Her light pink dress was studded with shining bright stones. She had long blonde hair curled into perfect ringlets that Kik would have gone crazy for, and a scar on her face. A burn mark. I recognized her crown immediately–the gently twisting vines, the moon and the stars, the sun set into it.

The queen of all fae. *Oh fuck.*

"Highness." I went to my knees and bowed my head. This was the position adopted when I spoke with mother, so it seemed suitable to adopt the same position for our queen. Especially since I'd just told her to fill her fucking boots looking at me. *Fuck, fuck, fuck.* What an impression to make.

"Well...you must be Silver," she said, her voice gentle despite my irreverence.

There was a firm quality beneath it, a tone that implied hidden strength. I liked her. Or maybe I just hoped she wouldn't kill me on the spot and stick me in a pot of bruadar. Kik had told me some stuff about her. He said he'd played an integral role during her quest to become queen of all fae.

"I . . .yes." Damn it, everyone was calling me that already anyway. Might as well accept it until the madness was over. "Silver."

"Thank you for coming to our aid, Silver." Her hand touched the top of my head, the waver of her voice indicating she was struggling with some emotion. "Why are you walking around with no clothes, child?"

I tipped my head to the side so that I could look up at her. "Shit clothes they gave."

Her boom of laughter was immediate. Her bright eyes lit up even more. "I see. Perhaps you will come and see me once you have found clothes that are not shit? We need to discuss the best place to start hunting for the missing children. As soon as possible, so more children aren't taken."

Her language seemed to catch everyone else around us off guard—and yes, we'd gathered a good group of people to gawk at me and the queen of all fae. Orry was completely silent. I could feel her trembling. At least she, too, had respect for our queen.

"Will hurry, my queen," I bowed my head. "Minutes."

"Call me Hyacinth. Now, move your bare ass and meet me at the main hall. I'll wait there with the regent. Don't make me wait long." She patted me again. I paused for only long enough to let her go first, then pushed to my feet.

I spun to my guide. "Asshole, armory, move."

Cormac stepped aside and jabbed a thumb toward a wide doorway. The tree of souls wrapped around its edges, but these branches were a deeper gold from mixing with the unnatural black seeping through. "We're there. At the bottom of the stairwell is the armory. There's no other door in and out, so don't bother trying to escape."

Had he missed the part where I'd chosen to be here? Imbecile.

I didn't wait for him to lead the way. I bolted past him, racing down the stairs as they curved around and around, down several levels. Gooseflesh rose across my arms and back as I descended, but I didn't slow. I had to hurry. The queen was waiting, and I wanted to make up for cursing at her.

At the bottom of the steps, the space opened into a massive room, three men high, full of armor and leather. The smell of fresh oiled weapons filled the air, and I breathed it in.

"Better." I padded to the stack of clothing to my right, digging around until I found a pair of leather pants that were my size. Soft, but I could see flecks of color in the leather. Dragon hide. What a find! I pulled them on, and they molded to my body. *Perfect.* I found a leather vest made of the same hide. This was worth more than all the jewels and gold I'd bargained for.

Though . . .

"Poor baby," I whispered. "Old Bastard be upset when he sees. Must not wear around him."

"What is that?" Orry whispered. "Who is the old bastard?"

"No mind." I worked my way through the room, finding a pair of boots that fit me well and laced up over my ankles. My fingers brushed over a few of the bigger weapons. With hunting you needed stealth, not big flashy tools. I'd never used a sword, and my daggers and arrowheads for my bows were fashioned out of the sharp and hard stone from Dragonsmount.

A smaller bow and arrow sat against the wall, covered in dust. I pulled it up and blew the dust off. The black wood was soft against my palms, and when I raised the bow up, the string was steady to pull to my ear and almost seemed to hum.

"Magic bow," I whispered. The weapon had the feel of my mother all over it, though I could not tell what it was made of. Likely she'd left it here for me, and my instincts said that the weapon was more than what it seemed. Maybe it was spelled to work with long-range targets ... or make the perfect shot every time? Guess I'd find out. I dug around near the bow, found the matching arrows and quiver. My focus fell on the tree of souls etched there, the branches and fruit wrapping around the case.

Definitely from Mother.

I was meant to be here.

"Knife," I said after taking a steadying breath. "Then to Queen Hyacinth."

I trailed my finger over the smaller bladed weapons. Again, I didn't need anything too big—that would not do me a lick of good. My fingers brushed against a handle made of a pearlescent white. Dragon bone. Probably from the same baby as my leathers. My jaw clenched. These fae were assholes. There weren't many dragons left, why did they think killing them was a good idea?

I found a thigh sheath and strapped it on, then slid the blade in. I was ready now.

"Your hair!" Orry finally found her voice. "Oh my goddess, you can't go and see the queen with your hair all wild and—"

"No matters. Lightning."

"Okay, okay, I'll do my best to fix it on the move!" Her tiny bat claws worked their way in and through my hair as I ran up the stairs.

Cormac wasn't there waiting as I'd thought he would be. Neither was Aaden.

I snorted. Asshole probably left me behind on purpose, hoping I would get lost and be late. I'd already figured out the trick of this castle. I touched the tree branches embedded on the wall. The tree of souls' branches shivered under my fingers.

I moved toward the center of the castle, following the branches as they thickened. "Stupid boy." I whispered. "Stinks too."

"He only stinks of lust and bedroom promises. I actually thought he smelled . . .wait, where is everyone? Did they all go to the main hall?"

"Maybe yes." I said, already aware of the subtle shift in the halls.

I drew a deep breath, tasting the air and not liking it. The surroundings had the feeling of a sunset in Underhill. A change was underway, and not a good one. "Darkness comes."

Orry shuddered as a distant cracking rent the air. "Did you hear that?"

I stopped. Closing my eyes, I tuned into my other senses, trying to figure out where the cracking had come from. The tree branch under my finger slid away, and I blinked my eyes open as it wrapped around my wrist and pushed me back the way I'd come.

A fissure of black ran through the branch. A droplet fell from the tip like a black tear before hitting the tile with a hiss. As urgent as the need to run toward the cracking was, I couldn't help pausing in dismay at the sight. What it meant, I had no idea, but I knew in my gut the tree was sick somehow. This confirmed my earlier suspicion.

Orry whispered. "I hear screaming."

I couldn't hear it, but I trusted her. "Where?"

"Back that way."

The same direction the tree had tugged me in. I spun on my heel and took off, drawing energy from the surrounding stone and earth so I could run faster.

Underhill was a ruthless place. Nature didn't always deign to claim only the old. I knew the sounds of a mother's agony, be that mother winged, hooved, or upright.

"Child," I breathed as I burst out of the castle and the screaming became audible to me too.

Someone was stealing a child.

Nine

The leathers I'd slipped into moved like a second skin as I blurred toward the tortured screaming ahead.

I raced through a small market and into the stone housing area just past it.

The screaming swelled. Ahead, magical bursts of vibrant color spliced through the blue sky. I inhaled, scenting the darkness from earlier.

"What is it?" Orry whispered, burrowing into my hair. She'd wisely stopped working on it earlier, after I launched into a full sprint.

No idea. But I knew what that darkness was here for. I pressed my lips together in a firm line and zig-zagged around a horse and cart to hurtle between two stone abodes. The missing occupants in the castle were now within my line of sight. I honed in on the queen and regent as I slowed.

Guards filled the narrow lane between the homes, their long spears and swords useless in such a setting.

"Can't see," I growled.

Jumping to the left, I kicked off the side of a stone abode, then flew through the air for a second before bounding onto the stone abode to my right. I landed in a crouch on the straw ceiling.

Cormac.

Aaden.

They stood fighting with twenty or so other fae guards, some of whom I recognized as my original kidnappers. But what they fought I couldn't say. Darkness wisped through the air high above them, gathering and dispersing in no semblance of a pattern. If not for the unconscious form of the sleeping toddler held by the creature, I doubted the shadow would have been spotted at all.

The guards flung magical blasts, not directly at the creature, but in its path.

Orlaith shivered. "The air feels cold and slimy."

I doubted there was a fae who couldn't sense the thing's wrongness at this proximity. "Need get child."

How was the question.

Running forward over the thatched roofs, I landed beside the queen and regent. Hyacinth was tense as she watched the battle above, but she spared a quick glance at me.

"The mother set off the alarm," the regent said. "We need you to defeat the darkness."

Was that all? "What it?"

Hyacinth answered, "No fucking idea. But that child cannot leave this castle." She cast a glance at the screaming mother, who was cradled in the arms of a man. Despite the terror and horror etched into every part of her being, she couldn't seem to look away. Hyacinth leaned closer to me. "The mother was shouting about how they hadn't found a child just to lose her now. Silver, the child is *three years old*. We've been searching for the next queen of all fae since her birth. She would be about three years old. You have no idea how many girls of that age we've checked since the Oracle made the prophecy. It could be her!"

The future queen of all fae? "Child next queen? What about your babies?" The queen had twins.

"No, no." She waved a hand. "The task of ruler is not meant for them, thank the goddesses. Just over three years ago, during Rubezahl's final attack on our main courts in Alaska, the Seelie queen consort was killed. She was pregnant. We mourned the loss of the babe, if not her mother." She added hastily at my grunt, "If you'd met Adair, you'd understand. Anyway, fast-forward six months, the Oracle has settled in and started to assess the paths. She finds a miracle. Somehow Adair's baby survived. Silver, the future queen of all fae is here somewhere. All we know is that she's female and three years old." Hyacinth grabbed my hand. "We must save her. The darkness can't be allowed to claim her. People like her are always in a tug-of-war between good and evil, and I can't go through times like Rubezahl put us through again. We need to reach her first."

The role of queen of all fae demanded a one-of-a-kind fae. She was destined and foretold for the job.

I had to find her.

I craned to look up as the darkness briefly condensed, the beautiful girl coming fully into view, too, before the shadow dispersed again, only to appear in a different spot thirty paces to the left. This creature was stealing children. My chest was already tight from the mother's screams, but now my resolve tightened it further. This child was too important to lose.

This must be why I was here.

This was what Mother needed me to do for her.

"Is there anything you can do?" the regent almost begged.

I knew about as much as they did, but unpredictability was everyday life in Underhill. I had plenty of experience adapting. "I try." Walking forward, I set Orlaith on a perch of a signpost.

"Be careful," she fretted, swinging to hang upside down as she watched me leave.

I ventured as close to the battling guards as I could without distracting them, then climbed onto the top of the stone abode that would give me the best vantage point. There, I crouched and *watched*.

The creature appeared. Gone. Five breaths. Appear. If it could stay gone for longer stints, then it would be doing that now. I could assume five breaths was its maximum before the creature's form had to condense.

The shadow could fly.

It could hold corporeal objects or people—like the toddler.

If the toddler weren't at risk, I'd just throw an entire house at it. But I'd have to settle for something that wouldn't hurt her.

I drew blue energy from the nearby stone, then whispered my silver power to my throat. Filling my lungs with a huge inhale, I blew out ice-cold air, moving my head side to side to ensure I covered the space where the shadow was being contained.

"What the hell is she doing?" I heard Asshole shout.

I ignored him. Snowflakes and icicles dripped from the air by the time I ran out of breath. The shadow appeared, and the black particles of its unusual form seemed to throb.

Gone.

Seven breaths.

The cold made it stronger. *Good to know.*

Drawing red energy from the surrounding thatch roofs, I pulled it into my throat and took another breath. I couldn't make this too hot. But ...

Blowing out a scorching breath that might feel like a mild sunburn to a person, I made sure to cover the entire space again.

A screech rent the air like a lightning bolt, the sound terrible and loud enough to drown out even the mother's screams.

Gone.

Five breaths.

Aaden landed in a crouch next to me. "It didn't like that."

Cormac hurled a ball of amber-rimmed darkness far to the right, then roared. "Do it again! Everyone, lets heat up our attack."

I released another scorching breath and was rewarded with a screech.

"It's working," Aaden blurted, releasing a green blast to the left.

Gone.

Four breaths.

Weaker. But not dead. And a cornered creature, even the gentlest of alicorns, was ferocious when it sensed its doom.

I swung my bow off where I'd slung it across my back. "Time see what arrows do."

Aaden shifted his focus to my bow. "They do something more than normal arrows?"

"Know special. Just not how. Will see."

Slipping an arrow into place, I centered my thoughts on a hay bale in the distance, then aimed wide toward the castle wall. Releasing the arrow, I grinned as it circled around to pierce the bale.

Aaden whistled low.

A grunt left me as sudden pain radiated through my stomach. Doubling over, I groaned.

"Silver," Aaden said frantically. "What happened?"

The pain began to ebb, leaving behind only an ache. I rubbed at the sore spot. If someone had been standing before me, I would have assumed they'd punched me in the gut. As it was ...

"Balance," I replied, glaring down at the bow in my grip. *Dammit, Mother.* "Nothing is good without bad."

Aaden's eyes widened on the weapon. "Shit. It hurt you?"

I had a feeling that the pain it caused directly correlated to how much magic was needed to correct the arrow's path. Pretty good incentive to work on my aim. Most importantly, I wouldn't hit the toddler.

Inhaling, I released another hot breath.

Screech.

Gone.

Three breaths.

I waited another two cycles to ensure the creature's rhythm didn't change. Setting my arrow on the notch, I drew back and focused on the shadowy, wispy form of the creature where it was not covered by the child's body. "One," I whispered. "Two . . ."

I released the arrow, holding the thought of the shadow strong in my mind as I released yet another heated breath.

Shocked yells erupted as fissures appeared in the ground, sinking houses and sending guards leaping for stable ground. The screech was deafening. High-pitched, like a dragon's nails being sharpened on diamond. Those not leaping to safety fell to their knees, hands clapped over their ears.

More prepared, I only had to hunch slightly as the bow took its toll from me. As predicted, it hurt less this time.

Which was good, because a ball of pure black catapulted toward where we crouched.

Shoving Aaden away, I pushed my silver power out and flipped backward off the home and to the ground. I only had time to see that the house had been reduced to a pile of ash before another ball of pure black careened toward me.

The creature was angry.

And it recognized who posed a real threat.

Running away from the crowds, I slammed down my power and surged into the air, nocking another arrow. *One. Two.*

Twang. I let it soar.

"The child," I bellowed to Cormac as the future queen toppled from the shrieking shadow's hold.

Asshole he might be, but at least he caught her.

Landing on a half-toppled stone house, I spread both arms wide and used my magic to sever a portion of the castle wall in the distance. "Protect me," I ordered the closest guard, who snorted in response.

A dirt-streaked Aaden joined me and gripped the female guard's tunic. "You heard her."

"I heard her," the guard hastened to say.

Sweat beaded on my brow as I dragged the wall closer. *Closer.* There weren't as many guards containing the shadow, but it was also injured.

Closer.

Drawing energy from all manner of stones, plants, and soil, I filled my cup until it was overflowing. Arms still spread wide, I brought my hands to meet before me, screaming as they clapped together.

Boom.

My power threw the castle wall through the area of air containing the creature. Any impact was impossible to hear over the earth-shattering explosion of stone and magic.

I sagged into Aaden, my knees giving way.

Bleary-eyed, I watched as Asshole passed the child over to the regent. As fae guards converged on the rubble and a dark, twisted form was dragged out and imprisoned in a case of Seelie fire.

"Silver," Aaden wrapped an arm around my waist and hauled me upright. "That was ... I've never felt so much power before. I—" He released a long breath. "Are you okay?"

"Should be. First time done. Big boom." I was more interested in his arm around my waist, in all honesty. Why did his touch feel so good when he was so ugly?

"*Big boom,*" he echoed, shaking his head. "That's one way to describe it. Here, I'm not a great healer, but I can help some."

An instant later, cool freshness entered my body like a balm as his green magic swept under my skin. I sighed at the soothing sensation. "Thanks."

Aaden cleared his throat. "I can't say it's ever worked *that* well before."

I glanced up into green orbs that searched my face as if for clues.

"What is it about you, Silver?" he said, nearly too quiet for me to hear.

What did that mean? I shrugged, then leaped down off the house to approach the mangled mess of darkness. "Dead?" I asked the nearest guard.

He nodded, fear in his blue eyes as he looked at me.

I smiled. The darkness was gone. The future queen had been saved.

Orlaith fluttered over and hooked her claws onto my vest. "Holy guacamole, girl! You looked so badass! Boom. Whoa. I mean *whoa*."

Her babbling recount of my attack was lost as evil choked me. Suffocating, I crashed to my knees as the sky turned black and all air was sucked from the sky. I distantly registered that those around me had done the same.

A ripping noise rent the silence of hundreds of fae reduced to helpless prey. Eyes watering at the awful iciness overtaking me, I glimpsed a tear in the sky ahead of me—like some kind of portal had been opened.

I saw the darkness reach out a hand to pluck the sleeping toddler from the regent's weakened arms.

I watched as the darkness carried the child back through its version of a portal without facing any opposition.

As air flooded my lungs once more, I remained still and could only stare in disbelief, in *dread*, at the thin air that remained once they were both gone.

Ten

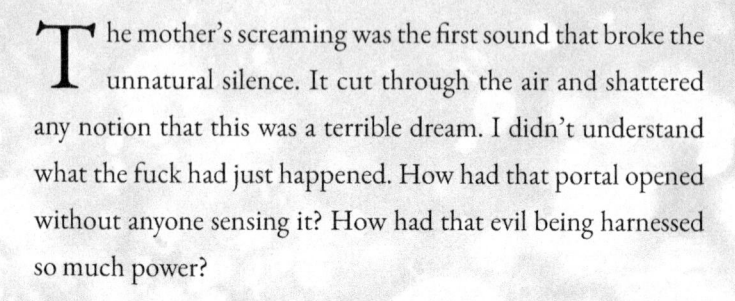

The mother's screaming was the first sound that broke the unnatural silence. It cut through the air and shattered any notion that this was a terrible dream. I didn't understand what the fuck had just happened. How had that portal opened without anyone sensing it? How had that evil being harnessed so much power?

Underhill was my mother, and *I* was shaken by what I'd seen.

Aaden staggered to his feet. "Was that a portal to Underhill?"

I shook my head. "No. Something bad." I just didn't know what.

Orlaith clung to me, shaking and gasping for air. Forcing my legs to move, I made my way to the regent, who was still on his knees, struggling to breathe.

The queen of all fae leaned against the castle wall, a hand to her chest, face pale. The future queen had to be protected, yes, but so did *this* queen.

This was why my mother had sent me. Not just for the children. My task was becoming clearer.

And there was no time to waste.

I circled around the regent, sniffing the air. I flicked my tongue out and gagged on the sulfurous quality that had lingered in a cloud. Shaking my head, I let out a low growl.

The regent stared at his arms. "She was right here, I had her. How ... how did this happen?"

"Evil," I grunted, circling around him, and moving further out. The rest of the fae remained on their knees–some were even flat on their backs. Aaden caught up with me, his complexion as pale as the queen's.

"Silver, what are you looking for? It was a portal, there's no evidence here."

It's like they only trusted what their eyes could see. What about their other senses? I flicked my tongue out again. Definitely sulfur—whatever creature had taken the child must have a big range of influence to have left such a mark. "Tracking evil."

Aaden frowned. I was quick to mimic the gesture when Cormac joined us. He crouched and slid his fingers across the stone before I thought to. I gritted my teeth.

"There's a residue here too. What are you smelling?" He threw the question at me. All business, there was no mockery in him now.

Maybe I could work with that.

Until I made him hurt.

My jaw ticked. "Sulfur. You?"

He bobbed his head, causing dark hair to fall forward over his face. "Sulfur."

The three of us spread out, testing the air and the stone until we'd found the edge of the creature's sphere of influence. We stood on what remained of the castle wall and peered back.

Thirty-three feet or thereabouts.

Thirty-three feet. That was ... Well, I'd *thought* a signature that large would be impossible.

Aaden and Cormac shared a look.

"Any ideas?" Aaden was the first to ask.

Cormac shook his head, eyes glinting. His voice was low. "I've not seen anything like this before."

My gaze slid to the regent. He hadn't budged from his knees. Why did they have such a useless leader?

The queen had pushed off the wall and was picking her way between her shocked and whispering subjects to reach us. "Silver," she said once she'd joined us on the castle wall, "do you know what that was?"

I wanted to say yes. I wanted to be able to solve this problem right here. I'd thought this was done mere minutes ago. But I could not lie to my queen. "No, maybe friend knows."

"You have a friend here?"

"I don't know anything," Orry whispered. "I h-have no idea what t-that thing was, I'm still s-shaking. I can b-barely speak!"

I placed a hand over the bat, calming her.

"Kik?" I hollered for the land kelpie, making the queen jump. He knew portals, and he'd been around a long, long time. He was my best shot at giving Queen Hyacinth an answer.

"Kik?" the queen muttered, a wrinkle between her brows. "You can't mean–"

His heavy hooves thundered across stone, and I peered over the edge of the castle wall. "Come to here."

Kik backed up a few feet, took a few running strides, and then leapt straight over the wall and landed next to me. His icicles tinkled like warning bells.

Show-off. He could've just trotted through the massive gap in the stone wall to our right.

"What's up, buttercup?" He butted me with his nose.

His Earth speak was still weirding me out. "Portal opened, child gone, sulfur taste, smell. What dealing?" I patted his shoulder and pointed at the area around the regent.

"What the actual fuck are *you* doing here?" Kik snapped.

I turned to see him glaring at the queen. I glanced between them.

The land kelpie stilled. "Don't suppose you brought any spoons with you? Or maybe some bruadar?"

From my friend, I knew that bruadar was a magical food that only the queen was able to make. The dish tasted exactly as a person wished and would be the most amazing food they'd ever had—or would ever have again. Their favorite meal that their mother used to make? Done.

There was an undercurrent of tension between them that I couldn't grasp. Did he know her personally? He had to if he'd asked her for bruadar. I couldn't believe he'd be so bold as to make requests of the queen.

I thumped him in the shoulder, hissing, "Not now!"

"It's fine." Queen Hyacinth pushed away from where she'd leaned on the wall. "Kik and I go way back. I beat him once, and I don't doubt that he remembers having my wooden spoon jammed so far up his nose that I could see it out his other end."

My jaw dropped.

She was *that* fae from his stories?

He'd never told me!

I glared hard at him while keeping half an eye on the queen. I wouldn't say I was afraid of her, but I also didn't want to fight her. If she could take on a land kelpie with a fucking wooden spoon and win, she was a goddess-created badass.

Still ... none of this was relevant.

"Kik, what makes portal?" Thumping him on the shoulder, I got his attention. "Kik!"

"Fine. Fuck me, you can nag," he grumbled and lowered his head to sniff at the ground. "Fucking stinks like a shart and armpits."

"Already knowing." I stepped out of his way as he backtracked in the circles toward the regent again.

Watching him go, I turned over the puzzle, part of me taking note of the relative quiet. Someone had caught the child's mother up and taken her away. The screaming was subsiding.

"Found baby," I murmured, my gut churning.

No matter that the child had been born to someone else, the mother's anguish told me that she considered the little girl to be hers. Would my mother scream for me if I were to be stolen away? I'd been with her for twenty-one years, not just three.

I snorted through the pulse of pain in my heart. Who was I kidding? Mother sent me into battle to save the queen of all fae. She'd *let* me be kidnapped. I knew where I stood in the pecking order. If there was one thing mother had taught me, it *was* order. Those lessons were only reinforced by her trusted underling, Lilivani, before her death.

Still, I had to admit that had served me well on Earth so far.

"Not sure exactly what this is," Kik shouted back at us, making fae skitter away from him in all directions. "Tastes of death." He tipped his nose toward the mangled body of the thing that had been destroyed by the wall. Though calling it a body was a stretch of the imagination.

In the horror of seeing evil rip open a portal to steal the child, I'd forgotten about the shadow I'd killed. The fight hadn't been easy, and the shadow was just a minion of the real problem.

"Idiot I am," I whispered, making my way around and over the broken slope of wall and scattered chunks of earth to halt next to the shadow's remains.

The creature was a mess, as though every bone in its body had broken and reformed in a grotesque, painful way over months and years. Its ashen skin was tight and scarred in areas. In other parts, the skin had stretched so thin, as if the shadow's very organs and brain had pushed outward to escape. The creature was puckered and bulbous. Disjointed. Unrecognizable as any two-legged creature I'd ever encountered.

I crouched near its head–or what was most likely its head–and used the point of my bow to push a clump of hair away from the face. The face had fallen in on itself, for lack of a better description, but I spotted a clump of long eyelashes. "Woman?"

Shoving away misgivings, I forced myself to touch her. Rolling the shadow over, I caught a waft of sulfur that was nowhere near as strong as her master's stench.

Thick limbs, no muscle. She was all-and-all average aside from her gruesome mien and ability to flick in and out of sight. Nothing exceptional stood out about her in terms of magic. She had no wings or horns or claws.

Cormac joined me on one side, Aaden on the other.

"She's fae, or was," Cormac muttered.

Really? I looked again, and could almost, *almost*, make out a form more like ours. If so, what the hell had happened to her?

The wolf pressed the tip of his dagger to the corner of her eyes where some rivets were visible on her ashen skin. "She's past childbearing years. Maybe she's become obsessed with filling a void?"

Fae creatures twisted by pain were prone to obsessions. There were fae in Underhill obsessed with building nests. Some with collecting any item of a certain color. I'd met one who'd appointed himself guardian of a spring bubbling from the side of Dragonsmount. Any drop spilled was like a dagger to his heart.

I shook my head. An obsession didn't feel right when it came to this ashen fae. "Too simple. Harder."

Aaden pointed at her clothing. "Look at her outfit. Threadbare, holes and tears, practically molding in places. Looks like she's been wearing it for a long time. She cared enough to dress herself once, but either that stopped years ago, or she has been badly mistreated."

Bits and pieces to contribute to the riddle, but no answers. I glanced back to see Kik watching the three of us. "Track stink-smell?" I asked him.

He stomped once. "Disappears after about thirty feet, kiddo. Nothing to track. Just fucking gone, poof, like a bad fart fading out of existence."

Dammit. Nothing more than what I'd discovered on my own. That meant Kik had never seen this shit before. That wasn't good. He'd lived a lot longer than I had.

There was a shuffle above me on the castle ledge. The regent and Queen Hyacinth's words floated down.

"No, let them go. She was the one that the Oracle believed could help," Hyacinth said.

"My queen, you saw her raw power. We should cuff her—"

"And keep her from finding the children? From finding the next queen of all fae? Are you out of your fucking mind, Ian?"

I smirked, then caught Cormac's searching gaze as he said, "They're right, you know."

I tilted my head, wondering what blows would most hurt him during our inevitable duel.

He quirked a brow, his voice teasing, "Daydreaming about murdering me, Silver?"

"Only a lot," I purred back.

Between us, Aaden tensed and moved closer to me. "Back off, wolf."

It was Cormac's turn to smirk. "Not in my nature."

Kik trotted to catch up as we left the queen and regent behind, moving toward the distant wails of the mourning mother. "I don't like her spoon wielding, but I can respect a mare with strength. Unlike her fucking bestie, Kallik of Fuck All."

Kallik of No House had been the queen's best friend? I never knew, though I was well acquainted with his hatred of Kallik in general. I shared his hatred. Not because of him, really, but because of what she'd done to my mother.

Lilivani had only given me bits and pieces, mostly by accident. Kik had filled in the rest.

Kallik had taken the throne, and had become the first Queen of All fae in .. .well, forever. But she'd split Underhill, destroying balance and order, and in doing so had made my mother a shell of her former self.

Not the time though, to rehash Kallik's sins.

I pulled myself up onto Kik's back. "Screaming one." The land kelpie took off before either of the fae boys could so much as think about leaping up to join me. I grinned at Cormac's shout of annoyance and Aaden's concerned call.

"Those two are trouble," Kik said as we galloped down a curving path that took us closer to the castle. "You best watch your scrawny rump around them."

"Fight the wolf again soon. Like Green Orbs."

He snorted. "You'll probably lose again."

"Won't."

"Whatever, kiddo. I know electricity when I see it. I hoped this day would never come." My bestie sounded sad. A little nervous too.

I didn't know what lightning had to do with me, Aaden, and Cormac–unless it was singeing Cormac's ass, which was a pleasant thought. "Kik?"

"Kiddo?"

"How speak Earth?" Orry was helpful in translating, but if I was going to be here for a while, then I'd have to use more fluff words.

Kik snorted. "It's simple. You just speak the way you think. In Underhill, we edit down what we say to save time and make sure all creatures can communicate. On Earth, they think in grunts, but fill the grunts with words to make sure *no* creatures can communicate except them. And stupid humans."

Speak the way I thought? What an odd concept.

One that would take practice, but I could see what he meant. In Underhill we did whittle down our thoughts to what was crucial. Guess it came from the frequency of having a predator at your heels.

The wails were growing louder. We followed the sound until I spotted the woman from earlier.

I patted Kik's neck, and when he slowed, I slid off his back. "Mother of child," I called after the small group, yelling to be heard over her hoarse, intermittent screams and sobs. The group was formed solely of women, not a single man among them. Five of them held the female in the middle, literally holding her up off the ground toward the castle.

They turned to face me, and the murmuring started. I squirmed. Even though I hadn't spent enough time with other fae to read them well, I could tell they were angry I'd followed them. They wanted to be alone.

"Orry, words," I whispered. Maybe Kik's advice made sense, but now wasn't the time to practice speaking my thoughts aloud.

"Tell them you want to help," Orlaith said.

"I want to help, Mother of Child," I lowered my tone, and kept my hands palm down, as if soothing a wild beast. "I help."

The woman in the middle—the mother—gazed woodenly at me, tears streaming down her face. "You?"

I tapped my chest. "Need know where child when taken. From sleeping?"

She shook the women off, and they set her on her legs. She wavered a little, as though she were waking from a deep sleep. "You?"

"I track, find child. Bring home to you." Again, I kept my tone soft, gentle. There was a wildness in her eyes that spoke of near madness. "Where taken from?"

The mother of the child launched at me, fingers outstretched. "The Oracle said you were supposed to stop this! You were supposed to protect her! You failed my baby!" Her slap caught me off guard. Kik made as if to get between us, but I wasn't afraid of her.

I also couldn't help her if she was going to be like this.

I slapped her back, hard enough to stop her shrieking. She slammed to her knees, gasping but no longer screaming.

"No help like this." I grabbed her by the elbows and lifted her up again, ignoring the sting in my own cheek. "Take to where child snatched."

Goddess, all these fluff words were a fucking struggle. The slap seemed to have done its work, though. The woman clung to me and led me back the way we'd come.

The pace was slow, but I didn't rush her.

Aaden and Cormac caught up, and I waved them off. They could follow, but they needed to stay out of our way.

The mother guided me into the castle and through a few halls to a room on the lower level. I peered out the window, right to where the fight took place. The child had been snatched and taken out the window?

"Here," she whispered, "Fiona was taken from here." Her voice broke on the last word.

There was a lovely, soft child's bed with blankets, pillows, and several stuffed creatures. The smell of sulfur was non-existent.

Aaden and Cormac trailed in after me.

"No sulfur." Cormac said, making me grit my teeth again. It annoyed me that most of these Earth-fae didn't use their senses, but that he *did* annoyed me more.

"There were two different creatures?" he said as though to himself. "The ashen woman, then another that initially took the child. That's the sensible explanation."

That was exactly my thought. And a follow-up question immediately came to mind. Had the first creature been working with the shadow creature? Or had the shadow creature taken advantage of the situation per her master's bidding? Was more than one force after the future queen?

I walked around the child's bed searching for a mark, a clue, anything that would push me in the right direction.

"Come. There is nothing," Cormac ordered.

I visualized cutting his ear off and smiled.

Aaden's voice was sharp. "Let her look. She killed a creature none of the rest of us could touch. Not even you."

Cormac stiffened, his eyes flashing, but Aaden's words gave me a warm feeling in my belly. Yes, I liked Green Orbs very much. I would find a way to make his face red again later.

Right now, I had a creature to track and kill.

My toes brushed something under the bed, and I crouched to look underneath.

What the..?

I tugged, and a branch of the tree of souls pulled free. The branch was curled as tight as a snake ready to strike, yet that wasn't what had caught my eye.

No. It was the dark fissure that ran the length of the branch. A gaping fissure that split the branch wide.

My gaze wandered over the branch as confusion filled me. This meant something. The tree was connected to what was happening.

Was it merely trying to protect the occupants of the castle, or was something far bigger going on?

"Find me bug." I demanded without moving from my crouch other than to hold out a hand to the two fae men.

"A bug?" Aaden asked. "Did I hear that right?"

Cormac grunted, but he was already sending out his amber-edged power.

A bug was placed into my hand a moment later, a beetle with a thick shell. Holding my breath, I placed it in the center of the branches, right on top of the black fissure.

And watched it disappear.

Eleven

"Anything?" Aaden whispered, close to my ear. He'd followed me all the way from the child's bedroom to my own, where I'd left a shivering Orry, and now to the central trunk of the soul tree.

He was taking his job as bodyguard far more seriously now.

I shivered, then pursed my lips as a tingle of awareness rippled through my body. Lifting my fingertips from a fissured branch of the soul tree, I turned to face him. Then, raising on my tiptoes, I gripped either side of his face. He stilled, and I cocked a brow. "No grope unless want it."

Amusement lit his green orbs.

Lifting my cheek to his, glad I'd deposited a sleeping Orlaith in my bed chamber earlier, I rubbed against his face, enjoying the scratch of the light stubble there. I hummed, lowering myself but leaving my hands where they were. "More tingles. I like."

The amusement died from his features that I, although knowing they were hideous to most people, had started to find alluring. I valued creatures of all shapes and sizes, so I was open to changing my outlook on his grotesqueness. Everything could be beautiful with the correct outlook. Even naked and wrinkly gugrallos had a song that could bring tears to the single eye of a hardened Wythn.

Aaden lowered his head. "The good kind?"

I thought about that. "Like way feels. Not poison." Not like a naga bite. "Grope me sometime."

He choked, but the arrival of Asshole took my attention away from Aaden. Why wouldn't he just go away? He seemed annoyed to be here too. We'd split up to search the branches of the soul tree after finding the black parts acted as a portal to . . .*somewhere*. I'd dared to hope Asshole would accidentally slip through a crack and be devoured by the child thief.

No such luck.

"Am I interrupting something?" Cormac bit out.

Aaden didn't back down. "What's up your ass?"

Cormac shifted blazing amber eyes to him. "Don't question your superiors, Seelie."

"Harder to contain the wolf today?"

The Unseelie's jaw ticked. "Yes." He turned his ire my way. "It's her doing."

"Didn't do shit, Asshole." I turned back to the tree.

"It's not what you've done. It's your presence and what you're not doing."

I rolled my eyes. "Then leave. No one want you."

A hand slammed against the wall next to my head, and then Cormac was staring furiously down at me. "The moment you get rid of me is the moment I find my niece, *Silver*. Until then, you can expect me to be breathing down that fragile thing you call a neck."

The insult to my neck was overshadowed by his admission. "Child thief has family?"

He turned away, shoulders tense. "Yes. Three weeks ago."

His constant, maddening presence made sense. His niece was gone. Maybe dead. Still an asshole, but I could understand his need to be present for the hunt. Even that he was so restless and full of rage. If someone hurt my mother or Kik, I'd be and do the same.

The tension grew, and a growl filled the air–Cormac's growl. Curiosity thrummed under my skin. "Have wolf in you. Shifter?"

Maybe that's what I could sense in him—the danger of a beast sitting just under his skin. It would explain why he irritated me so. The threat he posed chafed at my instincts.

Surprisingly, he answered, "Not a shifter. Power as dark as mine comes with qualities that ... must be managed. I refer to that side of myself as the wolf."

I nodded, then returned to the wall. "Anything your end?" We'd raised the alert with the queen and regent, who had then gathered the most skilled fae to execute a full search of the tree and its branches. I'd been sure we'd find another clue.

"Nothing." He set his hand on a tiny, new branch of the soul tree, petting it fondly.

The soul tree began to pulse with a happy hum, and the limb under my hand warmed. I sucked in a breath at its beauty, then nearly gave myself whiplash turning to stare at Cormac. "It likes you."

That was an understatement. The soul tree *loved* Cormac.

On my other side, Aaden's green eyes were wide, as if the beauty of the tree, of the moment, drew him in too. He set his fingertips to a gold leaf, and I gasped as gold shone from the soul tree like a beacon. A feeling of reassurance settled within me–a home-cooked meal, a roaring fire on a freezing evening, a refreshing dip in water under the blazing suns of Underhill. The space under my ribs vibrated with *rightness*. So much that I could barely breathe.

I was shaking as the three of us touched the tree.

But it wasn't just me. They were too. The entire castle even. Yet . . .pulling away from the tree was the furthest thing from my mind.

With a roar, Cormac ripped away, and I screamed as pain sliced through my palm, my chest. Stumbling back, I tripped and landed flat on my ass. Where the soul tree had warmed me, the pain in my chest was ice-cold. So cold.

"Fuck! Silver!" Aaden shouted. "No, don't worry about me. Look at her chest."

Shivers racked my frame. *My chest.* Lifting my head, I peered down through blurring vision to see the enormous black thorn embedded in my chest.

Cormac crouched on one side, and my head lolled until I was looking up into his eyes. I'd never seen them more serious. I coughed and something sharp stuck in my throat.

"Icicles," Cormac said in a tone filled with horror. "She's coughing up icicles."

My eyes began to close.

Aaden dropped down on my other side, ripping a thorn from his finger. "It's from the thorns. They're freezing. We need to get the big one out!"

Without preamble, the Unseelie ripped a thorn from my palm. "We need help with the other one. It's too close to her heart."

Their voices sounded so far away.

Aaden's voice was panicked. "*Her pulse is slowing.*"

"*The regent. Quick.*"

So cold.

Freezing from the inside out.

Masculine voices were replaced with a feminine one, and a wrinkle formed on my brow as the sounds and blurring sights of

Aaden and Cormac and the castle faded entirely, replaced with a room unlike anything I'd ever seen.

Wide-eyed, I clambered to my feet in the low-ceilinged chamber. Frilly cushions and tiered stands covered in sweet treats sat on every surface. Deep-cushioned–also frilled–chairs dotted the room. Statues and trinkets and fragile-looking cups and plates were set at uniform places on the higher, round tables.

"Me dead?" I asked aloud.

"The way you speak has ground on every last one of my nerves, dear," the feminine voice spoke again. "But I have learned to understand you at least. I can inform you that you are, indeed, not dead. Furthermore, you are currently in my tea-room. I like it rather a lot more than my last prison, I must admit."

I faced a woman in an enormous *dress*, which was apparently the word for the tent-like garments. Every inch of her was meticulously groomed and pinned and primped. Not a wrinkle in the myriad layers of material swathing her. Not a white hair out of place. She'd painted her lips with a red substance. She sat with her hands resting one over the other. Straight-backed and square-shouldered.

"Fuck are you?" I asked her.

Her expression pinched. "I do wish the kelpie had been killed in your youth. His influence on you has been atrocious."

I bared my teeth, then yelped to find her suddenly before me, utterly transformed. Her hair was wild–*snakelike*–her dress rags, and blood dripped from her mouth. "Do not seek to threaten *me*, young one. I will tear you apart."

My mouth shut with an audible click of my back teeth. A predator knew a predator, and this woman was a bigger predator than me. "Who you?"

Back in her seat and prim once more, the lady poured a strong-smelling liquid from a spouted pot. "I am Sigella."

"What you?" I edged closer to the table. She'd poured two cups of the concoction, but there was no way I'd drink it.

She lifted the cup to her red lips, deep in thought. "What am I? You know, child, I cannot quite recall. How amusing."

I peered around. She'd told me I wasn't dead. "Why here?"

"I would wager because you *are* dying." She kicked out a seat. "Sit."

I'm dying. I sat. "This interim?" Who would've thought I'd end up in this place before returning to Mother. My heart panged. Did Mother know I was here? If so, surely she had the power to save me. Though would she disrupt balance for her daughter? Bitterness filled my mouth as uncertainty plagued me. The future queen's mother would've done anything to save her daughter.

"I would assume you may like to know how to not die," the woman prompted with a weary sigh.

I perked up. *Thank you, Mother.* "How?"

She smirked over her cup. "Drink from the cup." Blood briefly flashed into view on her chin.

If she wanted me to drink, then she shouldn't have done that. My gaze fell to the steaming cup before me. My gut churned. The woman was powerful. Ancient. A goddess perhaps?

I didn't know her. Or what she wanted. Or who, if anyone, she answered to. There had to be another way out. I searched my surroundings, and jerked as a mirror on the wall shattered, a black fissure snaking through the place it had been. As I watched, it continued snaking across the far wall of the tea room, shattering everything in its path. My heart stopped as whispers started, echoing from the fissure.

Children's whispers.

"Hear that?" I stood and walked closer to the wall. The whispers swelled. They *were* from children. Many of them. "They afraid," I said sadly.

"Sit down," Sigella said in a quelling voice.

I reached out a hand to the fissure. They sounded so close ... "The children are in there."

She said in a deep baritone, "*In darkness they sit, in cold they tremor, in evil they weep as life grows dimmer.*"

A heavy thud disturbed the silence that followed, and I glanced back to see Sigella motionless on the wooden floor. Swallowing hard, I faced the blackness once more and drew closer, setting my eye to a wider part of the crack to peer inside.

I inhaled sharply at the sight of small, shadowed forms. I counted them. I couldn't see all of them–there were more whispers than there were children. Some were out of view. Where *were* they? So dark.

In darkness they sit.

Were they underground?

There was a dripping noise, and a screech rent the air. A black, clawed hand lunged out of the fissure to grab me, but at the very last moment a hand ripped me away from the wall and certain death.

Sigella, the blood-dripping version, loomed over me. "Drink the tea," she boomed in a voice filled with raw power.

The entire tea-room shook. Black fissures snaked over the ceiling and outermost furniture.

She dragged me to the table and forced the cup to my lips. I turned my head, kicking out at her legs in vain. "Why you help me?"

Her white hair formed snakes which hooked their fangs into the edges of my mouth to pry my lips apart. "I'm not helping you, you little shit. I'm helping myself. I need you alive!"

The very world was falling apart, shaking every fiber of my being with it, as Sigella poured the entire contents of the cup into my mouth.

The tea room disappeared, and her savage voice followed me through the darkness, muffled by two louder voices calling my name. Aaden and Cormac.

"I will escape," she said.

Hard stone.

Rough hands on my chest.

I grimaced at the sour taste in my mouth as I opened my eyes.

"Silver!" Strong arms supported me in sitting, and I found myself looking into green orbs. "You're back." He glanced at the regent, who was pulling his power back. "You figured it out?"

The regent lifted his gaze to mine. "No, that wasn't me; my magic could not touch what was happening to her. You had other help. Powerful help."

Sigella. She'd been real.

I will escape. A deep shiver ran through me.

"She's still cold," Aaden said, shrugging out of his tunic. "Here, wear this. We had to take your vest off." His face turned a delightful shade of red.

Movement stirred in the far corner, and Cormac the Wolf stalked closer with the slow movements of a predator. His eyes were fixed on my chest. "Just how I remember."

I glanced down to find my chest bare, scars on display. Aaden stiffened beside me before pushing the tunic over my head to cover my flesh. His fingers brushed my bare skin, and I yelped. *Ouch.* Was there another thorn in my back? I stretched a hand behind to check. *Nothing.* The tunic must've dislodged it.

He avoided my searching gaze and cleared his throat. "Are you okay, Silver?"

I rubbed my chest and then my palm. The iciness was gone. "Achy. But okay. What happened?"

Cormac snorted. "Like you don't know. You did something to the soul tree. It damn-well nearly brought the castle down."

I launched to my feet. "Not me," I spat.

"Sure," he said shortly. "I was there." Cormac addressed the regent over my head. "I don't believe we can trust her, sir. She did something."

Aaden rubbed his forehead. "I was there, too, and it wasn't her. It was a coincidence. The tree goes through the entire castle. *Anyone* could've set it off. For all we know it was one of the invaders."

"I don't trust her," the wolf repeated, rounding on me.

I briefly considered throwing away my decision to not fight him until after the job was done. Then I realized what I'd been drawn into. I didn't need to rely on these people or justify myself to them. They barely used their senses. Had forgotten their connection to Underhill. They'd kidnapped me, for goddess's sake!

Besides, I knew, as only a daughter unable to rely on her mother could, that a woman could only really rely on herself. Trust was for fools, and it was cold comfort when someone turned on you.

I smiled at Cormac, then at the regent and Aaden. Snatching up my dragon-hide vest, I turned on my heel, already hollering for Kik as I strode toward my chamber to collect Orry. I wouldn't learn more here.

The three male fae followed me.

"Where are you going?" the regent called.

Good question. "Guards on high alert. Every corner. Watch for shadows from black cracks. Will come again."

And we clearly couldn't contain the darkness here.

"What did you see while you were unconscious?" Aaden said from close on my heels.

Better question.

"Children in darkness. Whispering and cold."

A hand gripped my arm with iron strength. Cormac ripped me around to face him. A brief feeling of *home* hit me but was gone the next instant as he released me. Shoving the fleeting sensation aside, I pressed my dagger to his calf, but didn't strike after glimpsing his stricken expression. "You saw the children? A girl with russet hair. Curls to her lower back. Shorter than most."

I hated this fae, and he hated me.

But . . .

"Was dark. Not see good. Many are alive."

His breath stuck in his throat. "Where are they?"

Best question yet. "Underground. Dripping noise too." I tore away from amber eyes filled with rawness to green orbs that were more comfortable.

Growing up, I'd figured out the maze of shifting gold tunnels in Underhill to have them as an option for refuge from stronger predators. The task took me years, and during those years, the echoes of the tunnels became familiar. The soft sound of water as it collected on the ceiling to drip down. The darkness that the woman Sigella had mentioned. The cold.

I squared my shoulders, my ears picking up the thundering of Kik's hooves. "I think cave. Children in a cave."

In darkness they sit, in cold they tremor, in evil they weep as life grows dimmer.

We couldn't wait for the creature to come back. We had to hunt it, or the children would die, the future queen of all fae would be among the victims.

TWELVE

Kik wouldn't let me ride him.

"What the fuck is that on you?" He skittered away, nostrils wide.

I held out my hands. "Kik, need go now!"

"Nope." He reared sideways again as I stepped toward him. "Whatever's on you, kid, I can't have it touch me. Go get that golden mare for the job. Tell me if she's a good ride or not."

Aaden choked and coughed. "Land Kelpie—"

"Off you fuck, shit green eyes," Kik snapped at Aaden.

The fae jumped back. "Balor's left nut, man. I was going to point out that you could probably get the mare if you just asked nicely." Aaden stepped back and put a hand to my upper arm. "Come on, we'll go find good horses."

I could not believe what I was hearing. "Kik—"

"Not personal, kid, but there is something...wrong..." He backed away, unable to meet my eyes. "Maybe you need a shower or something to scrub that nasty shit off."

I looked down at my hands and at the black stain etched into my fingers and palms from the soul tree. Something about the substance infecting the tree was pushing Kik away from me. He was obeying his instincts. The same instincts I'd had about the black fissures too. They were just ... wrong. Still, I bit my lower lip, rubbed at my nose, and turned away from my one friend.

Cormac laughed as we walked away. "Figuring out that your asshole friend there isn't so much in your corner? Sucks."

I stopped hard and drove an elbow back fast enough that I caught the wolf off guard. The air whooshed from him, and I moved in to kick him in the teeth.

The wolf was already sidestepping, though, and he caught my ankle as my foot swept to where his face had been a split second before. Cormac's amber eyes blazed as he tightened his hold on me.

A countermove was robbed from me as a pulse of energy, that same feeling of home I'd experienced earlier, hit me in the chest again. The sensation swirled around us, and I had to assume that Cormac could feel it, too, with the way he gaped at me.

"Enough, the two of you!" snapped Aaden, breaking the hold between us.

I shook my head. I couldn't be interpreting that feeling between us correctly. That was the last thing I wanted to feel when touching Cormac. "Asshole is asshole. I am—"

"—a cun—"

"I said *enough*!" Aaden roared the words.

I scratched my chin. Damned if I didn't like this side of him. Made me want to get a little rough with him. In a delicious way.

"So. Freaking. Hot," Orry whispered. "I can feel your heart rate skyrocket, so I know you think he's sex-on-legs too. I wasn't sure at first. The bad-boy type is my usual fare. But I could totally go for Aaden right now. He has buttons I would totally push. Yum."

Unsure what a bad-boy type was. "Not ugly?" I spoke low.

"Ugly? Are you freakin' *kidding* me? You are literally traveling with the two hottest fae in the Irish court."

Huh. "Other people think…sex-on-legs?"

"Um, girl. Only everyone. Who told you about what's ugly and not?"

My gaze slid to Kik. Perhaps Kik had taught me what was considered ugly in Underhill. On Earth, they seemed to have different standards—which I agreed with in Aaden's case.

Walking up to Aaden, I gripped either side of his clenched jaw.

I yelped as a sharp pain speared my hands. He yelled and reeled back too. We stared at each other.

Cormac glanced between us. "What just happened?"

What the hell? "Defensive magic?" I blurted.

Wide eyed, he shook his head. "No. You?"

No. "Why hurt?" Touching him didn't hurt before.

"I have no idea," he said after a beat, then echoed my thought. "Touching you has always felt good."

I could second that. "Try again."

We edged toward each other. Whatever that was had fucking hurt. I touched him with a finger. We both yelped, and I whipped my hand back.

Cormac laughed. *Evil bastard.*

Aaden's brows furrowed. "Do you think it's from the thorn wounds?"

The theory was as good as any. "Maybe black on hands. Touch be good again when gone." Touching him better feel good soon. I had plans for Aaden and that roaring voice of his. I spun away. "Horses. Then search caves." I stopped short. "Where metal horses?"

Both men stopped and stared.

"Metal horses," echoed Cormac.

Aaden's brow cleared. "Cars. No, not helpful where we're going and with how thorough our search needs to be."

Shame. They were very fast.

"If you think," Cormac growled, "that you can just search all the caves in Ireland, then you are out of your fucking mind. There are thousands."

"Send out more people. Darkness in caves. We need to do big search." I called ahead, making both males whip to look in the same direction.

"No." The regent stepped off the walkway that intersected our path. "The oracle was clear that this was a job that only you could complete, Silver. She has warned us most seriously against dedicating more fae to the tasks, no matter how sorely tempted I am to go against her advice and the queen's orders. You will get no more help than Aaden and Cormac, who are only to act as your guides and protectors. The queen and I will remain here, waiting for you."

That made no sense. The oracle was a fucking idiot. There was a reason naga hunted in a pack. More hunters equated a higher chance of success. I stared at the regent, really looking at him. "Orry? What see?"

"Yeah, he's being a total dick wad, and I don't know why! One of his kids is missing. His youngest, Trevan. Sweet little baby, with lovely chestnut hair and green eyes." Her wings fluttered a bit against my skin. "He's cock-blocking your mojo."

I continued to peer at the regent. Approaching him slowly, I whispered. "Why you roostering me?"

"Rooster..." He frowned and backed up a step. "What in the world?"

Aaden made to grab my hand before stopping himself at the last second. Yeah, I wasn't eager for a repeat of that stabbing sensation either. "We will find the children, sir."

"Easier with more people helping." I yelled after the regent as he walked away. I strode after Aaden to the outside stables, fuming. "What his idiot problem? More people make sense."

Cormac's energy buzzed against my own. "I agree with her for once, Aaden. It's a fool's quest to think that we can check all the known and unknown caves. And that's assuming the cave is in Ireland and they aren't using portals. Assuming the cave is in this realm, and in this country, we would still need to check not just the cave entrances, but every length of them before . . ." he trailed off.

Before the children were killed? No matter that I'd seen them alive, none of us were stupid enough to think that it would remain that way. Sigella had suggested as much.

At the stable, Aaden headed inside. "I'll pack supplies," he called from somewhere within the structure. "Wolf, will you grab the horses?"

"On it." Cormac answered, making my brows shoot up. Was he being amenable for a change? Was it because Aaden had asked instead of demanding?

"I pick own horse," I announced. And I sure as shit wasn't going to pick the golden mare. If that was the mare Kik wanted, he could ride her himself. I understood why Kik had obeyed his instincts, but I also wished he'd trusted that I would never let anything happen to him. I'd needed his help, and instead of discussing the issue, he'd shut me down–and in front of Cormac, no less.

I walked the length of the barn, studying each of the animals from eyeballs to legs.

At the far end of the alley was a horse that was nearly purely white. Except that wasn't quite right. There was a distinctive sparkle to the ends of his coat. He was silver, like my hair. Big dark eyes turned my way, and he slid his head forward to be touched. There was a scar under his forelock.

"Hornless unicorn," I whispered.

He blew out a big breath and winked at me.

"No one knows?" I asked him.

Another big breath, and he shook his head.

"This one mine." I flung the door open. He was so beautiful. Kik was going to be *pissed*. Alicorns were stupid in his estimation. And I had to agree. *Uni*corns like this creature were smarter by a long, long shot. Maybe smarter than a land kelpie, though I'd never say as much to Kik.

"You take me to help find kids?" I patted his shoulder and ran my hands over his body, checking him for injuries.

"Oh, shit. Not the kids' pony," Cormac bit out. "That thing can't keep up with our horses."

"It fine." I didn't bother with saddling the unicorn. I climbed up on the side wall of its stall, balanced for a minute, then leaped onto his back. "Good boy." I patted his neck and bumped him with my heels. Not only would he outrun the horses if I needed him to, he'd damn well out stamina them as well.

"Screw Kik," I muttered under my breath.

My new ride stepped out of the stall and fell in line behind the horses. Cormac was in the lead, glowering. Probably annoyed by my choice.

Aaden glanced back at me. "Are you sure you don't want another—"

"No, best boy," I thought for a minute and patted his satiny soft neck. "New Bestie."

Aaden sighed. "We have the pack horse if we need to switch, wolf."

"She'll learn," was all Asshole said in reply.

I smirked, and New Bestie swung his head around, a twinkle in his gaze.

Cormac took off at a gallop. Aaden's horse followed. I bumped Bestie's sides with my heels, and we ran after them. I was used to riding Kik, who took no trouble to make journeys unpleasant for his passengers, so it was a pleasure to ride the once-upon-a-time unicorn. He stretched out, easily keeping up with the others, the ride as smooth as butter.

Aaden looked back a few times, but once he saw that we were keeping up, he kept his focus ahead. Cormac didn't glance back once, but he had to hear the third set of thundering hooves. I snorted, then turned my mind to the problem at hand. The problem that was becoming more complex and confusing at every turn.

Sigella. The soul tree. The missing kids. The shadow creature of unfathomable power. Even Kik spurning me. All the pieces floated around us like pollen bugs, clinging to my face and eyes, not actually visible but obscuring my vision, nonetheless. I let the motion of New Bestie soothe me as I replayed everything over and over. Yet no matter how many times I looked at the scenes I'd lived through, at the evidence I'd compiled, I couldn't figure out how it fit together.

What was the *why* behind stealing the children? If they were for food, they would already have been eaten. But the shadow was going to the effort of keeping them alive, which required food and water. No small effort for the number of young who'd been taken.

I frowned. "Orry, why someone steal child? What reasons could there be?"

"I don't know, Silver." She shuddered, tremors rolling through her tiny body. "If it was to get revenge, the kids would have been killed in their beds. And someone would have taken credit."

I hadn't considered revenge, but I agreed with her. There was only one theory that seemed to fit, but I didn't want to even voice it.

"Your heart rate changed, Silver. What are you thinking, honey?"

I grimaced. "Hope wrong. Bad if right."

Cormac held up a fist, and I copied Aaden when he slowed.

"We'll check this cave," the wolf said as we all crouched by the wide entrance that extended at least five kelpie spans overhead.

"One of us will split off at each tunnel fork. If the cave is empty, then we'll stay here tonight and continue at first light. If it's occupied, then...get ready for a fight."

"Bossy bitch," I whispered.

Orry let go and flew ahead of us. "I can help. I'll look in there. I'm a baaaaat." Her voice trailed away through the cave. She was gone before either of the boys noticed her.

I slid off my mount's back and thanked him quietly, scratching him under his jaw. "You keep watch. Call if bad comes?"

He bobbed his head and bunted me gently with his nose. I rather liked this quieter version of a mount. I would never have said so to Kik, but sometimes his constant comments grated on my nerves.

Cormac and Aaden lit three torches and handed one to me. I took it and started toward the cave, but Asshole grabbed me, yanking me to a stop.

"You can't just go in without a plan."

The feeling of home whomped me in the chest again, but I jerked my arm away and stomped on his foot for good measure. "I know if cave right quickly, dumb ass."

Aaden stepped between us again, speaking low to the other male. "Seriously, she's trying to help, wolf. Why are you being so hard on her?"

"You feel something when she touches you?"

Aaden's gaze shot to me, then back. "You feel pain too?"

"Pain?" Cormac tensed. "No, not pain. Something... pleasant and untrustworthy. She's doing something to both of us. I don't trust her." His jaw ticked hard, and hatred sparked in his amber eyes.

Yeah, well, right back at you, dick.

"I'm not doing things to you. You both doing to me. Since we all touched soul tree and the darkness attacked us." That was when this started. Prior to that, I'd been able to touch Aaden just fine. The two of us had even touched the tree together on another occasion and been fine, though we got pricked then as well. Whatever had happened either had to do with the *three* of us—or—more likely, had to do with an increased presence of the darkness in the soul tree. It got stronger between times and had done something weird to us.

"She's right. The pain when we touch only started after the tree," Aaden said.

"The good feeling started then too," Cormac admitted.

"Glad we figured out. Focus now. Touch be weird until touch not weird." Worrying about it now would only serve as a distraction.

The cave ahead was lit with the sun setting behind us. Reds and yellows seemed to slash across the dusty browns and grays of the stone. The opening was big enough for our mounts, both in height and width. I walked toward the mouth, inhaling the distinct smell of growth and plant life blowing out as the cave sighed, fluttering our torches. I didn't slow my steps, though I heard Aaden falter behind me. "Fine," I said. "Caves breathe."

"Caves do not breathe," Aaden replied, shooting an uncertain look at me.

I stepped over the threshold of the entrance and looked around the space. I was almost certain this was not the cave where the children were being kept. There was no sound or smell of water, there was no dank, deathly feel to my skin.

This was not the place.

"Not here." I turned to leave and ran smack into Cormac.

He whipped out a hand to steady me, then dropped my arm as though scalded from the intense energy pulsing between us. "We check it all."

"Okay, but fat waste of time when you could rest at camp." I shrugged as if it didn't matter to me whether the children lived or died. It wasn't true, of course. I wanted to get to them—and as quickly as possible. What I'd witnessed in Sigella's tea room had troubled me. I hadn't yet had time to consider *why* I'd even ended up there. Who and what was she? I knew what she wanted—to escape—and so I could assume that I was somehow integral to that. Otherwise, why would she have helped me?

Questions, so many questions. Earth was filled with them. It made me miss the brutal simplicity of my home.

Cormac led the way, and when Aaden tried to put me between them, I snorted. "I stronger. You middle."

At the front, Cormac laughed. "She's not wrong, Aaden, you are the weakest link here, lad."

I watched as Aaden stiffened at the challenge, but he didn't fight back. He breathed through his anger, and it flew away from him. That was a formidable strength in itself—the ability to keep one's mind clear and level regardless of distractions or aggravations. Interesting.

Would be fun to watch them really fight. I'd put money on Cormac, but perhaps Aaden wasn't as weak as he looked. He'd nearly kept up with me when they first kidnapped me. He was the only one who'd really tried to speak with me.

We walked deep into the cave until there was nowhere else to go.

"See?" I executed a full turn. "Nothing here."

"I wouldn't say that." Orry flew down from the ceiling and threw herself at my chest. Cormac focused on her, his narrowed gaze then flicking upward to my face.

"Up there," she whispered. "It's a narrow opening. There's a woman on the other side. Great hair. I don't know if the boys can get through, but you might stand a chance. It's just ... the woman. I think she might be a witch. She's not fae, anyway."

A witch.

My stomach churned. Fuck a saberduc, that was unfortunately in line with my sole remaining theory. Who would take a child and keep them alive and scared? A creature who had turned to darkness, and a witch was one such creature who could invite that kind of evil in. "I check something out." I pushed past Cormac—and was slammed against the cave wall before I had time to take another step.

Forearm against my throat, Cormac growled an inch from my face. "*Where* are you going? What did that bat tell you? You can speak to it."

His body pressed against me, pinning me to the wall, and I gathered my power, drawing from the surrounding stone. But another idea occurred to me.

Lifting my hand, I held his seething gaze and stroked my fingers softly down his cheek. The wolf shuddered, fleeting bliss blanketing his rage and stealing tension from his large frame before awareness slammed back to him. He shoved away from me, breathing hard. "She did it again."

I smirked, wiggling my fingers. My smirk helped hide that my knees were shaking and on the verge of collapse. It hid the feeling of rightness in my chest that had come from *him* touching *me*. It concealed my confusion. Because even though I detested Cormac, even though I planned to fight him soon, his body against mine gave me a feeling of . . .*home.*

Aaden stepped between us and cupped my cheek, letting go almost immediately as the stabbing sensation returned. It felt just like the thorns that had punctured my skin when touching the soul tree. We both winced. Like small pins pressed lightly against the skin.

"That feels shit," I said, my brows drawing together.

"It does." He sighed. "I wish it didn't."

Cormac scoffed. "You want to touch her?"

Aaden ran his thumb down the length of my neck, not quite touching my skin. My breath hitched. He hovered his hand over my chest, then dragged his gaze to mine.

"I wish it didn't too," I told him.

I was cursing the irony that touching the man I was attracted to caused me pain and touching the man I wanted to hurt felt glorious. If there was even a more obvious sign of balance in the workings, I hadn't witnessed it. And where there was balance, there was my mother standing behind it.

Aaden didn't move from where he kept me crowded against the cave wall. "You still don't feel pain when you touch her?"

I slipped away from him, more interested in Cormac's answer than I cared to admit. Because . . .what I felt when we touched was . . .personal. Not something I would have wanted to voice to even Kik or Orry.

Cormac grunted and turned away. "Not pain. No."

Looked like he didn't want to admit how nice our touch felt either. Good.

I swooped to pick up my fallen torch as Aaden continued to question him. Biting on the torch handle, I held it between my teeth as I climbed the sheer wall.

"Where the hell are you going?" Cormac lunged for me, but I was already too far up the wall. Orry was right. There was no way either of them would fit through the crack ahead.

"I will find out. You wait like good boy."

His angry snarl and Aaden's yells followed me into the tight crevice, a small tunnel, barely big enough for me to wiggle through on my belly.

I pushed my torch ahead of me and felt Cormac's fingers brush across the heels of my feet. *Home.* A sigh slipped from my lips.

But the way he made me feel didn't matter—Cormac wasn't getting what he wanted today.

I grinned as I wiggled along despite their yelled concern and fury.

"Careful, I don't know what kind of magic she might have," Orry whispered.

Good point. I slowed my pace. Should I put out my torch? I could always re-light it. Dousing the flames, I waited for my eyes to adjust to the dark.

Only then, in the sudden quiet, did I hear the soft chanting of a feminine, sweet-sounding voice.

Fae chanted sometimes. If they wanted added oomph. But they didn't chant like that.

Chanting belonged to witches.

Or another supernatural Earth creature I had yet to encounter.

I started moving again, creeping toward her. As the narrow tunnel opened into the next chamber, I could see down into the cave she occupied.

At her feet lay a large striped cat. The woman wore a deep-blue cloak covered with what *looked* like small glittering stars. She was young and had long golden hair, a slim figure, and muscular thighs. Kik would find her ugly but acceptably strong.

"Oka, our visitor is here," she hummed. "This is good. Good. I had grown tired of guessing which cave to occupy to put myself in her path. Would you bring her to see me?"

The orange-and-white striped cat stretched and yawned. "Really, Thorn. Do you have to help her? She stinks like darkness."

The witch laughed and spun toward me. Her blue eyes sparkled with a deep magic I could feel against my skin. Different than fae magic, it held an edge of darkness—a whiff of wrongness that seemed at odds with the woman's being. "Silver child, you may ask me three questions if you answer mine first. A trade of knowledge, for knowledge is power, and power is all. Are you game?"

"Oh, this is a terrible idea," Orry buried her face in my hair. "Terrible fucking idea."

THIRTEEN

There was no doubt she had a nefarious purpose for this game. So was she looking to trick me for fun? Or maybe she planned to draw useful information out of me while only giving me cryptic answers in return.

And yet, it felt like a sign from my mother that we'd found a witch in the first cave we'd searched, and that she'd offered to 'help'...

There were thousands of caves in Ireland. And as much as Asshole was...well, an *asshole*, he'd been right about one thing. We didn't have time to search them all.

I jumped down from the crevice and landed on light feet, then circled the witch, moving so I stood opposite the tiger lazily licking its paw. "May be game. What's the catch?"

The witch, Thorn, smirked, but again I got the sense that her darkness didn't quite fit her. Like a coat several sizes too small. "You understand balance. You understand imbalance."

I snorted. *Cryptic.* However, I understood what she was saying. She was a creature of darkness. Whether she'd always been that way was up for debate, but she'd embraced it now.

I continued to circle around the chamber, scanning the tiger as I passed behind it. "I do."

The witch's lips turned up. "Yet you consider yourself a creature of balance."

"I do not welcome evil forces, no, but balance does not need to be in the moment." Though I'd always found it best to consider balance as I went. When mother had to correct an imbalance later for a creature, she tended to do it when they least expected it.

A hum was my only answer. She announced, "Then we begin."

"Good," the huge cat muttered, making Orry go deadly still. "Let's get this over with quickly. Then she can take her stench and leave."

"Oka, we must be hospitable to our guest. Think of all she knows, a creature such as her."

Oka cracked an eyelid to gaze at me, then closed it, clearly not as impressed as Thorn.

"I don't like the tiger," Orry squeaked. "I don't like her."

I could second that. A predator of that size, with the ability to talk ... not a good combination in an enemy.

The witch seated herself on a boulder, arranging her dress, then tilted her head. The pretty image was ruined by those deep blue eyes whose expression could only disturb. She clicked her fingers and blue flames burst upward from the perimeter of the chamber in a roar before dying down to a flickering warning. I had a feeling that touching that blue fire wouldn't be a great idea.

I narrowed my eyes. "The answers must be truth." I was careful not to word it like a question, though I was sure I was skirting the line.

The witch gestured to the blue flame. "Naturally. The flames will know." She clapped her hands. "Guests first. Three questions."

A distant shout reached through the crevice toward us, and Thorn's focus darted over my shoulder. I smiled, imagining Asshole having a tantrum on the other side. I should hurry though.

Orry whispered, "What are you going to ask, honey?"

The first question was straightforward. "Where is map location of cave containing children I seek?"

"Ooo, nice one," my gold bat cheered.

Darkness flooded the witch's gaze, yet the blue was back before I could blink. Her lips pressed into a firm line. "Well asked, child of silver." Amusement sparked. "The cave you seek is in Connaught."

Connaught. My heart skipped a beat. The name of a village? That would greatly narrow my search. I licked my lips, more excited now I knew she would give useful answers.

Question two.

My instinct was to ask what the creature taking the children was. Some creatures didn't have names, however, and a name would only take us so far. If I asked how to defeat the creature, she might give me a vague answer like 'with magic' or 'with a sword.' I glanced up. "The creature stealing children I seek, what is the weakness that will be its downfall?"

The witch stood in a jerky movement as though agitated. She turned her back to me, staring—to my observation—at the blank, stone wall. I had an inkling she could see far more than stone there. She didn't look back at me as she answered, "The creature has no downfall."

Orlaith scoffed. "Bitch, please. That isn't an answer."

Agreed. I clenched my jaw. "I asked what weakness is."

"No, you asked what weakness will be the creature's downfall. The creature has no downfall."

My chest tightened as I was struck with a vision of the soul tree, completely black and shriveled, standing amidst the ruins of the castle. Dark creatures crawled from the black, feasting on the living. The very air surrounding the tree was poisonous.

If the creature had no downfall, that meant we would fail. My gaze flicked to the blue flames. There was a possibility the flames didn't do as she'd said. Thorn could be lying.

"I wasn't born in Underhill," I told them.

They flared red before returning blue.

Oka chuffed, and Thorn threw back her head in a full-throated laugh. "Testing my truth charm?" she asked afterward. "And how did it do?"

The creature has no downfall.

"That's not great news," Orry whispered into my neck.

A knot formed in my stomach, but I put aside the dread for now. I had one more question. I'd better use it well.

If I asked about the creature's weakness, she could just tell me what I already knew—that it was not affected by the cold.

Sigella's tea-room stretched its curious hand into my mind.

Did I dare use my last question to find out more about that? I didn't feel guilty about the idea—my life and the mysteries within meant no less to me than this quest. Sigella was also clearly linked to whatever was going on.

"Why does she take so long?" Oka yawned again, displaying teeth to rival a Vyf's.

The witch hummed again.

Who is Sigella? No. What is Sigella's purpose? I already knew—to escape. "Why does Sigella's escape depend on me remaining alive?"

The witch's brows slammed together. "*Sigella,*" she hissed.

Did they know one another? Did that mean Sigella was also a witch?

The witch spun back and settled herself once more on her rock. This time her movements radiated forced calm. She tilted her chin and met my gaze. "Her life is tied to yours," she said, then smirking, "as you are her vessel. It occurs to me now."

I stared at her. "Her vessel?" Suddenly the witch was before me. I held my dagger against her abdomen as the air crackled in the hand's width between our bodies.

"A fourth question? You may ask it, but the question will cost you something more." She appeared again, back beside her tiger. "Something you may not wish to give."

That was enough warning to me. Though it had just occurred to me that I should have asked whether she was linked to the child thief in any way. *Fuck.*

"Your turn, Thorn," the tiger drawled. "Her stench, remember?"

Thorn's voice rang in the chamber. "If your mother is gold, then why are you silver?"

The question hit me like a battering ram, drawing every feeling of neglect and insecurity to the surface. How she'd gotten directly to the core of me, I couldn't fathom, as my heart thundered against my ribs in an attempt to leap into those blue flames.

The thing is, I didn't know. I could only give the answer I believed to be true. "Because she has not fully accepted me as her own." With this test, if I succeeded, then maybe my magic would change.

"Is that so?" Thorn murmured, a cruel smile playing on her lips.

"That was your second question, and the answer is yes," I replied.

Oka snarled, surging upward with a speed that told me the tiger's size and obvious weight held no bearing on its agility. Thorn's hiss echoed in the chamber as she ran a hand down her companion's striped and orange fur. "My mistake, Oka. My mistake. The spirit of the game has been upheld." She checked the flames, sounding more murderous than accepting. "My last question then."

The witch contemplated me. I held her gaze even as the walls of the chamber started to shake. A deep sound emitted from deep underground, and I half-crouched in readiness for an attack.

She spread her arms wide. "Tell me, forgotten child of gold, what is the weakness that will be *your* downfall?"

I froze.

A predator never revealed their weakness. They knew it and hid it for everything they were worth. My instinct to hide my weakness was too strong. It was overruling my ability to consider other factors I knew were always at play.

There were consequences to forgetting those factors.

Dammit, I briefly closed my eyes. They were consequences I'd have to take on the chin. I spread my arms wide to match Thorn's, then answered, "I have no downfall."

The flames flared red.

Yet instead of anger, she let out another delighted, manic laugh. "No downfall, you say? My, my, quite the tab you just ran up with that lie."

I stumbled sideways as the ground underfoot shook with fury, stalagmites falling from the roof of the chamber to crash and shatter against the floor. "And you wanted me to do just that."

The witch had wanted to cause me future harm. I just couldn't figure out whether she was working with the dark creature or merely answering the call of her own darkness. Whatever the reason, I now owed my mother. I'd lied and created imbalance.

She didn't like cleaning up the messes of creatures who knew better. And she'd made certain that I knew better.

"Three questions asked, three questions answered," Thorn chanted, petting her tiger again. "Now run, child of forgotten gold. Run to face your end."

I was already wedging into the crevice.

Orry launched herself ahead through the crack. "Quick! The cave is coming down!"

The witch's laughter followed me, ringing in my ears as if she were in the very walls.

Around me, the stone seemed to pinch. I cried out and drew energy to me, bursting outward with silver magic curling around me.

Air filled my lungs again, and I dragged myself through the narrowing opening, cocooning myself in silver until two sets of hands–one clamping around each of my arms–yanked me from the other end. With Aaden and Cormac, I fell in a tangled heap of limbs to crash with brutal force onto the jagged stones below.

I groaned and, bizarrely, the groan wasn't just one of pain. I peered up into Cormac's amber gaze, fully aware of his body pressed along the length of mine. The feeling between us . . .it was growing stronger. So much stronger. Not like the feeling of home I'd felt from him lately. This was pure attraction.

I was at least as aware of Cormac's body above as I was of Aaden's body beneath me.

And I didn't feel pain though Aaden was touching me.

My cheeks flamed as the heat flushing my body swelled to an almost painful level. Aaden's hands swept up my sides, kneading. Cormac was caught in the bliss of whatever *this* was. Silver threads began to rise from my body, curling in wisps, stretching in the air around our forms.

"The cave!" Orry screamed overhead. "Not the time for a threesome, you idiots!"

I jerked to life as though through a river of mud. My hands came up as I mustered everything in me to shove at Cormac. He didn't raise so much as a finger in resistance as he thumped onto the ground beside Aaden.

Bereft of Cormac's touch, pain stabbed into my back in the few seconds before I rolled off the Seelie beneath me and popped to my feet. Cormac was on his feet, too, fury etched on his face now.

My fault again, was it?

Aaden wasn't far behind and soon led the way, racing through the tunnels we'd come through to arrive here. Orry was ahead. Cormac ran just behind me as I fueled my pace with silver power.

Green magic exploded ahead, sending a collapsed portion of the cave flying outward.

Air.

So close.

I threw myself headfirst from the cave mouth, rolling in uncontrolled chaos to a stand farther down the shingled slope. This time? The groan was all pain.

Tiny claw-tipped hands slapped my cheeks. "Silver? *Silver!*"

"Fine," I moaned, already drawing green energy from the soil to help sooth my aches and pains–and what felt like a puncture wound in my thigh.

Orlaith whistled. "Safe to say that cave is gone. You think the witch did it?"

"Yep." In slow increments, I made it onto my feet and picked my way down to Aaden and Cormac, who'd landed further away. Past them, the horses neighed and yanked at their tethers. My unicorn, untethered, calmly watched on.

Aaden winced, then circled me. "Are you hurt?"

I lifted the hand pressed down on my thigh. "Only this."

He sucked in a sharp breath and dropped to his knees, cupping his hands over my wound. Green magic flared, and I screamed.

"Sorry," he muttered. "All fixed though." On his knees, he peered up at me. "What's happening between us? When the three of us touched, I could've sworn..."

That it felt incredible? I opened my mouth to ask as much.

"What the fuck was that?" Cormac grabbed me, ripping me around.

I shoved him away. "Me getting answers from witch in cave. Know where children are."

That stopped him in his tracks. For a second, I thought he'd drop to his knees too. He grabbed my forearms in earnestness, not anger, stepping in close as he moved his gaze over my features. "Where, Silver? Where is my niece?"

"Connaught," I announced.

The word rang in the clearing. The wolf's gaze shuttered. "Connaught."

"Is it a village?" I asked.

He flung my arms away and swore loudly, spinning away and striding from me into the bush.

A sinking feeling hit me hard. I glanced back at Aaden. "Was I tricked?"

His expression was one of sorrow–and a hint of disappointment. "In part. Connaught covers over a quarter of Ireland. You've narrowed the search, just . . ."

I curled my hands into fists. "Just not very well."

Aaden gripped my shoulder and we both winced at the stabbing sensation. "Don't sweat it. We have more to go on now. You're sure the witch was telling the truth?"

I nodded. "Where Cormac going?"

"He's having a sexy rampage," Orry hushed in my ear.

"He'll be okay," Aaden said. "He just allowed himself to hope. His niece is his world."

The sinking feeling in my stomach intensified. "Right."

"What else did the witch tell you?"

I peered up at the Seelie fae.

The creature has no downfall.

Her life is linked to yours as you are her vessel.

I glanced away. "Nothing."

Fourteen

Nothing. The lie lingered in my mouth as we set up camp, feeding the mounts, brushing them down, setting a fire. I made sure not to touch either man. I mean, not that Cormac was coming anywhere near me. The pain that had shot through me though when Aaden healed me ... that still hummed just under my skin. I rubbed at my thigh as if it would make the sting go away quicker.

"You cold, hun?" Orry asked. "You could get nearer to the fire. Or even get those two boys to sandwich you again."

I was beginning to think the bat was laughing at me. "No." I grunted.

Aaden looked at me, and I shrugged.

"Can't blame a bat girl for wanting to live vicariously through her bestie." Orry sighed and laid her head against my collarbone. "It's been a long time. A long, long time. Other bats just don't do it for me."

My interest was piqued, but I had bigger problems than deciphering Orry's woes.

The witch had appeared to come to this cave just to meet me. I was guessing she'd collapsed the cave as she and her tiger left. We'd set up camp near the mouth of the cave so our backs were to the rock. That was smart when camping out in the wilds. Have your back safe so you could defend your position easily.

But how was I meant to defend myself against people *in* the camp?

Namely, Aaden. I'd started to care for him. That was bad.

"Are you sure you aren't cold? You keep rubbing your arms." He reached for me, and I jerked away from the assured pain of his touch, stumbling against Cormac and getting a zing of home before he shoved me off.

I pulled energy from the rocks beside us to buoy me up and stop myself from faceplanting. Silver tendrils swooped around my body and literally grounded me.

"I need walk. Alone." I held up my hands.

"You'd best not run off," Cormac snapped. "You have a job to do. Don't you fucking forget it. I will hunt you to the far corners of both realms."

I could have said a thousand cutting things in response—I had a vault of insults from Kik—but I kept my mouth shut and walked off into the darkness. On instinct, I closed my eyes and let my feet lead. The ground was mossy, soft, damp, and a light rain started as I walked.

Inhale. Water close by. Some smaller critters. Ancient trees. It was safe to let my mind wander.

Nothing ...

I'd lied to Aaden and Cormac earlier, and my mother's words about liars rolled through me like a vile drink.

The edge of the water beckoned me, and I found myself staring into the purple pool, a swirl of waves washing over crystalline black sand. I dipped my chubby fingers into the water and came up with a tiny fish. I held the fish cupped in my hands. No, not a fish, a tiny mermaid.

"Hello." I whispered. "Friend?"

The mermaid bit me, and I flung my hand with a screech, sending her way out into the waves. Or I would have if a black-tipped eagle hadn't swooped down and snatched her from the air.

"Daughter."

I froze where I was and clenched my hand into a fist, hiding the bite wound. "Yes, Mother?"

"Life force gave creation heartbeat. Where heartbeat now?"

I swallowed hard. "I ... don't know."

Mother, glowing with her golden magic, cupped my chin so that I was looking up at her. "Lie? From daughter?"

Tears pooled in my eyes. I doubled down. "I don't know."

Her form was womanly, but she looked different each time I saw her. This time her hair was braided into hundreds of tiny braids, then wrapped around her head. Her skin was smooth and dark as night, her eyes equally deep and rich with wisdom.

"Liar haunted by lies. Eat from inside. Pecked apart by black-tipped eagle."

I felt her disappointment so keenly that I could barely breathe. Tears slipped down my cheeks. She'd never hurt me. Not with her hands. Not with her power. But with her words and lessons? Yes. "I didn't know."

"Until do, you stay."

My mother's golden power locked my body to the rock I'd sat upon. The sharp edges bit into my skin, through my thin clothes. The sun beat down on me, and I closed my eyes against it, sleeping in fits and starts because the night never came, not for three days.

She gave me just enough food.

She gave me just enough water.

But her hold on me did not weaken or shift. What was I to do? Mother clearly wasn't letting me go until I found the answer.

I spoke to the wind, telling the whipping breeze what had happened. "Mermaid, she bit, I throw back to ocean, eagle caught first."

Over and over again, I repeated the words. First softly, then screaming them, then crying.

Mother's haunting voice echoed around me, in the wind, reverberating through the very rocks. "Speak true. I know lie. You know lie."

Was there something I'd missed?

Mermaid bit. I threw. Eagle ate. That was truth.

If that wasn't the truth, then what did the truth mean? What did the truth mean to my mother? Had I misunderstood what she wanted from me?

What would appease her? What would save me from this torture?

My mother's mouthpiece, Lilivani, who interacted with fae on Underhill's behalf, had taught me something—a way to find paths that were hidden. I closed my eyes, placed my hands over my ears and sunk into myself. The magic within me replaced my sight with a vision of the world in new colors and new layers.

Good and evil lay before me, their paths interconnecting. I frowned. The balance of Underhill was different than it had been. I didn't like what I was looking at. It felt wrong. Unnatural.

I replayed the death of the mermaid again, and finally understood.

The words came to me, slowly. "I ... kill mermaid before time. Imbalance," I whispered.

One death had caused the magic to feel wrong.

Mother's golden presence washed over me, soothing away the ache of my skin, blistered from the weather and bleeding from the rocks.

Her voice rang out. "In truth, path clear. In lies, cost high."

I tipped my face up to the rain, and let it wash across my cheeks to remove the tears that had come unbidden with the memory and the old pain I'd forgotten or pushed away.

"What the hell? Where have you been. . ." A light blazed, and I was standing there, staring into golden-amber eyes. Cormac frowned. "Are you hurt?"

My throat was tight. I was still so deep in the memory that I couldn't speak around the past. I shook my head.

He stepped closer, holding a fisted hand up. His power flared in his fist, the source of the light. "Why are you crying?"

I closed my eyes and drew a ragged, hard breath. "Old wounds."

When I opened my eyes, he was closer yet. I'd not heard him move. His jaw ticked, and there was a struggle on his face. "Who hurt you?"

Anyone else might have thought he was just ... asking. Yet there was a threat in his voice, one I recognized. I shook my head, inhaling deeper this time. "No matter. Long time gone."

"They're dead?"

Lilivani was. When I was around seven, but that wasn't what upset me now.

"Just . . ." I tried to push past the Unseelie, not rough, just to return to the fire. My hand connected with his, and the sensation was as immediate as if vines had wrapped around our fingers, binding us together. The feeling robbed me of speech.

We both reeled away from each other, and the light from Cormac's fist extinguished.

"What the fuck is that?" he growled. "Why is that happening? It must've been the tree. Did it mess something up in us? Switch how you and Aaden feel for how the two of us feel?" He lowered his voice and turned away. "And what the hell happened in the cave when the *three* of us touched?"

They were all questions I'd had. The current answer? No idea. And that was all the answer I could imagine us getting for now. Touching Aaden was painful. Touching Cormac was heart-warming. Touching both at once... *fire.*

My belly tightened, and my legs trembled in a way I didn't like. I was *not* feeling that for Cormac. For Aaden, no problem.

Cormac?

Nope.

Big.

Fat.

Not.

Happening.

My body wasn't listening though. I hurried away, back along the path I'd taken. Shit, I'd walked a hell of a lot further than I'd realized, lost in my memories.

A quick peek at the sky showed the moon was up. Hours, I'd lost *hours* in that place of my past.

Aaden stood as I made it back to the fire. "Are you okay?"

"Fine."

"Fucking bullshit," Cormac said from behind me. "Someone hurt her."

"Who?" Aaden's stance immediately changed. "Did you kill them?"

"She won't tell me." Cormac sat down by the fire and scooped something from a pot over the open flames.

Both watched me. I shrugged. "Old wounds. Old hurt. No matter now. Help with path ahead."

My unicorn bunted me from behind, and I sat down under his head and neck, taking a bit of shelter from the rain.

"Someone hurt you bad enough that you just lost time thinking about it," Cormac said, then shoved a mouthful of what looked like stew into his mouth.

He'd noticed I wasn't truly present during our ride? "Lost time, yes. And... yes, hurt. In a strange way. One that takes thought to unravel because some good was there too."

Cormac swallowed, and simply watched me for a time before saying, "Those are the worst types of hurts. The ones where you've got to separate the love and hate, the likes and dislikes, before you can understand how you feel."

I'd never thought of it that way. He was exactly right. "You've had to do it?"

"I wasn't always a lone wolf. It's only since my niece arrived that I've returned in part to my family fold." Perhaps feeling my gaze, he added quietly—too quietly for Aaden to hear, "My father."

He had struggles with a parent too? I'd never spoken with a person who felt the same. "I'm sorry you went through that. It can feel like," I searched for the right phrase, "you're a branch splitting away from a tree."

Cormac dipped his head. "You want to know the worst part?"

I really did. "Please."

"When you go through all that—separating out everything—and you realize what you dislike and hate about that person outweighs the parts you like and love. And yet it's inherent that we love our parents. So, does that child-parent bond eliminate the need to *like* your parent? Are we meant to forgive all just because we are wired to love them?"

My chest was tight to a near-painful level. I hadn't gotten this far with my thoughts about mother. In truth, I tended to lose time as I had today, then shove the thoughts aside due to some pressing need to survive. "What is the answer?"

"There isn't an answer, Silver," he said softly. "That's what makes it hard. Only you can tally everything and see how the sum sits with your heart and who you are and what you know is right."

I leaned closer. "But for you. Did you find answer?"

His jaw clenched. "When it came to my father, my dislikes and hate outweighed the good. I decided that being my father didn't excuse him from everything else. When I thought of him as a person, a stranger, then the choice to remove him from my life was a simple one. I deserved better. I chose self-respect. Only the love I held for him as a son had delayed the inevitable and muddied the decision.

We sat for a long moment, Cormac returning to his stew.

"Thank you, Cormac," I said to him.

He looked at me, frowning slightly. "You're welcome. Can I ask you a question?"

Who would've thought that I'd ever have this type of conversation with Cormac? From fighting him—and maybe killing him if I got a lucky hit in—to this. I just didn't share with people like this, and the easiness of our exchange hit me *hard*. I already respected Cormac as a warrior. I respected that he was one of the few fae I'd met who was aware of his surroundings. He tended to anger in this situation with his niece being involved, yet I could understand that more now after hearing about his father. His niece must be extra important to him.

Could Cormac ask me a personal question? Oddly, I had no qualms about that, and that surprised *me* most of all. "Yes."

He tilted his head. "Are you the only child of Underhill?"

I smiled at the thought. "No. There are many."

"And all of you have the same father?"

I grinned this time. "No. Nearly all different fathers, I would guess."

Cormac leaned back, appearing as stumped as the stump he sat upon. "Really? Interesting. She keeps...busy."

A weight pressed on my chest, but I didn't utter the cause of it aloud. Maybe one day, if Cormac and I continued down this interesting, and a little exciting path, then I'd tell him all. Aaden too.

Cormac returned to his stew.

Why was I watching his mouth? What was so fascinating about a man eating? And why did it make me want to squirm where I sat? That experience in the cave had felt so good that I couldn't help thinking of it now. A glance at Aaden didn't help. The rain had slicked his hair, and he'd smoothed it back with his hand. The urge to taste the water on his skin was . . .new. Intriguing.

I squirmed more, reminding myself that touching Aaden wasn't as pleasant as my mind was trying to convince me it would be.

"Change things," I blurted. "Where do we look in morning? What cave first? What plan will you two make that not work?"

The two of them exchanged a look. Aaden nodded, and Cormac waved a spoon at the pot. "Eat and we'll talk."

Oh, so they were friends now, were they? Or were they ganging up on me? That was more likely. They thought they should be in charge of what happened next.

I doubted they had a clue.

Using a tendril of power, I lifted a bowl and spoon and hovered them near the pot. Aaden's eyebrows shot up, but he spooned in the stew, and I floated the dinner over to my dry spot under my unicorn's neck. "Where do we start?"

"That's ... a good trick," Aaden muttered. "How did you get your horse to stand so still?"

He was trying to distract me. Why?

I snorted. "Not horse, hornless unicorn." I spooned some of the watery stew into my mouth and wrinkled my nose. They were terrible cooks. Even I could do better than this. I magically stretched to the surrounding plants, letting my power gently brush up against them until I found a few that would add flavor. I plucked them and floated them back.

"How is she doing that?" Aaden whispered as if I couldn't hear him.

"Not hard." I sighed as the stew absorbed the herbs I plopped into the bowl, then sampled it again. Better, that was better.

"Wait, did you say hornless unicorn?" Cormac spluttered out his mouthful of stew.

"Where we go tomorrow?" I waved my spoon at them. "Where do we start in Connaught?"

Cormac pulled himself together first. "There are a lot of caves, some we know of, and many that have been hidden by shadows and magic. We need a way to narrow the search further."

"You did good," Aaden said. "You cut the search to one section of Ireland at least. Wait ... I can't get past the unicorn comment. Is that really a hornless unicorn?"

I'd wondered when they were going to realize what a gem we had in my new friend. Kik would have been a help too, but a unicorn? He'd be a real help. "He senses imbalances." I scratched at my unicorn's chest. "He may let us know when a situation will be dangerous for us."

The two guys were staring at me like I'd sprouted another head.

"He didn't warn us about the witch," Aaden blurted.

I smiled and scooped up my dinner. "Because he didn't sense anything that concerned him—in that we would come out relatively unscathed. Unicorns rarely interfere. If they do, consider yourself very fortunate."

The guys continued to stare at me like I'd sprouted a second head.

Orlaith giggled against my neck. "Oh, you got them now."

I fished a piece of meat out of the stew and held it up for her. "Eat?"

"No, I need fruit."

I plopped the meat into my mouth. "Orry needs fruit."

Aaden stared at me. "Orry?"

"Bat girl." I motioned to her.

He fished a long yellow fruit from a saddlebag and tossed it to me. I inspected it.

"You gotta peel that one, sweetie," Orry said. "Quick. I don't want to drool in your hair. I got plans for it after dinner."

I peeled the skin off, and she crawled into my lap to eat, munching away.

The conversation with Cormac and Aaden had pushed away the hold of the memory, but the feelings edged back in now that silence had. *Why* had that memory come to me?

Because I'd lied. Lying did not sit well with me, but revealing what I'd learned from the witch didn't feel right either.

Only ... my mother had taught me something else that day too. The truth had layers, and what was visible on the surface didn't always hold true beneath it.

There were paths that could be seen, just like Lilivani had shown me on Mother's orders. Pathways that showed what had been and what could be. Though I'd been young at the time, the blood fae's lessons weren't the type a person forgot.

I could look at the paths now. Though I hadn't done so in a long time. Doing so scared me because of the rock-mermaid encounter, but mostly because I had to cut myself off from my other senses while looking. Or at least the two main ones I'd used to stay alive in Underhill all these years. It left me vulnerable.

I didn't want to try now, not on Earth nor in my present company, but I didn't see another way.

Wearily, I met the heavy focus of the two men sitting across from me. "I will ride in front, with New Bestie. Follow my feelings. Eyes closed. Ears plugged. Senses open to other forces. You two protect me. Keep safe. I will be weaker."

What I was suggesting was incredibly dangerous considering we were up against something so monstrously evil. A creature that knew more than me, and a creature that could have set up this moment to catch me with my weapons blunted.

Cormac's gaze narrowed. "What forces?"

"Forces my mother will reveal to me."

He leaned forward. "Underhill?"

I nodded once, my chest tightening. To close off every physical sense and try to track evil based on feel ... I was about to swim into deep water. "I am trusting you."

More than I'd like to.

"You can trust us," Aaden said softly. "I will protect you, Silver." His green eyes were steady on mine, full of belief.

An incredible calm put the swirling fears in my belly to rest, and I was left gaping at the Seelie, filled with the urge to put my hands on either side of his face and ...

I licked my lips, my focus dropping to his mouth.

"Speak for yourself," Cormac said, standing suddenly.

"Asshole protects too." I gritted my teeth. "You want to find niece. You protect me with your life."

Golden-amber eyes swung my way and stared me down. Hard. The moment extended, long enough for me to see that my breath was synced with his. Strange.

The Unseelie sat again. "To find my niece, yes, I'll protect your scrawny ass."

I dipped my head at them both. "Eat. Sleep. Tomorrow, we ride into darkness with these eyes closed."

Fifteen

Aaden brushed the back of my hand, and my stomach lurched even as my skin prickled with the unpleasant stabbing sensations. "You sure about this? You seem unsettled. There are other ways..."

I patted New Bestie, meeting Aaden's gaze. "Other ways take too long."

Too long for the children to survive. I knew that much in my belly—their time was running out.

Cormac stalked back to join us. "Nothing and no one for miles. Let's get this over with."

The Seelie watched him swing onto his mount. "You're so pleasant in the mornings, wolf."

He shot Aaden a dry look, then surprised me by winking my way. "That's what they tell me."

A snort was the response, and I ignored their light-hearted exchange to turn to the hornless unicorn. "New Bestie, I will need help with what is ahead." He would walk me through this plane and the others.

He bunted me gently with his nose. "I will be there, child of silver." His voice was a deep timbered bass, and both boys had their mouths flapping open. Even though I'd told them, they hadn't really believed New Bestie was a hornless unicorn. Until he spoke.

"Is this going to mess up your hair?" Orry asked, her voice edged with panic. "I accidentally did it upside-down. I was disorientated hanging that way—got things confused. But I really like how things turned out!"

She'd braided my hair from the base of my skull upward and circled the strands into a loose bun at the crown of my head.

"Be riding slow," I assured her.

Taking a steadying breath, I mounted, not meeting the men's searching looks. "One in front, one behind."

"Who's in front?" Aaden adjusted the grip on his reins, his shoulders tensing.

I glanced at him. The question seemed loaded. Did he want to be in front? The answer was a simple one. A person couldn't trust a wolf at their back. "Cormac."

His brows drew in, and he jerked his head in a nod, circling his horse back.

Cormac nudged his mount closer, drawing alongside me. I studied the smirk playing on his lips.

"Don't worry, feral," he said in a conspiratorial tone. "He's used to being second."

I tilted my head. "In what way?"

The wolf grinned. "I've never met someone so eager to prove themselves, so capable at their job and position, who's never been promoted to a higher rank."

"That just means the people around him are idiots."

"Maybe in Underhill. Here it just means his family isn't good enough."

I glanced back over my shoulder and allowed my gaze to roam over the Seelie's stiff posture. Really, despite the fact that I far preferred Aaden's company to that of anyone else on Earth—except maybe Orry's—I suddenly realized he hadn't divulged a lot about himself. That he possessed sound qualities, I knew. But otherwise, *bizarrely*, I knew far more about Cormac.

Which was laughable.

"I know who I want at my back," I murmured to Cormac, half-noting the grin slipping off his face. I walked New Bestie toward Aaden, whispering to the golden bat on my neck. "You not with me in what follows, friend." A certain amount of power was needed to exist where I was going. Orlaith didn't have enough to survive the journey.

Orry exhaled as I gently pried her loose. "I don't like this. I don't like this one bit!"

Neither did I. "I'll be okay."

She clutched either side of her head. "Just promise me you won't get drawn in."

Drawn in? I frowned. I didn't recall anything about that. "In what way?"

"I don't know," she fretted. "I just remember my father mentioning it once. Some of the magic tied to Underhill can break a person's soul into pieces."

I pursed my lips. "It will be okay." Pausing next to Aaden, ignoring the slight pain as our thighs brushed against each other, I held Orlaith out to him. "Could you protect her while I am ... away?"

Aaden's face softened. "Of course, Silver. Sorry, I poked fun at Cormac for being pleasant in the mornings when really I'm the one in a temper."

Why did people dance around the truth here? Would I ever understand it? "I do not think you are second. That is why you protect my back. That is the first position with me. I see your worth."

His inhale was audible. Checking Orry was safely hooked onto the neckline of his tunic, I paused before reaching over to squeeze Aaden's hand for good measure.

We both winced.

Then smiled.

I circled New Bestie around him again. Really, we had to figure out this painful touching business. I had plans for Aaden when this was done. Before I returned to Mother.

Maybe he could visit sometimes too.

Cormac didn't wait to move ahead of me. I stopped in the middle of the Seelie and Unseelie, then wrapped silver power around my throat. "Adjust as needed. I will find our direction."

I hoped.

Letting my power drop, I patted the unicorn again—more for my own comfort—then swallowed hard.

Nothing for it.

"Now," I whispered.

Closing my eyes, I pushed away the sensation of wind on my skin. I covered my ears to block out the birdsong and rustling of leaves. I rid myself of the feeling of the unicorn beneath me. I became numb to the knowledge of the sky and sun above. The soil under.

The very air.

My body.

I removed my very soul from the landscape I physically inhabited. For nothing physical belonged in a place of magic and fate.

Suspended in this layer of the living, I lowered my hands, opened my eyes, and licked my lips at the explosion of color dancing and weaving before me.

I could count the number of times I'd been here on one hand since the mermaid encounter. Even then, I recalled strongly the feeling of wrongness which had been the drive behind me not returning here in many years.

That remembered wrongness had nothing on *this*.

Outwardly, ribbons and threads of color twisted in a seemingly joyful manner. Inwardly, I choked on the atrocity of what I felt. The ribbons were land eels writhing over one another in search of raw meat. Shadows flicked across their lengths, dulling their vibrancy.

I didn't know what these ribbons were. In my previous visits, they weren't here. Or maybe my younger self hadn't noticed. But no, I was certain these hadn't been present. The way they weaved ...

They weren't weaving at all.

I peered closer, swallowing down the bile that wished to rise. "They're branching."

The ribbons were connected.

Magic didn't do such a thing. A fae drew energy from their surroundings to fuel their power. Power didn't lock end to end unless two people wished to battle to the death. Even then, a battle lasted a finite amount of time, until the stronger fae drained the other.

It would not just *exist* like these threads did.

This was not magic. I could not say what the ribbons were ... but they were *wrong*.

So wrong I felt my place in this layer shaking and fading, my very being trying to wrench free of it.

"Focus," I hissed.

There had to be something from what Lilivani said on one of our two trips here. I cast my mind back, but that detail—if she'd discussed it with me—had been lost.

I peered more closely at the shadows rippling over the ribbons. They seemed to be central to the unnatural feeling of this plane. Where were they coming from? A visual sweep didn't give me the answer.

Fuck.

Steeling myself, I walked forward against my better judgment. The ribbons shied away like opportunistic savages when faced with a threat.

I was no threat.

Not in this sorry, dreadful place where I could only observe and not act.

I walked. And turned. And walked some more.

Finally, stopping, I planted my feet, then braced myself before reaching for a ribbon. The blue thread reared back, then raced away, becoming lost in the general tangle. My head felt like it was in vise. Keeping down bile was growing harder. My instincts had been screaming for so long and so hard, they were starting to whimper and beg.

I could not remain here.

And I couldn't leave without learning *something*.

Drawing on my silver magic, I tentatively released the tiniest wisp of power. It shone like nothing else in this layer, a beacon—and it summoned something from the depths of this place. A thick golden ribbon reached toward me, extending so far back its journey seemed to cross time itself, centuries and millennia, to reach me. As it came toward me, its shine extinguished mine with its eye-watering brilliancy.

"Mother?" I asked.

I touched my silver wisp to the gold ribbon. An explosion rocked my ears as I was propelled through the plane, sent flying by an invisible blow of giant proportions. I rolled to a stop and dragged in a painful breath. Broken ribs.

Note to self: Don't touch the ribbons.

Hauling myself upright, one arm pressed against my ribs, I froze. Millions of ribbons surrounded me in orderly circles, their ends pointed upright, like cobras ready to strike. They hovered there, each swaying in an individual rhythm.

I didn't dare move.

I didn't dare breathe.

A deep, agonized scream reverberated upward, and I saw something that I'd missed in the original tangle of ribbons. On the floor of this plane lay limp black ribbons. They resembled the rotting leaves of a plant touching wet ground.

In jerking movements, the black ribbons began to rise.

I screamed, kicking off a thin one that wrapped around my leg. My head rocked to the side as a *huge* black rope hit me. What were these? Why were they here?

For lack of any better ideas, I gathered my silver and pushed it out around me in a barrier, then paused as the thick black ribbons beat against my bubble of power, retreating with each strike. These ribbons were the source of the shadows. They were branching and seemed to be causing the other surrounding ribbons to branch also.

They were the wrongness here.

My knees shook under the weight of their blows.

I still had no answers, but I had to get away from them.

I ran, barrier raised in front of me, and the pressure eased slightly. Enough for me to spot a red ribbon plucking away a black one before it could strike against my power.

They were helping me?

"I need your aid," I shouted.

The sweetest song floated through the air, lifting my heart. The ground started to leap and buck, throwing me high, and as I spun through the air, I looked directly down.

Color shot upward from the ground like lava from millions of tiny volcanos. The color pinned down the shadows and darkness, and hope seared me at the sight.

The view from up here was so different.

Saddening.

Black snaked out in every direction like a network of water. It was *everywhere*. A low moan fell from my lips at the horrible sight. This was like the soul tree in the Irish court, but *so much worse*. The black was thicker off to the left in the distance. The area I'd entered held the most color, and I shuddered to think that I might've accidentally entered right into the shadows.

I landed in a crouch and was shoved sideways by the darkness. A gold ribbon tried to help, but five dark ribbons strangled it, pinning it to the ground.

My entire body shook.

I couldn't stay here.

This place was infiltrated with vileness.

Tears fell from my eyes as I backed away, my voice hoarse. "I'm so sorry I can't help you."

The apology was lost to the furious and futile battle stretching around me.

I opened the doorway to my physical form once more. The sky returned. The sun. Wind rushing in my ears. Thundering hooves.

A branch slapped my cheek. Roars filled my ears. Bellows.

Woodenly, I stared at the hundreds of animals bearing down on me from all sides. Stampeding. Murder in their eyes.

I swayed, and my head thumped to my chest. I blinked at the back of my unicorn, at the blood dripping onto him.

From me?

Shouts echoed in my ears. I listed sideways, my mind already shutting down into a quiet, unknowing bliss. Cormac's face filled my vision, etched with rage.

Off.

Down.

Out.

Sixteen

Hands and voices. Prior to that it had been hooves and feet jammed into my middle, snapping bones, shoving me hard into the earth.

All I could feel and hear were those hands and voices ... and a pain that was weirdly distant. Maybe it wasn't that bad?

My eyes felt like they were glued shut, sticky with something warm. Blood?

As if the word unleashed my senses, a coppery tang slid up my nose and down the back of my throat. I gagged and choked, the movement of my chest sending waves of agony through me. I couldn't breathe.

My body didn't feel right. It was bad. Something terrible had happened to me.

"Turn her over!"

Hands touched my skin, the resulting pain like thorns driving into my flesh. Screams built in my chest but couldn't burst past the blood, and I didn't dare move again.

I was flipped around, and the blood poured out of my mouth and down my chin. I still couldn't breathe. The position may have taken care of the pooling blood, but it had done nothing to help the immense, roaring pain.

How could so many places hurt at once?

"I can't fucking touch her."

"Give her to me!"

One set of hands hurt, but the other set felt too good, as if they were luring me into a trap.

I fought them both. Weak, futile attempts, for every move I made pushed me toward blacking out, but I still hit something soft.

A grunt, and then no one was touching me. I was on the ground, my fingers digging into the soil as I pulled energy into myself, drawing on the surrounding world to ease the agony.

Or at least I tried to.

I pressed my face into the ground, damp moss cushioning my cheek as I struggled to get my bearings. I'd been in the in-between, and when I came out, a stampede of animals had been rushing down on us. On me.

And now, there was something terribly wrong with me.

"Idiots!" A woman's voice snapped through the air. *Mother*.

The errant hope was gone as soon as it arrived. Not even with me on the cusp of death would my mother interfere with balance. If I was to live, I'd live. If I was to die, then die I would.

Still, I hoped she'd come for me and would soothe away the hurt as I'd seen other mothers do with their young.

"You'd let her bleed to death? Internally, externally, it's all a terrible idea!"

Bleed to death? I was injured that badly? Maybe that's just what I thought because I was dying. I reached for my magic again and pulled more energy from the plants and trees. The stones and soil. Even though I couldn't see them, I could feel their energy. The burst of vitality stirred my mind, though it didn't really help my wounds.

Injured ribs, I knew that much. I kept my breathing slow and drew in a little air, then unstuck one eye so I could look around.

I found myself staring at a mottled gray, felted shoe that curled at the point. Rolling up my head, I looked at the person standing over me. A woman dressed in a gray-ish robe that swirled and danced all around her as if it were alive. No . . . that wasn't quite right.

"Idiots," She shouted and waved four wrinkled hands at the boys.

Four? I blinked slowly, then looked again. The image didn't change. She had four hands, four arms, and her skin was the same gray as her felted shoe. *Unless*.

I reached for the shoe and found myself touching skin. Fuzzy skin.

Troll.

Those hands reached down and scooped me up, somehow holding me without pressing in on my ribs. Or what was left of them. My body sagged strangely in the middle. Not broken, *shattered*. My ribs had been demolished.

"Like a bag of ice," she muttered as she balanced me carefully. I gazed into her face with my one open eye. She squinted down at me, then spoke louder, as if my ears were broken and not the rest of me. "Your ribs ... it's like a bag of ice inside your chest, and those bits have cut your insides. You're bleeding out. We need to get you healed and that's going to take some time."

"No time," I mouthed the words even as Cormac yelled, "We don't have any time."

She sniffed and shrugged. "To my hut first. We will discuss time and what it means and why you must have it, or you must not."

Was this the oracle? She spoke oddly, and coming from me, that was saying something.

A flutter of wings sounded over our heads, and Orry landed on the woman's shoulder. When she tried to creep closer, the top right hand of the old woman pushed her back. "Leave her alone. You cannot help her, bat. Barely alive, she is. Good thing that she has big magic to pull on. Good thing she thought of it while two oafs are dancing about flapping gums."

Orry sniffed, and a tiny tear slid from her. "I won't hurt her."

I had no strength in me to reassure her. Between the injuries and whatever had happened in the in-between, I had nothing left to give.

"Is she going to be okay?" Aaden hurried alongside us, and I caught glimpses of his drawn face and the worried pinch to the skin around his green eyes. Scared, he was scared for me.

I didn't like seeing that. He was usually so quietly certain. Steady as a tree. I *needed* him to be steady as a tree.

"She'd better be," Cormac snapped.

Orry shuddered and crawled as close as she could. "Hang on, Silver, please!"

I was looking at Orry one moment, and the next I was being lowered onto something soft and enveloping. Above me were objects suspended from the ceiling by strings. Little items. Some I recognized like flowers and rocks and feathers, and a few of them I couldn't place. Items made of a creamy white, carved into different shapes.

"You're part troll," Aaden spoke. "You're a collector."

"I am both those things," the woman agreed. "A child of a human and troll liaison. To the human's, I am a witch in the forest, and I am a monster to those of you in the fae world." Hands brushed over me carefully. "It is good that I am a monster, for I am what those animals ran from. Not you and your puny swords. They'd have killed her for the disturbance she caused in our delicate balance within this forest."

Orry had managed to tuck into the crook of my neck. "She's not lying. All the animals seemed to come straight for you, it was crazy!"

"Why?" I whispered the word, though not much sound came out.

"Why?" The old woman leaned over me. I could see more hints of troll in her face now. Her irises were oriented the wrong way, and her ears were large and pointed. "Because you touched the darkness and showed it another path into our world, little fool. Lucky for you, it didn't follow you out. Anyone less powerful would have been killed twice over. Once by the darkness, and once by these injuries. You are a gem. A treasure. Even if a foolish one." She leaned back and sighed, then said to herself, "Perhaps you were preordained to be a fool at that time, who can say? Surely not me."

She spoke of the black ribbons in the in-between. I could feel them again, wrapping around me, so full of violence and rage—of the desire to destroy everything they touched.

I'd nearly set them loose on the world?

The urge to vomit surged, and the best I could do was turn my head. I couldn't even roll to the side of the bed.

"There, now you see how bad it almost was. But almost is not 'is.' So we are still safe here in my hut," the old woman cooed as she wiped my face and arms with a cool cloth. For a half troll, she was rather kind. Nothing like the trolls I'd encountered in

Underhill. Her kindness made me wonder what she'd want in exchange for helping me.

Orry buried in closer and lowered her voice. "Silver, I don't think it's safe here. She hoards things. Things of power."

I peered up at the objects dangling over our heads. There were gemstones here and there amongst the other items, and a few flickered with a light that didn't seem to come from anywhere but within. Her hoarding habit made me think of dragons. Dragons were neither good nor bad, but they were powerful.

How much power did this woman have, or was she the kind of being that stole power?

"Do you have a name at least?" Cormac came around to the top of the bed, near my head.

"Sadhbh." With her two sets of arms, she worked a mortar and pestle, the scents of fresh herbs and sharp spices overpowering the smell of vomit. The other arms snatched at tinctures and powders on the table. Pungent scents. Liquid that hissed. A bottle of something that rung like chimes when the contents were added into the mixing bowl.

Orry squeaked. "She's dangerous." With a louder voice she said, "My father said that she's the one ... he said she . . .souls could be ... I thought she was dead." Her words were stuttering and full of fear.

Sadhbh glanced over. "Most think me dead, aye, and I like to be keeping it that way so you and your bat and your boys can pretend like you never did meet me once you be done and healed and gone. That be the deal-ee-o."

Lie. Her eyes and mouth didn't match up as she spoke. What exactly was she lying about though?

Cormac moved between me and Sadhbh. "We need her healed fast. Not weeks, not days. Lives depend on her." He didn't seem happy about that either.

Sadhbh paused in her preparations. "Healing her faster would hurt her. You're willing to cause deep pain to this silver-haired woman whose touch you yearn for?"

He held her gaze before glancing away.

Though I didn't want deep pain, I was in agreement with Cormac. We needed to hurry.

"Don't hurt her more," Aaden said from behind where I lay.

Sadhbh watched me closely. "What about you? You have one for and one against."

"Heal me," I whispered the two words with difficulty. I could handle pain. I couldn't handle waiting around to see what this half-troll was going to do.

With one of her hands, she pried open my mouth and dumped the entire contents of the mortar into me, then shoved my mouth shut.

Ten long seconds passed as the cordial sank in.

My eyes bugged as the heat in the spices hit me suddenly, like dragon fire crawling down my throat, burning its way to my belly and coating my insides. I couldn't get away from it.

My body was still in some sort of state of paralysis from the in-between.

"How bad is it going to be?" Aaden was at my side, his fingertips brushing close enough that I'd probably be flinching away from him if I weren't dealing with the fire ripping through my body.

"Oh, it'll hurt her bad, but not just body pain, some deep soul pain. You two really are idiots, aren't you?" Sadhbh shook her head. "The animals trampled her and would have killed her if not for her hornless unicorn friend there standing over her. The animals thought she was on the side of the dark one that has been roaming these lands. They crushed her ribs, so we must create new ones. But rebuilding a body means we need some of her deepest tissues, and then payment for giving her new bones, and that don't come from nowhere."

"Like Harry Potter! Is it like the stuff that grows skeletons?" Orry squeaked and flapped her wings. "I've read all the Harry Potter books!"

"Bah. Nothing like that at all, bat! It doesn't taste horrible, but the melding cordial is incredibly hot. The pain comes in waves after." Sadhbh waved one of her hands at Orry.

My other eye popped open, but I couldn't get my mouth to do the same. Lava, I had lava inside of me, but my mind circled away from that and to what the half-troll woman just said.

Sadhbh knew something about the creature of darkness we sought? I tried to unstick my jaw. We needed information.

Surely one of the boys would ask her the pertinent questions. *Surely* they understood that this half-troll woman could help us? She was dangerous, though, and we needed to take what we could and run. Just like stealing from a dragon's hoard.

"It will take a few hours to get the ribs to a fragile but usable state," Sadhbh murmured. I tracked her movement. "Moments from now, she will sink into a deep, healing sleep. When she wakes, then you may go."

She smiled at me and gave a soft wink that set my heart pounding. Predator. She was a predator and we'd walked into her lair.

"I thought you said she would be in great pain?" Cormac said. "She's hardly moving."

Of course he'd be *hoping* that I'd suffer, the great asshole that he was.

"Don't worry about her," Sadhbh patted him with three of her hands, gripping him with her fingers as if ... testing how thick his muscles were? Was she going to *eat* him? "She will be in immense pain. Might not look it, but that's why I put her to sleep. That amount of screaming is nothing any of us needs. Bringing the locals down on us is no good."

As she spoke, the cordial sunk deeper into my blood and my eyes drooped. My belly sunk, and the first lance of true pain shot across my chest. Like a ghost rib being jabbed back into place, through my skin. Then another and another.

If I'd been able to scream, there would have been no holding back. I wanted to arch my back, to writhe and dance away, to fight this agony that built inside my chest.

"It works in our favor to have her sleeping and unable to move, as strange as that may seem." Sadhbh patted my head, scratching at my scalp with long fingernails, hard enough to draw a little blood, though the scratch itself was nothing compared to the state of the rest of my body. "Now you two, shall we get you something to eat?"

Don't eat the food. My gaze sought out Aaden's, then Cormac's. They were focused on the half-troll.

Sadhbh smiled down at me as she spoke, then leaned in close as she stroked my hair. "You will heal, my pet. But those two, those two will give me trouble."

Pet.

I swallowed hard as she stood and clapped all four of her hands. "Food for the two of you."

I couldn't speak. I tried to. I tried to reach for Cormac as he turned away. He was the more distrusting of the two.

But I had no control over my body. I was trapped as I sunk down deep into the unknown, my consciousness buried under waves of sleep.

"You little moron, what kind of shit have you gotten yourself into this time?"

I almost sighed with relief. "Sigella."

Seventeen

The tea room was different this time.

My pain was gone in this in-between place; I stood and perused the savage tears in the wallpaper on the far wall. "I like what you've done with place."

Sigella paused her tea pouring mid-flow, and regarded me with a mild expression. "I see your sense of humor is still intact if nothing else."

"Bad shape?" I strode closer to the tears in the wall and peered through them into the darkness, hoping to catch a glimpse of the children. Alive.

Sigella sighed, and I listened to her quiet swallow as she sipped her tea.

"Obviously I couldn't leave my tea room open to any old riff-raff. There is a seal on the room," she said. Her expression darkened. "Though will it hold? Now, after centuries, will my efforts crumble?"

I half-turned, unwilling to give the tears on the wall my back despite her reassurances about the seal. "Your efforts to escape?"

She sipped her tea again, watching me over the rim of the dainty cup. "You know, you're sounding almost civilized. If I knew you were capable of learning, I might've invited you here more over the years, and not just when you were on death's door."

I walked slowly back to her, scanning the room, but everything else appeared the same as it had last time. There had to be a clue in here somewhere though. Powerful people liked trophies. Old Bastard, my dragon friend, collected naga skulls. He had a neat row of them that stretched about half his length. I always kept a tooth when I took down a tarbeast.

This woman was too powerful not to have a trophy of some kind.

"Why didn't you?" I asked on my way to a cabinet against the far wall. "Invite me."

She set down her teacup and flicked at an invisible speck of dust on her voluminous skirt. "I rather think because I hate you."

My brows rose. "I have never knowingly done harm to you. Why do you hate me?" I reached the cabinet, then answered my own question. "Because I am your prison." That was essentially what the witch had told me.

The tea room darkened as though thick clouds had shifted overhead.

"Thorn. She wasn't always such a cold-hearted bitch," Sigella announced in a menacing voice. "Yes. You are."

And she needed me alive to escape.

"I'm only twenty-one. I can't be your first prison." She'd mentioned *centuries*.

Tea cups rattled in threat. "No. You talk and move a lot more than my last prison though." Her remark seemed to amuse her.

She'd had a prison before me? I peered into the cabinet, shaking my head at all the teacups and pots and tea-related objects that I would have no idea how to use. "Have you considered that I would be more helpful to you if you told me what you needed to escape?"

I walked to the next glass cabinet.

"I have considered past lessons."

More tea cups. "Past lessons," I mused. "In that you no longer trust others?"

Silence.

Another cabinet. How many fucking tea cups did one person need? "Then I guess we'll keep meeting like this each time I nearly die?"

I strode past a half-toppled wooden cabinet, then stopped abruptly as Sigella replied, "No."

She'd risen.

"No?" I ventured.

"Saving you will come with a price tag this time."

"Yet you need me alive to escape."

Her gown flickered to dirty rags before flickering back, and I tensed when she appeared directly before me.

"Escape *alive*," she breathed. "There is escape in death, too, and as the years pass, death does hold a growing appeal."

I considered that. "Centuries, you said earlier. Does a person hold on for centuries only to give up when their escape grows more likely?"

Sigella watched me through narrowed slits. "More likely in what way?"

"More likely in that I can help you."

She scoffed. "Help. No one *helps*, little girl. People only exchange and take."

I couldn't argue too much with that. "I would like to help if I can."

Sigella scoffed again and, in a swirl of fabric, marched back to her table. I quickly crouched and opened the half-toppled cabinet behind me. I would've walked past if she hadn't done so much to distract me from it.

Inside was a sole object. A heavy, square wooden board etched with a large circle. Smaller circles were carved at each corner. Rings and lines filled the largest circle in what was clearly a pattern but resembled a maze to my eyes.

Footsteps sounded behind me, and the hairs on the back of my neck prickled.

"Is it a game?" I asked her.

"It was meant to be a game," she answered quietly. "And that is a game, yes. Similar to chess, called Fidchell. I should have known better, perhaps, than to try to beat him at his own game." The woman laughed bitterly. "Close the case."

My fingers itched to explore the board further, but I closed the cabinet once more. "Who–"

"If you wish to leave here alive, then you must make me a promise," she announced, gesturing to the empty seat across from her.

I crossed over and sat. "What kind of promise?"

"The binding kind."

"And what is it?"

Her eyes glittered. "If you wish to survive the half-troll and your injuries from the scale realm, then you must promise me blood from the Oracle's soul."

Scale realm was her term for the realm filled with ribbons? The name did fit the feel of the place. And should I be happy she didn't want my firstborn? "How do I collect blood from a soul?"

"The Oracle's soul does not reside within her body. It has legs." Her gaze swept to the cabinet containing the Fidchell board. "It is *his* blood I need."

"And if I refuse?"

"Then you can remain here. The children will die. We will follow." A wide grin stretched across her painted lips. "I do not choose death as a rule, but I am vindictive enough to choose it to prove a point."

That seemed like a bluff. Her actions until now—despite hating me, despite being stuck in this place for so long—countered her words. "What will collecting his blood do to me?"

"Why, nothing I would say, if you are fast enough. In my experience, though, not many people like to bleed."

"If the Oracle lives up to her name, won't she see me coming?"

Sigella poured tea into an empty cup, and I eyed it with distaste. Somehow, I had a feeling that was for me and that I wouldn't like what it did.

"Paths open and close with a blink, a breath, and a sneeze, child. The Oracle knows this better than most. Understands it better than most. There is little point in staring at the future that could so readily change. Besides if you could see all, would you not choose to be surprised?"

No. "So you have no idea if she'll know I'm coming."

Irritation flashed in her gaze, but she set the pot down and recovered her mild expression before answering, "Best be prepared. Don't let the cloak fool you. She's a fighter." Her lip twisted into a snarl. "And she lowered herself enough to become involved with that line."

I picked up the tea cup and sniffed. She'd just pour it down my throat anyway. "One more question. If I collect this blood for you, then what will you do with it?"

Blood was important. Blood was powerful. She could do any number of things to the Oracle. Or she could take revenge on this man for the actions of his forebears, whoever they were.

"I will break my bindings," she hissed.

"Will that kill the man or the Oracle?"

The paint on her lips began to run down her chin like drops of blood. "They will live on as they are."

I nodded. "Then you have a deal. Blood from the Oracle's soul for my survival."

She wiped a long, black fingernail over her chin and scooped up some of the liquid. Holding my attention, she held her finger over my tea cup. Drip. Drip.

Sigella leaned back, her savage form gone again. "Do drink up and stop wasting my time." She poured more tea into her cup. "If you fail to fulfill our bargain, then I will not hesitate to kill you and everyone you love in a most horrific way."

I gulped back the contents.

The blow to my forehead was invisible, a mallet slammed with vicious force to push me from the tea room and back to the living world. I fell back off my seat—and bolted upright in bed in the troll's abode.

I took a few breaths, allowing my mind to settle and take in that the blood previously covering my naked body was gone. I couldn't recall being washed ever. Maybe mother did it when I was really young—more likely designated the task to Lilivani—but those memories weren't present. In their place were those of edging closer to the river to clean while wondering if a creature lurked in the deep ready to lunge.

Aaden and Cormac! I swung my legs over the side of the bed and didn't bother with my clothes. Snatching up my bow and arrows and dagger, I left the room that would have been *my* prison, I was certain, if the troll got her way.

At the end of the hall, firelight flickered against the wooden walls. There should have been three voices speaking. The silence spoke louder than words.

I spun my dagger in my grip and held it high to walk into the chamber.

Relief poured through me at the sight of my companions intact and sitting in armchairs by the fire. Except a closer look showed me they appeared locked there, immobile beneath a mobile of trinkets and gems similar to the one that had hung over my bed. Their eyes were glazed and fixed on the slowly spinning objects.

"They are not as powerful as you yet," the troll murmured from a table in the far corner. She'd picked them clean of their belongings and was inspecting her haul. She glanced back. "But even you should still be under with the dose I gave you." The troll frowned. "And still quite injured." She fully turned. "Who aided you?"

"Unlock my companions from your spells and return their things, and choose to live," I told her calmly. "Fail to do those things, and choose to die."

She turned back to the table and held a small painting high. It was of a young girl, set in a gold frame. The portrait had to be of Cormac's niece. "I could look at what I am, at how I can exist amongst neither humans nor other supernatural beings as anything but a curse. Or I could see myself as a creature who can survive in the light or the darkness." The troll faced me. "I care not if the darkness wins or if you are the victor. There is no stake in it for me. I will simply continue living on."

"If you are alive."

The troll tilted her head. "While you are precocious and will be formidable, there is much that yet stands in the way. You will not win an exchange between us."

I'd fought trolls in the caves. Though they were slow, their skin was near impossible to penetrate. But nature demanded balance. Strength always required a weakness. For a *full-blooded* troll, that weakness was behind their left ear.

The half-troll charged without warning, roaring loudly enough to shake the walls.

I dodged out of her path, then spun, pushing silver power out to shove me in a circle behind her. I leaped, arrows rattling in the quiver across my back as I drove my dagger into the space that would kill her full-blooded brethren.

The air rushed from my lungs, and I grunted as I hit the wall above the fireplace and crashed to the wooden floor.

Cormac's finger twitched as I hauled myself upright.

"You have fought some of my ancestors, I see," she said gleefully. "And how do I compare?"

That blow should have killed her. So she didn't compare, as she well knew.

Where was *her* weakness?

"You are trying to figure out where my vulnerability is," she sighed. "Unfortunately, your vulnerability is plain. Or should I say vulnerabil*ies*?"

The troll charged from the doorway toward Aaden and Cormac.

I cast my dagger aside and swung my bow off my back, digging into my quiver. The troll paused in her attack; her eyes gleaming as they landed on my weapon.

"What is *that* treasure?" she breathed.

I drew out an arrow, an arrow far heavier than those from the quiver I'd already used. I set it against the bow and drew back. *This is going to hurt.* I had no idea where I was aiming. "It's your end."

Releasing, I didn't blink as the arrow shot straight forward, then executed a tiny circle in front of the troll to angle in under her ribs to her heart.

My knees gave way, and I slammed to the ground as pain swept through me.

A shocked gaze rose to mine. "How very human of me."

The troll toppled backward to the ground, sending dust out in a wave.

I wheezed through the pain branching through my body. Then, staggering to my feet, I dropped my bow and found my dagger, making quick work of severing the mobiles from above the men and casting them into the fire.

Aaden dragged in a huge breath, clutching the armrests of his chair.

Cormac blinked a few times, his chest rising slower but just as much. He broke the silence. "The troll is dead."

I grabbed my other weapons and crossed the room to jab the end of my bow into one of the troll's open eyes. No reaction. "Dead."

Crouching, I studied the arrow jutting out from under her ribs. Given the troll's power, I would have expected the toll of shooting the arrow to be a lot worse. I rubbed the feathers between my fingers, and they crumbled in my grip.

To tea leaves.

Sigella. I stood and met Cormac's questioning look.

"How are you healed already?" he asked.

I strode to the table. "I had help. We must leave now. Grab your things." I picked up the portrait of his niece and walked to him, holding it out.

Cormac's accusing amber gaze dropped to the small frame. He took it and slid it into the breast pocket of his tunic, then swept past me toward the table. "You *will* answer my questions one day, Silver."

I focused on the magic threads in the room, following a small golden one to a painting of a shiny red apple on the wall. Standing before it, I pushed it aside and opened the cupboard behind. I hooked the shivering bat on my finger. "Are you okay, Orry?"

"I thought you were a goner!" She flung herself against my neck and held on tight. "She put me in there after Aaden and Cormac went all frozen. She said she was going to use my blood!"

I stroked her back. "It's all okay now, Orry." Well, not really, but it was temporarily true. "We must go."

She shuddered. "The sooner the better. But . . ." The bat took flight and landed on the troll's clawed right hand. Orry hooked her claws under the troll's fingernails and scraped them clean. "Blood is power," the bat explained in response to my look. "Best not to leave it lying around. We should clean up the other room before we go." She glanced up at me. "And get your clothes too. If you want these guys capable of actually doing anything."

I looked back at Aaden and Cormac. Aaden looked like a starved beast ready to devour a meal. Gone were his red cheeks, and I felt a sudden and strong surge of hunger as I took him in. Cormac looked about as furious as always, but I noted he was taking particular care *not* to glance my way.

"We leave as soon as possible," I told them. "We have our direction."

Aaden dragged his focus up from the apex of my thighs. "You do?"

"*You* do," I answered. "What direction was I riding in just before the animals came?" I'd been facing the darkness, the black ribbons, in the scale realm. The position of my body would have been mirrored on Earth too.

"North-west," he replied after a beat, then looked at Cormac, who nodded.

So much had happened in the last few hours. I hadn't even begun to process it all, but the memory of the writhing darkness in the scale realm caused my skin to rise in small bumps. That darkness contained many things, and one of them was a cave filled with children.

North-west.

"That is where the cave resides," I announced. "That is where we must go."

Eighteen

There wasn't much time left in the day as we rode from the half-troll's home. Around us, the forest settled down into the last bird calls as the sun lowered behind the horizon.

"We need to put distance between us and the troll's hoard," Cormac barked. "A full troll would have booby traps laid out, to spring in the event they're killed. We have to assume that's the case here."

I agreed with him, silently, but I didn't say so. For one thing, I wanted to keep his ego in check. For another, my reserves were low. I couldn't take another attack without a good night's sleep and some food in my belly. Not a physical one, and not an exchange of barbs with Cormac.

Aaden spurred his horse forward. "Then we go for as long as we safely can."

The forest was thick, and the brambles tore at my legs, but New Bestie kept forging his way through it, seemingly impervious to cuts and scrapes

I leaned into his neck and pressed my cheek to his mane, less worried about booby traps than I was about my deal with Sigella and the darkness that was enveloping the world.

"You are quiet, new friend." I said so only he could hear me. "Why?"

If he'd been Kik, he'd have told me to take a flying fuck into the trees if he wasn't ready to talk. But a unicorn, even a hornless one, was a gentler creature than an ancient land kelpie with an attitude problem.

He blew a snort as we loped along, covering the ground with ease even through the thickest bits of undergrowth, almost as if the plants and trees parted for him. "As a being that would protect you, I watched you in the scale realm. I saw what you saw."

I shuddered. "Unnatural."

"Natural," he countered. "But concerning."

"The black is similar to the black on the soul tree in the Irish court."

The unicorn was quiet, probably tallying up the balance of the moment. "Do you know what the black is doing to the tree?"

Not truly. But my instincts said one thing. "Killing it."

"Yes, child of gold."

I blinked. "The black is killing the ribbons in the scale realm like it's killing the tree of souls." I took a breath. "New Bestie, what does it mean if all the joyful ribbons are overcome?"

"Then the scale realm is no longer a scale," he said quietly. "More, I am not able to say without affecting balance."

I'd never understood the ribbons and had left the scale realm with the acknowledgement I *still* wouldn't understand. Yet for the scale realm to die...

There had to be ramifications to that in all realms. Huge ramifications.

"There is something tugging at me. I first sensed it while waiting on your return from the scale realm. It is tearing at my senses, and I have come to believe it will be useful to your survival. Though something about it worries me."

"What kind of something?" I asked.

The hornless unicorn tossed his head, forcing me to sit up. "It is an item of great power and great chaos, an object best kept rooted at all times."

That one took me a moment. "This thing of chaos might help us? How?"

He pulled far ahead of the two fae men.

The plants that had opened for us closed behind New Bestie. Aaden and Cormac's surprised shouts were lost as we cantered ahead.

"When unrooted, this item needs to be fed," New Bestie finally said. "Its appetite is darkness. Do you understand?"

An object that ate darkness? That sounded perfect.

"So it will search out a big hunk of darkness like a divining rod?" Orry offered, lifting her head from my neck.

New Bestie bobbed his head. "I believe so. Which would lead you to the children."

I glanced over my shoulder. The two men pushed their mounts hard to keep within sight of us through the gnarled branches. I'd pay for running off later. More questions. Less sleep. "Why did you take me from them to tell me these things? Are they not friends?"

New Bestie slowed. "Together, they present an unusual symmetry. Apart, not. I have never come across such a phenomenon. One male wishes to save all, valuing none above another, and hopes to prove himself in the process. The other wants to save a single child, with no regard for any other and believes he has nothing to prove. That his family name will absolve any choices he makes. They are driven by different motivations. I wish to see how they'll react in this moment without preparation to increase my knowledge. You are my rider, which means I will protect you. But will they?"

Ouch.

"In other words, her taste in men is shit." Orry sighed. "Girl, I feel that all the way to the tip of my wings."

"I have no taste in men," I muttered. "I did not taste them."
Yet.

Orry snickered, and New Bestie shook his head again but slowed his pace. "Be warned is all. While you are drawn to them, they are not merely here to protect you. In the end, you could be just another tool. Or another weapon. They could view you as replaceable if your path is ever at odds with theirs. I do not wish you to be hurt in any way."

I patted him on the neck, unable to stop myself from chuckling. "Oh, I know my value to them lies in what I can do for them. That's how I like it. Keeps things simple."

And I did. Still...his words stung.

"Oh, sweetie, you're worth so much more than a business transaction. If they don't see that, then they're plain ol' dumb." Orry snuggled her furry head under my jaw. "You okay?"

I shrugged and the words slipped out before I could capture them and hold them back. "Tired of being used, is all."

Behind us came the crashing of the two men and their mounts through the thick bush. New Bestie slowed to a walk. "Your mother?"

Double ouch. Kik may not be able to tally imbalance like the unicorn, but that had its benefits. There was no hiding truth from this creature of Underhill. I didn't answer, couldn't. Nope, I wasn't going to answer that. My tongue tangled. "We have job ahead. Save queen of all fae and all children. You have direction?" I slid off his back and walked next to him, feeling my cheeks warm.

He bobbed his head. "Yes, we will continue on. I think ... perhaps we will go to ... no, let us hope that is not the place. *Near* to it is bad enough."

I didn't press my friend. I was exhausted. Wrung out from the day's events. Funny how nearly dying could make a person vulnerable to their emotions.

As the sun fully dipped behind the horizon and night took over the sky, we stopped under a massive oak tree. The leaves spread wide and thick, giving us a good canopy that would keep the worst of the weather off.

"Here," I said. "Good choice, New Bestie."

"I'm so tired, I don't think I could even be interested in the glossiest, most luscious hair right now," Orlaith whispered, snuggling in.

I stroked her back a few times. "Orry?"

"Mmm?"

Things were feeling hopeless right now. I wanted to pretend that I wasn't likely going to die for a minute or two. "Can you tell me something about you?"

The golden bat froze. "Mmm, what?"

"Something about you. Where you're from or just something small. If you don't want to tell me about you, then how about your father?"

She seemed to relax slightly at the mention of her father—hard to tell with a bat.

Orry snuggled in again. "Father came into my life about fifty years ago."

"Huh. Not your blood father?"

"Nah, that's what everyone called him who ended up there."

"Where?"

She sighed. "The punishment zone."

My brows shot up. "I've never heard of it."

"It's where Underhill sends people when they really rack up some imbalance but when they're not *bad* as such. More like... careless about what they do. I go to sleep between seven hotties one night, then *bam!* I'm in the punishment zone. Oh, and I'm a golden bat that only one person understands." Her voice lowered. "I think your mother makes us gold so we know she hasn't ditched us. Like she's still rooting for us to make the right choices, you know?"

I snorted. "Sure. Probably."

"Yeah.... Guess she's your mother and all. So that's me. Father took us all under his wing. He'd been there a long time. Always felt sad that she'd never let him out. But we all did things to get there. Anyway, he got a memo from the big girl to drop me off with you. And you understand me, too, which made my decade."

We were silent for a time as I processed that this tiny, golden bat had committed a list of imbalances so extensive that she'd been put in... "Fae Jail."

"Fun fact, that's where the word 'Fail' comes from," she murmured.

I bit my lip. "What was it like there?" I wanted to ask what she'd done, but that felt too personal when I could tell she was already reluctant to talk about it.

She took so long to respond that I thought she'd fallen asleep. "Your mother is, can be," she shook her head against my shoulder, "*needs to be* ruthless. Realizing the enormity of her job took me a few decades. But I discovered a love of everything hair while there, so things weren't all bad. And now look at me." She chuckled sleepily, and I stroked her back again.

"Thanks for telling me." I felt better.

For now.

Aaden and Cormac burst from the trees behind us, their horses slicked with sweat.

Neither looked ... happy.

"What the hell was that?" Cormac barked. "You can't just take off into the dark without us."

"I did though, didn't I?" I lifted my chin and stared back at him. "New Bestie brought us here. He is trusted. He is good. He is *my* friend."

Orry slurred sleepily, "Me too."

"And Orry, too, is my good friend." I touched her again.

Aaden slid off his mount first, his voice tight, anger lacing each word, "Let's get the mounts cared for, then we can make a meal. Figure out tomorrow."

My stomach churned at his reaction. I always expected anger from Cormac. Not so much from Aaden.

We set up camp in absolute silence. Furious silence. The tumult felt like the beginning of a storm. Waiting for everything to explode.

Best get it over with.

"Why angry?" I asked as we sat around the merrily crackling fire, the heat soaking into my bones. Above us, the sky rumbled, and I hunched closer to the flames.

"You ... you don't understand that running off after nearly dying might freak us out?" Aaden stared across the fire at me, his green eyes wide. "Our job is to protect you! How can we do that—"

I held up a hand, stopping him. "I protect you, Aaden. I save you too. Goes both ways."

"Then why did you take off?" Cormac asked, deadly quiet. His voice was smooth, but his energy was off the charts furious.

I looked between them, back and forth. "New Bestie wanted discussion without your ears hearing. So. He took speed. We discuss and now we have a plan."

"And that is?"

"Divining rod." I pulled my cloak more firmly around me. The temperature was dropping, I didn't like it. Snow wasn't unknown to me, but I hadn't expected such weather in the spring season.

"Divining rod," Aaden repeated. "How? Where?"

I pointed in the general direction we were headed. "That way. We find, then it leads to the darkness, which leads to children."

Neither man had taken even a scoop of the stew that they'd thrown together. It smelled unseasoned. Again.

I quickly sent out threads of my silver magic, pulling at the plants and herbs in the vicinity until I found those that I liked. Quickly plopping them into the stew, I fed my magic into the flames below the pot and heated the meal until the liquid was at a rolling boil.

"You know, hun, I think they both care for you," Orry said softly. "Maybe you scared them when you took off? I mean, you had just almost died. Maybe they started out using you, but . . ."

I frowned and made myself look first at Aaden. His face was tight with worry, and he held his lips together as if he were biting back words. Then to Cormac, who looked as though he would snap me in half given the chance. I doubted he'd been afraid but ... "You afraid for me? Is that why you are angry?"

Cormac broke first, shocking me. "Lugh's limp dick! Of course we were afraid for you! You were on death's door, and a troll was about to eat us, and then you just fucked off into the dark! We couldn't see you in the dim light, and how were we to know you hadn't galloped into a fucking booby trap?"

I looked at Aaden as Cormac's words stopped ringing in the air. "Truth?"

His jaw ticked. "Truth."

I grimaced, not understanding the strange flutters in my belly and those lower that came with their admission that they'd been afraid for me. I didn't know why their confession made me want ... something I couldn't put my fingers on.

An image flashed in my mind. Skin on skin, hands and mouths, the heat of other bodies pressed against mine. I swallowed hard and bolted upright—I needed space to breathe. Cormac and Aaden burst upward too, looking ready to chase. Perhaps I'd earned that reaction after the way I'd left earlier. I wasn't going to get away from them this time, I knew that. And ... maybe I didn't want to?

"Oh fuck," I whispered, locking my knees and squeezing my legs together. Why was this burning so strong? I didn't know how to ease this sensation that demanded *something* happen. It was an aching pressure. Almost a pain.

"Are you hurt?" Aaden's voice wrapped around me, and I took a half step toward him. But I knew his touch hurt.

The feeling ramped up further, and a sigh left my lips.

"Grab her, she's going to pass out." Cormac leapt for me first.

His hands scooped under the cloak to grab hold of my upper arms.

I wanted to say I was fine, but a low moan left me instead. Breathless. His touch was doing things to me. Making the sensation worse, but also promising to make it better.

Orry laughed and flew off my chest, spun through the air, and landed on New Bestie's back. "You are burning up, girl! I can't promise I won't watch you three beautiful people. It might be the most action I get in a long time."

New Bestie trotted away with her, protesting loudly.

Watch what action?

Where Cormac held me, my skin tensed and prickled, the sensation of vines curling around both of us, binding us together ...

"I don't like you," I whispered, and then I was looking up into wolfy amber eyes, seeing a hunger there that I just didn't understand. My body wanted him, and I swayed closer until my body brushed against his.

Hard, he was hard. The same heat that I was feeling radiated off him.

He wanted me.

Aaden slipped behind and captured me around the waist. With both of them making contact, the feeling of home instantly swept to something hotter. Something urgent.

I struggled to breathe past the growing sensations rippling through my body, up and down like long stroking hands. Last time, a cave had been falling down around us. This time I had longer to assess the exact sensation, a strange pleasure and pain I couldn't escape. For every stabbing sensation, there was a cooling balm and caress to soothe the hurt. Pain, caress. Pain, caress. The back and forth was constant. I could barely think through it.

"Aaden, what is this?" Cormac's whisper was hoarse. As though he too were in agony.

Only this wasn't a bad agony, not completely. This was unlike any pain I'd experienced.

Aaden's body was flush against mine, his mouth buried in my hair. "I don't know. *Fuck*."

Their responses cut through some of my own reaction. "Booby trap?" I whispered the two words, and that was all it took to break the spell.

Cormac stumbled back, and as he let go, I was able to step away from Aaden. All three of us went to our knees.

I pressed trembling fingers to my lips, eyes wide.

"Shit." Cormac shook his head slowly, as if he could shake off the spell. "Of course it's a booby trap. We can't stay here tonight. *That's* not happening." He turned away. "Not with Aaden present."

My brows drew together. *Just* because Aaden was present? I was far more concerned about the booby trap, personally. We may have started something similar in the cave, but that happened when I'd literally fallen on the pair of them. The way I'd been burning up before... magic was afoot. Sexy magic. What better way to capture someone than to render them unable to think? It'd be better if the trap hadn't left me acutely uncomfortable between the thighs.

His voice was still hoarse. Thick. My focus dropped to his ass before I remembered myself. I cleared my throat, my body still tingling all over.

"A stupid spell," I said, pushing to my feet. "A spell to make us stupid."

Orry laughed from the treeline. "I like the denial! The effort is good."

New Bestie bobbed his head, stepping back into the clearing. "Orry speaks truth. The half-troll had no part in what happened."

"She did," I snapped, and my two friends laughed. "Cormac, Aaden, that was spell to make us stupid, yes?"

Both nodded in agreement. Several times. Emphatically.

I folded my arms. "See?"

New Bestie sighed. "I suggest the three of you sleep away from one another. You are in no danger here. Idiots."

I blinked. He'd sounded a bit like Kik right there.

Aaden had his back to me. "It's late. The hornless one is right. We should just go to sleep. Things will be better in the morning."

Would they though? I took a bowl of the stew even though I wasn't hungry, forcing myself to shovel it in my mouth.

The meal warmed me. Wrapping myself in my cloak, I curled up underneath my New Bestie, the way I would have with Kik. Orry joined me, snuggling into the crook of my arms.

"You would have had fun with them," she whispered.

A bolt of heat shot low in my belly at a vision of me writhing between Cormac and Aaden, working to rid myself of that painful burning.

"Didn't feel fun," I muttered back. "Felt strange and weird."

And dangerous and new and exciting.

She burrowed in close. "Trust me, if you get the chance again, take it. You won't regret the things you do, but you will regret the things—or people—you don't."

I already did, and that . . . that was *crazy*.

I didn't want to hear about regret or fun. This day had been too much by far.

I pulled my cloak over my head and pretended to sleep, while Aaden and Cormac ... from the sounds of their ragged breathing and tossing and turning, tried to do the same.

Nineteen

"*Come back to bed and play.*"

Aaden turned from the window and looked back at the tousled-haired blonde beauty in his bed. Moonlight washed over his bare skin, and his teeth glinted as he half-grinned at her. "Again?"

"Anything to tear you from your thoughts of the animal."

"Her name was Silver."

"Was it really? She didn't have a name."

Aaden chuckled. "That's true enough."

"Barely spoke too." The beauty shuddered, her breasts shuddering with her. "I mean, her own mother didn't want her, right?"

Aaden snagged her ankles and jerked. The gorgeous fae female squealed in delight, then proceeded to drag her nails up the sides of his torso.

She hooked him around the neck with both arms and pulled him close. "But maybe you prefer someone who doesn't talk much." Reaching down, she stroked between his thighs. "Mmm?"

Aaden moaned low. "She didn't do that either."

"No," the woman purred, stroking faster. "And that's why you're with me. I love you, Addy."

Gasping, kicking, I startled awake and shoved at the thin blanket that covered me. Sweat coated me, beading on my forehead and on my top lip. I clutched the sides of my head through the knotted mess of my silver hair, breathing hard.

Aaden with another woman. Clenching my fists on my lap, I glanced over to Aaden's slumbering form. He mumbled softly and rolled to face me, and I surveyed his face in the moonlight.

Moonlight that had licked his skin as surely as *she* had in my dream.

How she *would* lick his skin for all I knew. How had I ever labeled him as ugly? He was beautiful.

Cormac shifted onto his back, and I glared at him for good measure. Aaden had nothing on his 'nocturnal activities'.

The burning was back–or maybe it had never left. My skin was fire. *Why was I so damn warm?*

I couldn't breathe.

Bursting to my feet, I at least had the presence of mind to untangle a dead-asleep Orry from my neck and hang her on a passing branch before I picked my way silently from the others.

I drew in slow breaths. Slow breaths that did nothing for the rage trickling through my system, into my chest and mind.

In fact, the rage was growing worse. All of it directed at Aaden and the woman. I'd never had a prescient dream before. My dreams had always just been that. Dreams. But how had I visualized her in such perfect clarity? She'd been my opposite in every way. Soft and welcoming. Refined. Likely from a loving family. A family with status. Well spoken. No stranger to the bedroom.

An image of her on top of Cormac flashed in my mind, and a growl fell from my lips.

The ground underfoot was springy and damp, muddy in areas, but perhaps for the first time since childhood, my senses had abandoned me. I was walking dumb.

When I arrived at the small lake's edge, I simply glowered at the gently lapping water and the far silhouettes of the trees on the other side.

Crack.

Whipping my dagger free, I crouched, teeth bared.

New Bestie joined me on the shore, seemingly unfazed by my aggressive display. "There are not many who can resist the draw of this lake."

I wasn't angry at my unicorn friend. I was angry at Aaden and Cormac ... angry because I felt inadequate.

I forced myself to lower the dagger.

"I believe the males will arrive in due course," he mused. "You are only here first because you are . . . how shall I say . . . fighting a battle on *two* fronts."

My tone was withering. "What are you talking about?"

He looked out across the still surface. "Loch Éad. The object you require lies in its depths. You must simply retrieve the object to find what you seek."

That did reach me through my simmering, churning fury. "Is it guarded?"

"Nothing of power is without protection," he replied, then swung his head to look at me. "Including you. Enter the water without fear of coming to harm while in its embrace."

I watched him closely. "And once I'm out of the water?"

A soft chuff left him. New Bestie turned and walked toward the trees.

I'd rather fight on land any day. "The object. Will I know it?"

"You will, child of gold. I assure you. You and your male companions."

Left alone once more, I gritted my teeth against the building resentment in my chest. How had I let myself grow feelings for either of the men? Especially the wolf. I *hated* him. But this feeling inside ... I wanted to rage at him and hurt him for entirely different reasons.

Because he'd hurt *me* when he had sex with the blonde fae.

I rubbed my forehead. Or was that Aaden? *Both of them.*

A rustle of leaves caught my attention through the thick haze cloying my mind. I glanced over my shoulder as Cormac stumbled out of the treeline, his face a thunderstorm.

"What the fuck are you doing out here?" he demanded, searching the shore and trees. "Who were you speaking to?"

I faced the lake again. "None of your fucking business."

"The hell it isn't."

My jaw was clenched hard enough to snap my teeth. "You have business *elsewhere* if I remember correctly. *My* business is in this lake. The object that will lead us to the darkness is contained within."

"The darkness," he said, almost in confusion.

Warmth heated my back, and I turned to look up at the wolf, letting every inch of my fury show. "I'm going in."

Shadows crept into his gaze. "Who were you speaking to? Was it Aaden? He's not at the camp. Do you two meet behind my back often?"

"He's probably with *her*," I spat back.

Cormac sneered. "Don't tell me you're jealous over him."

I lifted my hands to my leather vest and worked at the knot. Loosening the ties under Cormac's watchful attention, I slipped free of the garment and stood bare chested before him. His hands rose, and I stepped back, bitterness slapping me like an icy wind.

"Don't touch me with those hands," I snapped at him.

His inhale was slow and audible. "Are there other hands you'd prefer on your breasts?"

I untied my trousers and stepped free of them too. I was too hot, too bothered, and so furious I was about to make a rug out of the wolf's pelt. "I'm going to get the object."

"Good," was his hissed answer. "Maybe that will wash away the traces of him on your body."

I shook my head at his senseless words and strode into the water. The lake floor dropped away quickly, and I pushed off the shelf to submerge myself in its cool depths. If I'd expected the temperature of the water to help, I was mistaken. Images of Cormac with the blonde fae battered me from every direction, leaving barely enough of my mind behind for me to focus on swimming across the surface. I cut through the water with angry strokes, and drew in the cool, nearly white energy around me to sharpen my vision.

New Bestie hadn't been wrong.

The object was literally on a shining pedestal under the surface. Right in the center. The pedestal was unmarred by the algae and weeds covering the rest of the lake floor, yet I hadn't been able to see it until just now. That indicated a charm *or* a guardian. I peered more closely at the object, nearly able to feel curiosity through the storm whipping and pounding through my body. It was white. Pure white. Round and small.

Dagger in hand, I studied my surroundings. Any number of predators could be lurking. New Bestie had assured me the battle would arrive once I exited the water, but though nearly every piece of me was occupied with Aaden and Cormac's betrayals, old instincts died hard. I cast my silver tendrils out to the pedestal and brushed against the engravings snaking up the sides.

Nothing.

Next I touched my hand to the pedestal.

Nothing leaped from the depths of the lake.

Facing the beaming object, I looked over the engravings again, following the criss-crossing lines down to where the white stone became a tree limb and disappeared into the lake floor. The criss-crossing lines were its branches, knit together to form a throne for the treasure.

I touched my fingers to the small white treasure, noting its complete smoothness. "Seed pod," I said, my words disappearing in bubbles to rise to the surface.

That's what this had to be. I could feel the tree's magic within it, so like the soul tree in the Irish court. Was this a soul tree too? Maybe even part of the same tree? Black cracked the tree at its base, traveling up toward the pedestal. Tree and pedestal disintegrated before my eyes.

The tree had gifted me a seed at the expense of its life.

Thank you.

Taking the precious seed in hand, sorrow heavy in my chest, I pedaled back in the water.

I swam from the darkness, seed tight in my grip. Light poured out from between my fingers, flaring out ahead and illuminating the way. But the small bubble of sadness I'd felt when taking the seed fled as surely as the tree.

I choked on the dark anger as it returned triple-fold, surging to impossible heights. I screamed under the surface as a new image came to the fore of my mind. One of the blonde between Aaden *and* Cormac. The three of them were moving together, both men entirely focused on her.

On her.

My opposite.

Perfection.

I staggered from the lake, clutching my chest and sobbing hard. Water ran from my hair and down my frame in large rivulets. "How could you both do that to me?"

A roar was my answer. Such was my state that I didn't immediately raise my head—nor, once I did, did I immediately understand what was happening.

Aaden was trying to kill Cormac.

Cormac was trying to kill Aaden right back.

"What were the two of you doing before I got here?" Aaden bellowed, sword hurtling through the air. "Why is she undressed?"

Leaping back, Cormac bolted forward, twin blades gleaming with the same murderous light as his amber gaze. "She'd come from you. The two of you were here, speaking. Laughing over my ignorance of your affair."

My brows slammed together. They were fighting over her. Not just bedding her. *Fighting* over her. They loved her.

I swiped up my bow and arrow and set two arrows across its taut string. "Give me one reason why I shouldn't kill you both." Power sent my voice booming toward them in a wave.

They turned as though hypnotized.

"Silver," Aaden growled.

Cormac stalked my way.

Mere feet from me, they seemed to collect that I was aiming a deadly weapon right at them.

"These arrows never miss, you know," I told them quietly. "One for each of you. For betraying me. For choosing her."

"I choose you," Aaden said, walking closer. "There is no her."

"I saw you together!" I shouted.

"There is no one else. On my part." Aaden frowned. "But why are you shooting Cormac if you love him?"

I screamed, "Because he loves her," just as Cormac yelled, "Because she loves you."

Cormac blinked. "Why are you going to shoot Aaden though?"

Seething, I tightened the bowstring as the two males exchanged a look. A look of lies. A look they'd probably shared while pleasuring the same woman. At the *same* time. Tears trekked over my cheeks.

"Silver," Aaden said slowly, reaching out to touch me. "Put down the bow and come to me."

Cormac's shoulders bunched, and he reached for me too. "There is no one else."

It's like they thought I was an idiot.

But maybe I could show them that I was the worthier choice. If I killed them, it would kill *me*. Literally, yet also . . . my very being was crying at the idea of the light fading from their eyes, even as I was in agony at the idea of them with another.

Discarding my bow, I gripped Cormac's tunic and yanked him closer as I popped up on my tiptoes to set my lips against Aaden's.

Pain.

His touch was pain, but the pain inside was worse. The pain of potentially losing him to another. Gasping, I wrenched away.

Because there was another that inspired that same pain.

Cormac threaded his hands into my wet hair and briefly rested his forehead against my temple. His body was tense behind me, and as he trailed his nose along my jaw, every muscle in my body relaxed. The stabbing sensation from Aaden's touch melted away.

I sighed.

"I hate that he can do that to you," Aaden hushed, his voice catching.

Opening my eyes, I rested a hand against his cheek. Whatever this was, my soul was demanding I stay and see it out.

Strengthen whatever this was with them. Not live in regret as Orry had said.

"Touch me," I told him.

The direction of his green orbs lowered immediately to my breasts. He moaned. "With pleasure."

Cormac tipped my neck to the side, and I was lost to the feeling of so many hands roaming my body, alongside the heat of two men and the warmth of their tongues.

"Darling," Cormac said, his voice low. "Have you been with anyone?"

"No, but I'd like to have sex with both of you right now," I answered solemnly.

Aaden chuckled, and I jerked against the vibrating sensation on my nipple. "Never one to shy away from what she wants."

"That's why I can't look away from her," Cormac answered, adding a short chuckle of his own. His hands slipped across my stomach, and I arched. The burning may have lessened, but an acute ache had been left behind.

"May I?" the wolf asked, pausing at the top of my thigh.

I squirmed. "Yes. Now."

Aaden paused to tilt my chin. His gaze shifted over my shoulder. "I don't like it."

"You don't have to." Cormac said.

Grabbing Aaden's chin, I forced his focus back to mine. "What don't you like?"

His cheeks reddened. *My favorite.* "That he gets to touch you first. The very first. That's special, Silver. I want to do that for you. Think of how you'd feel if I hadn't yet experienced that kind of touching and chose to do so with another woman."

My brows drew together.

"You did," Cormac said dryly.

True.

Aaden snarled, "Then how about you step aside?"

I glanced back and up to watch storm clouds gather on Cormac's face. This was my favorite too, my favorite of *his* looks.

"How about *she* chooses?" Cormac shot back.

Aaden gripped my forearms. "Silver, I don't know if that's possible for me. It would always be between us that you chose to share some experiences with him instead of me."

"Not if she's with me—"

"Stop!" I yelled.

Their anger was almost palpable as I rested a hand on Aaden's cheek, then a hand on Cormac's. Stepping between them, I rose on my tiptoes again and pressed their faces on either side of mine, their foreheads to my temples.

We all sighed in unison, and I felt the tension drain away. "Please. Don't fight." Drawing up my silver tendrils of power, I sent one to each male to lend them some energy. Something to soothe them.

"We're touching and there's no pain," Aaden murmured, his lips whispering over my skin.

My eyes nearly popped open, but the utter bliss coursing through every bit of me won the day. "Then we'll enjoy it."

Because as only Underhill herself truly knew, nothing good could last indefinitely. Happiness demanded sacrifice. This, right now, was happiness.

Green magic rose to hold hands with my silver.

I smiled, eyes still closed, and watched as Cormac's amber-edged dark tendrils rose to join ours. He hesitated, holding his magic an inch from mine. He pressed his mouth close to my ear. "I don't know what this is. But I'm willing to find out."

And so was I.

Wiggling my silver tendril in front of his power, I grinned at his resulting chuckle.

He wound his magic around mine, and hands slithered over my body anew.

Different.

I frowned. The touch was cold and—

Aaden's yelp of pain only just beat mine. Cormac's curse came an instant later. I wrenched away from them.

Tried to.

Something sharp, akin to a blunted dagger, punctured my stomach. I screamed and peered down, but whatever it was *held* me to Aaden. A vine. Or a rope.

"It's fucking thorns," Aaden groaned.

My eyes widened. He was right. And they were wrapped around us both. They *crawled* their way up our frames, binding our mouths together.

Aaden's gaze rounded as he gaped over my shoulder, making me aware Cormac was melded to my back.

And struggling.

I listened to the stuttering sounds and my horror grew. "He's choking!" I screamed into Aaden's mouth, only to feel the coldness creep up to my own neck, where it tightened.

The same force, whatever it was, was choking me. I reached for my silver magic, only to find it lost in a mess of green and amber-edged darkness.

Brilliant white flared.

A deafening explosion threw me through the air, ripping thorns from my body and burning away the cold. I hit the sandy shore and rolled to a stop.

I plucked my cheek from atop a mound of washed-up twigs and stones at the crunch of hooves.

New Bestie nudged me. "The battle is done. This is where I leave you."

"Is she okay?"

I managed to get up into a crouch and took in a tearful Orry.

"He wouldn't let me help you," she sobbed.

"You would have died," the hornless unicorn replied. "That is not your fate, as you are aware."

His white magic pulsed outward, encompassing me and the others. Aaden and Cormac staggered to join us, and I blanched at the welts around the wolf's neck, then blanched all over again at the puncture wounds spotting Aaden's body. They both paled at the sight of me.

"What was that?" I asked the unicorn. "What happened?" I wasn't referring to what had happened with the thorns. It was as if a cloud had lifted from my thoughts. The burning was gone. The pain and what could only have been all-encompassing jealousy were gone—like a mist burned by morning light.

The anger. The sense of loss and betrayal . . .

My stomach churned as I glanced back at the lake. "What does Loch Éad mean?"

The unicorn replied, "Lake of Jealousy. The charm on the water is very powerful and seeps far from the actual shores. It has had you in its thrall since yesterday."

When the burning began. "Why didn't you tell me?" I ... I'd felt so many things that weren't true or real. Had I declared to Cormac that I loved him? Because I'd sure felt it.

I felt the weight of twin gazes on me, but I didn't have the courage to look at either man.

"And I told you to go for it," Orry whispered. "I'm so sorry, I didn't know. I thought your feelings were real."

Cormac dropped to one knee, rubbing his neck. "What are you saying? The lake was behind all of that?"

"The lake can only work its magic if feelings exist," the unicorn mused. "Unfortunately, once the charm initiates, there is only one way to survive. That is what has protected the seed of life for millennia."

I rubbed my face. "Your light."

"That is not what I refer to. I had no part in saving you from the lake."

"But the thorns when we kissed," Aaden blurted.

Cormac lifted his head. "When the three of us *touched*. Not when you kissed. That happened before."

Aaden glanced at him. "And the silver chains choking the both of you to death?"

Silver chains? That was the cold slithering sensation?

I swallowed. "You *did* save us," I said to New Bestie. "With your light."

"Only from yourselves."

I wanted Kik back. He may be an occasional piece of horseshit, but at least he wasn't a cryptic piece of horseshit.

"Now the seed is in your possession, you have no need of me or my protection," the unicorn said. "Farewell, child of gold."

I stood on shaking knees. "We may have a direction, but we still need help." I'd never believed that more. I had less understanding now of what was happening than when I'd been aimlessly wandering around Ireland, for fuck's sake!

The unicorn didn't immediately answer.

He lowered his nose to touch my shoulder, and slight sorrow infused his voice. "May balance smile upon you in what lies ahead." Then, almost as if to himself, so quietly I just managed to catch his words, he added, "Thorn kissed and silver chains."

Twenty

The next morning dawned with a strange, hard frost across the ground—strange, because the weather until this point had been anything but frosty. Not that the cold had woken any of us up. I didn't think any of us had truly slept after the incident at the lake.

We'd moved close to ten miles away before stopping for the night. Just to be on the safe side.

Lying awake as the surrounding air dropped in temperature despite the rising sun, I forced myself to sit. Bits of ice fell from my dragon scale tunic and clung to my hair and skin.

Cormac leaned against a tree about twenty feet from my left, his eyes not leaving me as I moved. I twisted to glance the other way. Aaden sat twenty feet away in the other direction, his back against a rock that jutted from the soil. His eyes were closed, his face pinched as if in pain.

I grimaced and stood, dusting myself off. "Let's go then."

Orry shuddered, shivering hard against my neck. "Why is it so dang cold? It's spring going to summer."

I fed her a piece of the yellow fruit we had in the bags and mulled over her question. It was a good one. "Why is it cold?"

Which one of the boys would answer? We hadn't talked about what had happened at the lake. Were they feeling as torn about it as I did? If we didn't feel anything for one another, then the lake wouldn't have affected us. That it had, that we were unable to deny what had occurred, was almost worse.

Cormac spoke first. "We triggered something yesterday."

I snorted. "Not news."

He rolled his eyes, but something about him had ... softened, I guess. Like a razor edge behind a curtain of silk now. Progress, I could go as far to say. Except the razor could cut through at any second. Pretty much the same way I felt about him.

"The item you took, there was a cost to the world," Aaden said quietly. I turned to him. Whereas Cormac had softened, there was a different change in Aaden. He looked tired, as though he were fighting his own battle within.

I tried not to think of the woman I'd seen in my dreams with him, and with Cormac. Maybe the whole situation was haunting him too, though?

I let myself reach a hand to him, but he flinched.

"Don't."

Just that one word. Like a slap, it shocked me out of my worry for him. Right. "Thank you." I spat the two words out.

Orry let out what almost sounded like a hiss. "That little bitch. Did he seriously just shut you down when you went to comfort him? Goddesses! Some men are so out of touch with their own baggage."

She had a point, yet I'd realized Orry had a story too, one she was keeping quiet for reasons of her own.

"Thank you?" His confusion was heavy. I didn't care. The blonde woman who'd been with him and Cormac in my dreams had clearly been part of an illusion from the Lake of Jealousy, but even with her out of the picture, my mind was occupied with the belief that Aaden didn't want me as I wanted him.

I went to Cormac. "I will ride with you."

His dark brows shot up. "You don't want to find another mount?"

I shrugged. "Your horse is strong enough for us both."

I could run beside the other horses, but that would have wasted energy that I would need to fight the darkness. Yes, I would have preferred my own mount, but New Bestie had fucked right off, leaving me without anyone to carry me. I mean, I couldn't really blame him. Riding into unknown darkness without a way to win was pretty much a death sentence.

With one quick leap, I was up on the horse that had previously belonged to Cormac. I patted the stallion's neck, and he pawed with one foot. *Acceptable.* Cormac pulled himself up behind me.

His arm brushed mine and . . .

"Fuck!" I threw myself off the horse, scrambling from Cormac as the sensation of choking vines started again.

Orry clung harder, tapping at me with a tiny claw. "You'll need a horse, honey. No matter how you look at it, no matter how fun they are to imagine naked with you, you can't touch the goodies right now. They bite."

Looked like Orry was right. Whatever there was between me and the boys bit harder than a dragon with a week-long empty belly.

I sighed. "We need to find me a horse."

***

The first village we came to was small, and the humans there were just as confused as we were by the frost coating the land. Confused and *despairing* as they assessed their entire fields of damaged crops. Even with the sun high above, creeping towards the noon hour, the frost crunched under foot.

Their eyes followed us as we walked in, leading the horses behind Cormac and Aaden.

"You should have just ridden." I said for about the tenth time.

"It's not right for us to ride and you to walk," Aaden said stiffly. "We'll find you a horse here."

I was just surprised that he'd said something halfway polite for the first time today.

I pulled some green energy toward me from the ground, wanting to twine the tendril with my silver magic so I could send the power out in search of a horse to ride—or at least that was what I tried to do.

Nothing. There was nothing when I tried to pull energy from the ground.

"Hang on," I said. "Something is wrong. Try to pull energy from the ground."

I watched as the two boys did so. Aaden's green magic and Cormac's amber-toned magic curled around, tugging on the earth.

Nothing.

Cormac grunted. "The frost?"

I nodded. "I think so. Frost is a response to us taking the seed pod, I gather. Balance."

Is that what's happening, Mother?

I knew better than to ask her for help.

I blew out a breath, and it lingered in the air in front of me in a clearly visible cloud. How much colder would the children be in their cave now?

We had to be running out of time.

Sigella's voice whispered through me. *In taking the seed pod, there was a cost to this island of green. Just as there is a cost with any Unseelie magic. Death follows that seed pod. Now, that death is creeping toward the children.*

"How much time?" I broke into a run.

Sigella was quiet, so quiet that I thought she wouldn't answer. She'd never come to me before like this. But I'd never possessed the seed of life before either. Maybe the pod had weakened her prison. Or maybe she wasn't speaking to me at all, and the stress of this quest was finally pulling at my seams.

A black horse stood on the other side of a fence in a long, green pasture. I didn't pause to ask the humans that were in the house attached to the pasture. I leaped over the fence and ran for the horse, sending out a thread of my silver magic to tap into the horse's heart.

Good heart, strong and willing, but more than that, she was bored. This horse craved adventure.

"That I can give you, Beauty." I leapt up onto her bare back without looking back to see if the boys had kept up. The mare under me snorted and lunged forward, but my magic kept me seated as she took off at a gallop.

Before the day ends.

Sigella's voice cut through me as surely as any knife edged to kill.

I gasped. Before the day ends ... twelve *hours*?

"We have to ride hard," I yelled to the boys.

The seed pod I'd taken from the Lake of Jealousy was safely tucked inside my hip pouch, but I could feel it ... humming? I reached for it and pulled the blinding white pod free.

Was it smaller now?

I touched the mare's neck. "Easy."

As much as I wanted to continue galloping at full speed, we needed to go in the right direction.

Cormac slid to a stop next to me, and Aaden on the other side. Just like last night, barring the horses. *Focus, Silver.*

Great, now I was calling myself that too.

"Is this a crack?" I rolled the seed pod over so they could both see, dread unfurling in my gut. I wanted to be wrong about the feeling of the seed pod growing smaller.

"How is it going to lead us to the cave?" Aaden said in a low voice. Then, "it's not glowing as much as last night."

He was right about that. Still an asshole. But right.

"Too high of a price to waste." I had an idea of what to do, but it scared me. Scared me like nothing I'd ever done in my life, like nothing I'd ever faced in Underhill. Not even my terror upon seeing all the black ribbons in the other realm could compare.

Even as we watched, the seed pod grew smaller, shrinking until it was nothing more than the size of a peach pit.

If we didn't do something, we'd lose our one chance at finding the children, and of stopping the darkness ...

"What the fuck?" Cormac growled. "How the hell—"

He hadn't finished speaking as I shoved the now grape sized seed pod into my mouth and swallowed it down.

I closed my eyes as the boys started yelling. "Shut up, both of you," I yelled back. "This is the only way."

"That thing ... it was in the lake!" Aaden shouted. "You don't know what it could do to you!" He sucked in a breath. "To *us*."

I opened my eyes as the seed pod hit my stomach. I wove my magic out, and the silver threads were joined by a faint white wisp. The magic within the seed pod? I sent the combined threads of magic out as if searching for herbs, or horses, only this time I was searching for the children—for the darkness.

The twining magics tightened around each other, and I gasped, finding my voice, then thumped my mare's sides. "We ride!"

I didn't wait to see if they would keep up. I could feel the magic that wasn't mine clinging hard to my silver threads. I didn't want to know what would happen if I ran out of the energy, or tried to untangle the two threads.

The horse underneath me galloped across fields and alongside roads, where the human's motorized vehicles honked and blared. She leaped over fences and hedges. Through it all, the seed pod's magic stayed steady.

Whatever had been cannibalizing the magic, the seed was now protected inside of me.

There will be a cost, you little fool. One greater than you could possibly understand with your pea brain.

Once again, Sigella's voice was there, tugging at me. The worst part? She was echoed by someone else.

"What will this cost?" Orry asked, her words whipping up around us. "I mean, it's working, I get that—even I can see that the pod is leading us—but . . .I don't want it to hurt you. What if you turn into a tree?"

I'd laugh but . . .there was a decent possibility that could happen. "I know there will be a price, and I will pay it."

We galloped the horses as far as we could before taking a break.

Cormac's voice was tight. "We keep walking. The horses need to catch their wind."

"Why are you angry?" I asked, studying him.

"Because I can't fucking pull from the ground or the world around us, which means something is blocking us from using our magic." He grimaced.

"Ease off," Aaden muttered. "It's not her fault."

"I'm not yelling at Silver," Cormac spat out. "I'm pissed because we keep hitting barriers. Whatever we're hunting has power. We make some headway, then the rug is pulled out from under us."

I frowned. "There are no rugs here."

"Manner of speaking, honey," Orry whispered quickly. "It means something unexpected happens."

Why didn't he just say that then?

My horse walked beside me, her coat slick with sweat. I kept a hand on her so I could feel when her heart rate settled enough to go again.

Aaden dared to walk closer to me. "Are you okay? Is the seed pod hurting you?"

I shrugged. "I'm unsure why you're concerned after how you spoke to me this morning."

"Silver." He rubbed a hand through his hair. "It's . . .I had an idea of how things might be, a hope. Since the lake, another path seems to be opening, and I'm struggling to get my head around it."

Did he think any of us had taken what happened at the lake in our stride? "Pushing me away is not the answer."

He frowned. "That may be true, but it's nothing more or less than what you've done since arriving in this realm. And the ease with which you do it suggests keeping others at a distance is how you've coped for a long time."

I sucked in a sharp breath, my eyes widening as a stabbing sensation hit me under the ribs.

Something flickered in Aaden's gaze, but he pressed his lips together, glancing away.

Did I do that? Push people away? I wasn't sure the accusation was entirely fair. I'd grown up alone, aside from Kik and a few friendly creatures in Underhill. To invite a being close was a silent agreement that the two of you would help and care for each other. That wasn't a promise a lot of creatures could make, myself included. Even my mother couldn't make that promise, and if a parent couldn't make the promise to always protect for you, then no one could. If I pushed others away, I did so because I was realistic, not out of resistance to forming deeper connections.

At least, I'd thought so.

Cormac pushed past my mare's head, so the boys were once more flanking me, jarring me from my thoughts.

I ran a hand over my face. What a fucking mess.

"How are you feeling?" he asked. "Has the seed done anything to you?"

"Not yet."

"What do you mean 'not yet'?" Cormac's question was delivered in his most deadly tone. The one that made me shiver.

I shrugged as if his question didn't matter. As if I weren't concerned. Maybe that was what I had to convince myself of too. "There must be balance to everything. This is a gift, a power that is tangled with mine. There will be a cost, but … not yet. I think," I chewed my bottom lip, voicing my fear aloud, "after the children are found."

I could feel that the time was ticking, sliding away. The seed pod was shrinking even inside of me. Slower than it had done in my hand, but it was still shrinking. Dying.

Which meant we might have to run the horses into the ground.

I put my hand back on my mare's side. Her heart rate had calmed. I jumped back onto her. "We go until horses drop."

Just saying it out loud made my gut twist. I didn't want to hurt the horses. Certainly not this one.

Cormac nodded, and when I looked at Aaden, his face was grim as well.

"End of day," I repeated, and leaned into my mare's neck, urging her forward with my heels.

Hours, we had hours to find the children before the darkness and frost took them.

Goddess be with us, I'd never thought Kik's stories of Lugh very impressive, but if there was ever a time to have his luck, then that time was now.

Twenty-One

My teeth chattered. I wasn't the only one. The three of us were making so much noise, there'd be no need to alert the darkness to our presence. Or any predator close by.

That was, if any predators had survived this frost.

Everything was dead. I'd thought it would be the pace that killed our horses, but just like the trees and shrubs, the animals small and large, our horses had succumbed to the freezing temperatures. We couldn't even draw energy to warm ourselves, let alone other creatures. They'd been left behind, dead.

"We can't go much longer," Aaden said between chatters, the sound muffled by the way he'd tucked the bottom half of his face under his tunic.

Our reservoirs of power could only bring us so far. That was why fae always drew from their surroundings.

Cormac sandwiched me from the other side. "What's the seed doing? Is it shrinking again?"

I shivered and shook my head. "Still the same." Around an hour ago, the seed had stopped shrinking. In fact ... "I think it's growing stronger. Larger."

Aaden cursed.

"Tell me about it," Cormac said. "When all this is done, I'd like some damn answers."

I snorted.

"Answers?" Aaden said the word slowly as though trying it for the first time. "What are those?"

"Exactly," the Unseelie muttered in reply. "Yet that's exactly what will be demanded of us the second we return to the court."

Orry's voice was barely audible from where she was buried under my vest. "They can shove their demands up their rich buttholes."

Couldn't argue with that. Not like any of *them* were out here freezing off body parts in search of the villain. My stomach turned for another reason, however.

I licked my lips. I still hadn't divulged the witch's words to Aaden or Cormac.

My reasons for keeping the information, whether true or false, to myself now seemed ...

Paltry. Or dishonest, perhaps.

Somehow, some*where*, I'd started to care about their feelings. *Damn.* Kik would roar with laughter over that one. Earth surely was more complex than Underhill, and while I yearned for the ruthless simplicity of my home, the sudden vision of us returning to the courts only for me to depart was creating an ache in my heart.

I staggered up a rise of shingled stone after Cormac. Panting hard, the three of us stopped just inside a copse higher up.

There, down the hill, I could see our destination through the trees. The black maw of a cave, the edges dusted with frost and shimmering with fresh ice. The boys had not seen it yet. They were doing everything they could to stay warm, and their heads were down.

Rubbing my hands together, I gritted my teeth. *May as well get it over with.* "I have something to tell you."

"What?" Aaden blurted.

The pair exchanged a suspicious look, each male sizing the other up as though I'd be spilling the details on some passionate encounter the other had missed out on. If we survived, then maybe my departure would be for the best. Aaden was right. Maybe he'd focused on who got to touch my vagina first, but the *idea* behind the concern was sound. That resentment would build. I could only foresee a cycle of their hurt, my guilt, their anger, then mine.

I didn't want that for myself nor them.

"Put your penises away," I said, sighing.

Cormac's brows shot up. "Believe me, all parts of my genitalia have run screaming from this weather."

My lips twitched, then I frowned. "The witch said something to me at that first cave. I've kept it to myself until now, but it wouldn't be fair for me not to say anything before we reach the darkness."

Aaden rubbed his face, then stepped closer. Blazing green eyes met mine. "I will spend my life convincing you that your secrets are mine to hold."

"I'll just drag them out of you," Cormac drawled, shuffling in place to stay warm. "Spill it, sweetheart."

How to put this nicely ... "The witch said we won't win. The darkness is too powerful." I swallowed at the resulting silence. "So, obviously I'm telling you both because if you want to return to the courts, to your families and lives there, then now would be the time to do it. I have the seed, the weapon needed to overthrow the darkness. That means I don't need—"

"If you're about to say that you don't need our help," Aaden said pleasantly, "then I'm going to tie you up and go into that cave by myself."

My mouth shut with a click of my back teeth. "You can't do that."

He tilted his head. "You think?"

My gaze swept down his body. Honestly, Aaden seriously underplayed his abilities and power. I might always have underestimated him if not for this journey. Could he manage to tie me up?

Yes.

I think he could.

"I can't return to my family without trying to get my niece back," Cormac said. He lifted a hand close to my face and drew it down as though mimicking the act of stroking my hair. "We've all felt this thing's power. We knew what we were getting into. I'm walking in with my eyes open." His gaze lifted over my shoulder. "But my reasons for coming on this quest were different from yours."

I glanced back at Aaden, who was watching Cormac.

"Furthering my career was only one reason for embarking on this mission," he replied after a beat. "That's still important to me. But we *did* all feel that thing's power. There is something in me that cannot rest until I do my best to defeat this darkness and help the children of our courts. But—" he shook his head, "—it's more than that. You both must feel it too. Something is ... wrong. Altered. This darkness—I can't fathom how no one has noticed the way it's rooted."

My head jerked up at the word. "That's how you see it?"

He lifted a shoulder. "Yes. That's what it feels like to me. Perhaps because we first noticed it in the roots of the tree of life. I suppose if this entity has taken up residence in the tree, then it would follow the paths of its limbs."

True. I lifted my chin. "I don't care what the witch said. I will kill the darkness and end this."

"*We,*" Aaden said.

"I second that." Cormac cleared his throat. "Now, if we'd like to save lengthy chats for when we're in front of a roaring fire, that would be ideal. I don't have much left in my reserves."

Aaden's reply was a grin. "Neither do I."

My focus lifted from their faces to what lay behind them. And up. Then up some more. The seed was noticeably bigger in my stomach. Bigger even that a few minutes prior. "We don't have long to go. The seed is getting stronger again. We're nearly there."

I walked between them and resumed our climb.

"But why is the seed strengthening?" Orry whispered.

Good question. I repeated it for the others. "Any ideas?"

Cormac grunted, but Aaden pushed ahead of us and crouched, then glanced up. "Anything to do with this?"

We looked over his shoulder at the dead plant. The icicles that had frozen the plant stiff were melting. Water dripped from its yellowed, withered leaves.

"It's melting," I said.

Cormac peered up at the sky. "It does feel marginally warmer."

So did the seed. The sensation wasn't painful, though. The drained feeling I'd initially felt after swallowing the pod had disappeared once it stopped shrinking.

"*Why?*" Aaden said in a low voice. "If we triggered the frost when we took the seed, why is the frost breaking?"

"It's regained strength," the wolf offered.

"Things don't just regain strength without sacrifice," I countered.

Their gazes fixed on me, and I raised my hands. "It wasn't my sacrifice." *So far anyway.*

Orry poked her head out from my vest. "It *is* getting warmer, Silver. I can feel it too."

I grunted, then hooked her feet on my hand, striding to the nearest tree. "Orlaith, I need you to do something for me."

"Nuh-uh. This sounds like a final request type thing. I don't do those. I'm coming with you." The gold bat crossed her arms.

"I need you to deliver a message to the queen in case something happens to us. The lives of more children are on the line."

"Don't like children."

"You need to tell her what transpired on our journey."

Orry's snickered. "Even the threesome part?"

I cast a look at the others, feeling heat creep into my cheeks. "Leave that part out."

"What about all the sexual tension and angst? The jealousy and tears? The—"

"Just say that the darkness is rooted in this cave," I growled.

The bat narrowed her eyes. "Nope. This bat doesn't leave when the going gets tough. She gets going."

"Where?"

"It's a saying. I'm sticking around."

I blew out a breath and lifted her closer. "I need you to do this."

Her defiance melted away as surely as the surrounding frost. "Dang, girl. Why you gotta get all earnest with me? Damn got through my defenses, that did."

"Thank you." Even if we died today, the truth would be passed on to another. If anyone had the resources at her disposal to crush this darkness, it was the queen.

I hoped.

"Wait. Don't get ahead of yourself," the bat sniffed. "If I do this for you and allow you to save me—because let's not pretend you're not also trying to do that—and when you get back to the court, I will have the exclusive artistic right to do your hair. Care regime. A trim. Daily hairstyles. The works."

Aaden shifted. "Will she do it?"

"Negotiating terms," I replied, then extended my pointer finger to the bat. "Deal."

She squealed, shaking my finger between both of her claws. "You won't regret it."

"The queen, Orry. No one else." I threw her into the air before I could see her excitement turn into sorrow. I wouldn't say goodbye.

I'd survived a childhood in Underhill.

I'd fought nearly every day of my life just to survive.

If there was a way to defeat this monster, then I'd find it, and I'd see Orlaith again.

"Please be careful," came her whisper on the wind.

Careful. Being careful was often the opposite to what delivered success. But this Earth was an emotionally complex kind of place.

My chest tightened as I whispered the lie to comfort her, "I will."

Twenty-Two

Aaden made the first move to head down toward the cave that he *still* had not noticed was even there. I grabbed his sleeve, making sure not to touch his skin. "We need a plan first."

I tugged on him and then took hold of Cormac's tunic sleeve to tug on him, too, until the three of us were crouching and looking down at the cave. I let them go and pointed through the trees. "We're there."

"Lugh's left nut, I didn't see it." Aaden shook his head.

"The cold," Cormac grunted, "It's numbing everything, all our senses."

Only it wasn't as cold as it had been. Around us, the ice that had tightened its fist around the world was melting in a steady drip of water falling to the ground even though there was no rain. The seed pod was growing within my belly, pressing upward toward my throat. I swallowed hard to push it back down. The little bastard wanted out, but I wasn't ready to deal with that yet.

THORN KISSED AND SILVER CHAINS

"First the children," I said softly. "The future queen of all fae is in there. We have to get the children out and safe before we deal with the darkness."

"You say that like it will be easy," Cormac said. "Like nothing will try and stop us. The darkness had its friend, the gray fae. There could be more like her."

"One of us stays back," I replied after a beat. "Fights whatever is there. The other two go in. When the next group of enemies shows up to fight, one stays, and the other continues." I'd seen saberducs use this strategy. Leave traps, lead prey to their doom to take down the numbers, and then get to the nests where the jewels were hoarded.

"I'll take the first fight," Aaden said. "Cormac, you go with her. Your niece is in there."

Cormac extended his hand to Aaden, and they quickly shook. "Be safe. Don't leave me alone with this one."

He tipped his head to me, and I frowned. "What do you mean?"

Aaden laughed, then sobered as he glanced my way. "Yeah, maybe it will take both of us to handle her. Not what I'd thought, but here we are."

"What are you talking about?" I spluttered. What kind of handling did they think I needed? Because now I definitely knew what type of handling I *wanted*. This would be a great time for Orry to be around to translate.

Aaden shook his head. "We can talk about it after. There's a lot to...figure out. I don't really know how things will work, if I'm honest, but I want to see if there's a way." His face colored.

I didn't want to wait to talk about it, but he was already moving down the slope, ghosting between the trees. Cormac started out next, and I found myself watching the two boys.

For all Aaden's kindness, he moved as stealthily as any hunter without a twig snapping underfoot. Cormac slunk like a predator, every flexing muscle as he made his way through the trees.

My cheeks grew hot as I thought about them both touching me. "Not the time," I whispered to myself, shaking off the whispering sensations that were just there, out of reach.

I followed them, feeling the seed pod push up again inside of me. I touched my throat, and something pushed my finger back with a surge of power. My eyes widened. *Vines.*

The seed pod had sprouted.

I hurried my ass up as fear spiked inside of me. The sensation of vines increased, spreading through me. "Fuck." I whispered the word, but Cormac turned.

"What?" he mouthed. I shook my head. Between the seed pod growing within me and what lay ahead, I had no words.

Because Cormac was right. There was a guardian at the front of the cave.

Fuck my life with a prickly pear.

The beast lifted its head and snorted once, bigger than any hog in existence as it towered over us. A hulking male tarbeast. Solid black with coarse hair that could attack you like little darts if you got too close. I'd never seen one this big. Not in all of Underhill.

The beast opened its long toothy mouth and let loose a snot-filled bellow that sent a shiver of primal fear down my spine.

This was so much worse than the gray fae.

"What the actual fuck is that?" Aaden snarled as he pulled his sword.

"Tarbeast. Change of plan. We must fight this ugly bastard together." I unsheathed my sword too.

Cormac grunted. "Aaden and I will take this on. You go get the kids." He spun his weapon around and leapt toward the beast, landing a solid blow on its shoulder.

"The hair is deadly too!" I shouted.

The tarbeast screamed and kicked out at Cormac, connecting with his gut, and sending him flying.

Aaden was up next, his sword locking with the tarbeast's hooked tusks that curled back towards its ridiculously small eyes.

"Eyes, go for the eyes," I yelled.

The tarbeast swung its head toward me, and a laugh burbled out of it. "I know you."

I pulled my bow from my back, already wincing, knowing full well that I'd pay a steep price for making the arrow land where it was needed. "Can't say the same."

The male tarbeast smiled . . .yes, *smiled*. I smiled back even though I was quaking with fear, and my throat was tight with climbing vines. "Hog for dinner tonight, boys?"

I let the arrow fly, aiming as best as I could for the left eye in the hopes the toll wouldn't be quite so bad.

The arrowhead sunk deep into the left eye of the tarbeast, and the cost slammed into me. I gasped and tumbled to my knees as the world swayed. My face hit the dirt, so I was looking across at the trampling, oncoming feet of the tarbeast as he rushed toward me.

Ouch.

Sure, I'd gotten his attention, but would it be enough for Aaden and Cormac to kill him? If I could have rolled out of the way, I would have.

The tarbeast still had one eye, one furious eye, and he regarded me with it. "Death is your only option."

He scooped his tusks toward me and lifted me off the ground, throwing me high into the air over his back toward the cave. The moment of weightlessness passed, and I struggled to care that I was falling.

The cost of using the arrows, the binding of the seed pod inside of me ... I almost wished that I'd land wrong and end it all.

I was not so lucky.

I hit the ground and rolled to a stop just on the inside of the cave, a rock 'softening' my landing. The smell of blood and shit filled the air, and I managed to lift my head to see Aaden and Cormac, one on either side of the massive tarbeast, their blades buried deep in its belly.

The tarbeast tried to throw them clean, but only succeeded in slicing its own body further, a chunk of intestine falling to the ground, followed by a gush of blood.

"I am . . ." the tarbeast muttered, then crumpled to his knees and went still.

I drew in a breath, dust coating my mouth. But we were alive.

The vines inside of me were nearly to the back of my throat as I pushed up to my feet. What was fueling it? My energy wasn't dimming. I wasn't losing strength.

But the seed pod was rapidly growing.

Sigella's laughter was there in the cave, her voice calling to me. *The seed pod is drawing off the darkness. Eating it. You only have to get close now to finish it off.*

My mouth dried anew.

Hope surged in me for the first time since my encounter with the witch. Was there actually a chance we could win this fight?

"We have to go. Hurry," I called. Aaden was limping badly, an arm around his middle, and Cormac was roughed up, but both were on their feet. "I know how to stop the darkness."

Sigella's laughter tugged me forward. I held up a hand, drawing from the last of my reserves to make light. The cave curled around and around, steadily descending, and the three of us staggered down. Probably a good thing we couldn't move any faster.

I wanted to run.

I wanted to get the children out and then escape myself. But charging full speed into a cave was beyond dangerous—it was stupid.

Casting my light back and forth, I scanned the floor and the walls upon entering the cave. No one seemed to be waiting. Could the tarbeast have been the only guardian of the cave? The theory wasn't impossible. Not many people would have survived that monster. I only knew to go for the eyes because of my own experience with the tarbeasts in Underhill.

We walked into the cave. Down. Our footsteps rang against the stone, and I quickly gave up trying to muffle the sound.

This cave was endless. And freezing.

"There's a light ahead," Aaden said, his voice echoing.

I dropped my own light to conserve energy. The seed pod lurched inside of me, the vines breaking out and up from my throat.

The light didn't bother me. I was bothered that the light cast shadows that were being used by a suffocating, unnatural presence. "Darkness," I blurted the warning around the vines.

"I see you, daughter of Underhill," The voice was oily, slick, and cold and arose from the shadows painting the cave walls ahead. "You think you can stop me? In this form, what you carry is unstable. The cost you will bear ... it will not be as you think."

Yeah ... I'd already gathered that swallowing the seed of life would have serious consequences. Didn't take a genius to put that together.

I hurried forward, feeling the pull from the seed pod and the darkness itself. "Get the kids," I ordered Aaden.

His eyes were wide as he took in my face. No doubt it was the vines climbing out of my mouth? Not exactly the look he was expecting, but he managed to respond, "We can't leave you."

"Go!" I snapped the word and pushed as much strength into it as I could, forcing him to move his feet.

I turned to face the darkness. I hadn't known what to expect, really—if it would have a tangible form or just exist in the shadows. The darkness was somewhere between the two, shadow and form. As it stood on the far side of a small fire, I peered at its flowing darkness and could at times discern more of a body, only to have that vision interrupted by moving shadows.

Far to my left, I could hear the cries of the children that had been stolen. *Babies.* At least some of them were alive. Thank fuck for that. "Why did you take them?" I needed time to feel this creature out.

"Because my master requires it of me." The darkness moved as if to circle behind me, but I mirrored its movements.

I'd thought the darkness *was* the master. Or was this just another servant like the gray fae?

A shuffling of feet, and four of the gray fae stepped up beside the dark form, two on either side.

"I've got this," Cormac said, joining me on my left. "Aaden will get the kids out. You kick the darkness in the nuts."

Sigella's laughter rippled around me. I thought I would be the only one able to hear her, but the figure in black tipped its head. "You keep unusual companions for one seemingly against my work."

The seed pod pushed its way up and out of my throat, and I reached up to help it along, pulling it out. It glowed like a tiny moon, vines reaching for the darkness before I could do anything. I held on tightly as its tendrils raced to the monster.

Yet the darkness didn't fight back. Didn't twitch.

It just stood there and let the seed pod's vines strangle it. I stumbled forward, yanked closer by the frantic spinning of the seed.

The sound of Cormac's blade, the screams of the gray fae that he faced, all of it faded as I found myself reeled in so close to the darkness that I could see into his eyes. Green eyes, light green eyes with flecks of silver. *His.* Male. The darkness was not just an entity, but a real person. A fae like any of us.

"Who are you?" I whispered.

"It does not matter now," he whispered. "My own creation will destroy me. The seed of life *and* death lies in your hands.

What will you do with it when the darkness is not enough? When it wants more?"

He wasn't talking any sense. But I couldn't look away from his eyes. The darkness flowed around us. Cormac and Aaden were yelling. I couldn't move. This was not the fight I'd anticipated. Not one of swords and muscle, but one of invisible forces and inner strength—of so many damn things I didn't understand. How was I meant to act when I *didn't understand*?

There was only one person who understood all things. My mother.

I blinked, then felt my quailing insides steady again. My purpose was not to understand all things. I was just another creature, subject to Mother's forces and powerless to stop the toll of balance. She was everywhere, always watching the paths that could and should and *must* be. Even here. All I had to do—all I *could* do—was make a choice and make a move and let everything fall where it would.

The darkness cupped his hands around mine. "Now, which of us has the strength to take the other?"

I already knew the answer. This fae was old, and as such, he'd gathered great power.

Still, I would not go down without taking him with me. "Why did you take the children?"

"Ahh, you wish to talk while we battle?" His sigh was ... sad? "Their lives would have ushered in a great new realm. One of true balance. One where darkness could reign in freedom."

He might be sad, but he also sounded fucking crazy. "Darkness cannot reign."

"Come now. You fathom balance more than most." he asked. "There must be dark for the light to glow strong. There must be death for life to continue. Surely, as a daughter of Underhill, you of all people know this."

I clenched my hand around the seed pod. I did know that. Balance was precarious. Ruthless. Unrelenting. To balance, there was no right and wrong, just light and dark. Life and death. Seelie and Unseelie.

I'd asked my mother, once, how she knew when things were tallied correctly in the realms, when balance had been achieved. She'd smiled that golden smile of hers—the mysterious one that could nearly make me forget she was Underhill.

She'd replied, *Balance has a certain ring to it.*

Having her for a mother, being raised the way I had, to respect and notice such things, I could almost hear that sound sometimes. Like now.

Which was how I knew what I had to do.

Forgive me, Orry. I won't be keeping my promise to you.

I nodded and dug my fingers more tightly into his. "Yes, I understand balance. I know it. I live it. Which is why I give my life to the seed, so that yours will also be taken."

TWENTY-THREE

I'd never given my life to anything. Clearly. But every fae knew *not* to overextend their power. Doing the opposite seemed like a good place to start.

His hands over mine, I gritted my teeth and focused on the seed in my iron grip.

The darkness just met my gaze. His expression almost accepting.

I hadn't come to this realm to die, hadn't been *dragged* to this realm to die. But now there were more people I would die for.

It meant I'd never see Mother again.

Or Kik.

Or Old Bastard.

But it was a toll I was willing to pay. Steeling myself, I brushed all thoughts aside, entering into the hunting quiet I'd perfected over the years.

Feed the seed.

Let it grow and eliminate this evil.

Opening the floodgates of my remaining power, I funneled every bit of it to the seed in my hands. My ability to draw energy from my surroundings was still cut off. I wasn't sure if what I had would be enough.

My knees shook, and I squeezed power from my core toward the seed. The pod had already germinated while within me. Now its roots shot to the ground, puncturing the earth and sending rocks and dirt slicing through the air.

"Silver!"

I ignored Cormac's shout. More pointedly the panic contained therein.

"You will do it?" the darkness asked, tilting his head.

My arms shook so hard, even he could not hold on. Black smoke congregated around my glowing frame. Waiting for when I failed. For when there was not enough.

That couldn't happen.

Crying out, I fell forward between two branches, my leg giving way. The small tree was now taller than me.

My eyes closed.

I pushed harder.

Every last drop had to go into the seed so it could devour the darkness.

"It's attacking the darkness!" Cormac's shouts filled my head. Peering through slitted eyes, I watched him attack the black smoke surrounding me as the seed—now a tree—sucked in the darkness as if drinking through a straw. Past him, Aaden plunged his sword through a gray fae.

Get the children out.

I coughed pathetically, feeling the cold seep from the tips of my toes and fingers, creeping inward to my heart. The chill was a final type of cold, and those who felt it, like me, were probably too weary to be afraid of what it meant.

A hand latched onto my ankle and yanked.

Cormac dragged me up, yelling in my face. My head lolled as I stared into his beautiful eyes. *He* was beautiful. A tear trickled down my cheek.

I peered past him, slurring, "The darkness."

"Gone. You did it, Silver," he said, then his smile disappeared. "What the fuck was that?"

He was always angriest when I put myself in danger. "You know it had to be done."

Cormac clenched his jaw and looped an arm around my waist.

We turned to face the new tree of life.

The darkness and all traces of the black smoke were gone. We were safe.

"What happened?" I croaked.

"I thought you were gone," he said. "The seed grew into a small tree, then started to absorb the darkness. Eat it. That's what it looked like anyway."

Stepping closer, I squinted at the tree streaked with black. "The darkness is contained." And I was alive. I couldn't believe it was over. "Didn't think I'd make it."

Cormac's lips were white with fury as he leaned down to glare at me. "And we will be talking about that later. For now . . ."

My face softened. "Let's go find your niece."

He closed the gap. "The only thing I want to do right now is kiss you."

"Back at you," I whispered.

He cocked a brow. "Might be worth death by strangulation?"

A laugh startled out of me. But . . . the temptation was strong.

Cormac would have his niece safe. The children would return to their families. And me, Aaden, and Cormac... who knew what would happen there, but I was excited to venture down that path at least.

"Uncle Wolf!" The scream hitched with sobs. A dark-haired girl, thin and filthy, hurtled across the cave floor to reach Cormac.

He caught her in a one-armed hug, hugging her tightly as tears fell freely from his eyes. He tucked a finger under her chin and lifted her face. "Lissie Bear. I'm *so* happy to see you."

I listened to her stuttering reply.

"I'm okay now," I told him, forcing my legs to work. Cormac thanked me with his eyes.

I staggered over to Aaden to give them some privacy.

"Your eyes look wet," Aaden said, shrugging out of his tunic to wrap it around two of the smaller children.

"Allergic to bullshit," I replied, sniffing. "How many?"

"All are accounted for," he said, frowning.

"The future queen too?"

"Over there."

I followed his look to the blonde-haired toddler in the far corner, then released a long breath. We weren't too late. "The darkness was waiting to sacrifice them. Waiting for us, I think."

"Sacrifice them to who?"

Good question. "He mentioned a master."

Aaden inhaled, and we exchanged a look that was as weary as it was unnerved. There was something stronger out there. We'd barely come through *this* encounter alive. That was someone else's problem though. I'd found the future queen of all fae and the children. We'd contained *this* darkness. Someone else could take a fucking turn.

I anchored my thoughts in the here and now. "We need to get these children back to their families. Guess we'll have to wait for Orry."

Aaden nodded. "Let's get a fire going first."

"We'll take the children further out," I said, eyeing a few. "They shouldn't be trapped down here any longer."

"I'll take them," Cormac said, then to Lissie. "Go join the other children. I'll be there soon. We're going home."

Lissie sniffled and in a wavering voice replied, "I'll see Mama, Uncle Wolf?"

"We will, Lissie bear."

"Aaden?" A child called, a small boy. "When are we leaving?"

Aaden left to attend him, and Cormac asked me, "Can you draw from your surroundings again yet?"

I stretched my senses. Not that I'd have any magic for days—maybe a week—after my stunt. "Nope. It's like the energy here is tapped out."

A low whining cut off his reply.

We faced the tree as its leaves started to pulse a dark gold. The humming swelled. The pulsing spread down to the smaller limbs. A huge crack ripped through the cave floor without warning, drowning out the renewed screams and cries of the young fae.

Heart in my mouth, I rose from my crouch once it became apparent that the cave wouldn't stop shaking.

"None of the children are hurt," Cormac reported.

Not hurt, but Cormac and I had been split off from them. At least they were on the entrance side.

"Aaden," I yelled. "Get them out of here!"

He nodded, somehow hearing me over the din. I could see the pinch in his expression.

"We'll find another way out," I shouted. Without magic, we weren't jumping that yawning cavern. Not a chance.

The pulsing had nearly reached the base of the trunk. The shaking ramped up. Aaden and the children disappeared down the tunnel.

Please get out safely.

I squared off with the tree.

"What's wrong with it?" Cormac called from beside me.

I shook my head, raising my voice. "Add that to the list of things we don't know."

He snorted.

I peered closer at the pulsing gold now spreading across the ground. First the gold extended into the far-left corner of the cave chamber, then moved along the back wall. Retreating to the trunk again, the gold spread toward me.

"Careful," Cormac warned as the gold touched my boots.

The gold retreated again, moving toward him.

"It's searching," I murmured.

He hummed low. "For what?"

The dark gold touched Cormac's boots, then erupted in a blast. Rock sliced through the air, and the very walls of the cave shook as every one of the tree's limbs burst in Cormac's direction.

A scream tore from me, the entire world pausing for a breath, as a thick branch punctured through the middle of his chest.

Shocked amber-gold eyes found mine.

His dark-edged aura started to drain into the tree. The tree was eating his power. The truth punctured my chest as surely as the tree had my wolf. The tree had been searching for more power, a food source. There was none in this cave after the darkness's occupation here, and I didn't have any left.

Still didn't.

So it was taking it from Cormac.

Racing forward, I drew my daggers and slashed at the tree of life. "No!" I screamed.

Blood poured from Cormac's mouth. He hadn't just been punctured by one branch. But I could fix him.

I could save him.

I had to.

"Hold on," I cried out.

"Sweetheart," the garbled word was accompanied by a fresh wave of blood over his chin.

I'd only just opened to him—only just accepted that we could have something more. Maybe things between us would've ended in disaster, but they may have been incredible. *Unshakeable.* I wanted to live in that world. I wanted *him.* I wanted our possibilities before me, not dead and buried. "Wolf," I managed to say. I couldn't reach his face through the lattice of branches. Only the cold tips of his fingers.

That chill. I'd recently felt it myself. I hadn't minded it so much then. Face pressed against the branches; I didn't move as a branch wrapped around my neck in response to me touching Cormac. I couldn't leave him.

There were times, when we touched and when we both forgot our warrior pride, that Cormac felt like a part of me.

That was how I knew he wouldn't die now.

He *couldn't* die. It felt like part of me would die too.

The branch stopped tightening around my neck. Cormac's fingertips were so cold. The tree of life, now shining a vibrant gold, loosened its death-grip from my neck and chest. The branches fell away, easing back.

Satiated.

I couldn't look up at him.

I couldn't confirm what I already knew. My heart—maybe something deeper—begged me to exist in denial for a moment longer.

To refuse to believe that Cormac was gone.

Twenty-Four

A howl erupted from outside the cave, a scream that came not from one of the children, but from Aaden.

My body was moving before I could think straight, taking Cormac's sword and stumbling away from his lifeless body and toward the screams that tore at the *other* half of my heart.

I could not lose them both. I would not survive it. My instincts had kept me alive thus far, and maybe I didn't understand what the fuck was going on between me, Aaden, and Cormac, but I trusted the hell out of my instincts.

"Aaden!"

"Silver, get away," he roared, his voice thick, as though blood coated it.

I burst from the cave, and the scene that awaited drove every last bit of sanity from me.

The tree of life had sprung out of the dirt and pinned Aaden to the ground by his shoulders, its branches driving through his flesh.

"No!" I screamed, and launched at the tree, slashing with Cormac's sword, knowing only one thing. The tree had taken one man from me. I would not allow it to take both.

The branches splintered under my blows, sending tiny shards of the tree spraying across the open space. The children screamed and backed away as I fought to free Aaden.

The two main branches that pinned him pulsed, flexing and pushing harder into him.

Screaming, I cut through one with a single blow, snapping it clean in half. The roots of the golden tree jerked away, pulling Aaden roughly to his feet before retreating.

I caught him as he buckled to his knees.

"Aaden, please don't die, please don't die!" I was crying, I didn't care that Kik would have had a field day making fun of me for it. All that mattered was that Aaden didn't die. He leaned into me, and his forehead touched mine.

"I'm not dead. I'm not dying on you, Silver. I promise." His lips found my skin. I waited for the telltale prickle of thorns, but there was nothing but heat, warmth, connection.

I didn't understand, but I also didn't care. I clung to him.

"Cormac ... he ..."

"Where's my Uncle Wolf?" Lissie came up to us, hands on hips, eyes challenging. As bold as her uncle would have been had he been there with us. *Would* have.

I shook my head, fighting for the right words. This moment would stay with her forever—the moment she found out her uncle was no longer alive. "He died protecting us all. He saved us. He saved you, Lissie."

Her eyes went wider yet, wobbling with liquid until it slid down her cheeks. Her lower lip trembled, and she shook her head. I reached for the child and pulled her in against my side as sobs wracked her tiny frame. "You're lying!"

She jerked from me and ran toward the cave.

I let go of Aaden. "Stay with them, I'll get her." Not that he had much choice. He slumped to his knees as I turned away.

Back into the infernal cave I went, following the path down to where the darkness had waited—knowing we would come.

Lissie's sobs drew me forward.

I found her at the base of the golden tree, but there was no body.

Cormac was gone. Even his clothes. All that was left of him ... I clutched the weapon in my hand. The sword was the only thing that the tree hadn't taken.

"He's not here," Lissie cried. "Is he really gone?"

I crouched, unsure of how to proceed. Because as much as my heart ached for Cormac, as much as I could feel the tightness in my chest and throat and the desire to scream at the fact that he was no longer with us, his niece was grieving too.

"He ... he—"

"He would not have wanted you to be sad, Lissie." Aaden approached us from behind, limping heavily and clutching his side. I glanced up at him, and he whispered low to me, "The queen of all fae has arrived with her forces. The children are safe."

Lissie looked up at Aaden. "How do you know Uncle Wolf wouldn't want me to feel sad?"

"Because I would not want anyone I love to be sad, if I had to die. Especially if I had to die to save them. I would want them to live." He reached out and touched the girl's face gently, tipping her chin up with a single finger. "It will be okay, Lissie. You can trust me, and you can trust Silver to look out for you. Okay?"

Her head lowered very slowly until her tiny chin touched her chest. "I don't want him to be dead. Please . . .bring him back."

It was a child's plea to make time go backward, to change what could not be.

I understood it completely. "None of us do, Lissie. None of us do. And if we could bring him back, we would."

The tree of gold shivered, and the branches whispered as they rubbed against one another.

Whispered?

I grabbed Lissie, scooping her into my arms as I backed away. "Do you hear that, Aaden?"

"Yes," he growled, hefting his sword in his hand as we backed away.

The whispers were growing louder, even as we put distance between ourselves and the tree.

"Run!" Aaden yelled, and I spun, clutching Lissie to me as I bolted back up through the cave. I had no energy left, yet

I found the strength to carry Lissie away as fast as I could, knowing that Aaden had my back.

We burst from the cave, entering a scene of utter chaos. There were fae everywhere, soldiers mostly, carts, and children being loaded up to go back to the castle.

I clutched Lissie as I slid to a stop, spun, and stared at the opening to the cave as the tree roots burst out toward us, grabbing at the rock and earth and starting to pull the mountain down on itself.

Lissie was crying hard, face buried against my chest. My legs buckled as I went to the ground, exhausted but unwilling to let go of the last connection I had to Cormac. His precious niece.

Aaden crouched beside us and gently put a hand on the side of my face. "Silver. We need to get you back to the castle. You need to rest."

I looked at him, my eyelids so heavy. I was scared to close them. "Don't leave me, Aaden. Promise." *Not like Cormac.*

His smile was sad. "Never."

The ride to the castle was made over a few days to not put more undue stress on the children.

Apparently the queen of all fae had followed us at a distance, with the carts and soldiers, believing that we'd find the children. That was how they'd reached us so quickly.

The children bounced back from their ordeal with food and a good number of soldiers to chase them about and protect them.

Two soldiers for every missing child. Just not when they were actually missing, only when they were found. This Oracle had a lot to answer for in my fucking opinion.

Kik had come with the contingent from the castle, but ... I found myself avoiding my old friend. My bestie. The friend whom I'd thought would always be my friend.

"What the fuck are you doing, ding dong?" Kik forced his way in front of me at the end of the first day, making me look at him. "I came all the way here to help—"

"You can fuck right off with that bullshit." I slapped him on the nose, maybe shocking myself more than him. I'd never struck Kik before, but right then ... "When I needed you most, you ran from me. Left me to fend for myself. That's not friendship. That's shallow."

Kik stared hard at me. "And if I'd died?"

I glared at him. "You wouldn't have died. Cormac died." I choked on his name, and the tears started again.

Kik snorted. "You're not the strong girl I'd thought you. I knew a death waited on your journey. I didn't want to see you die. And *I* didn't want to die. So I let you go on your own. And it worked out. You're alive, and so am I."

My jaw dropped as I stared at the one creature I'd always trusted, the one that I'd always believed would tell me the truth.

He was not my friend.

Hurt tore through my chest. "Go fuck a dog, Kik."

"Why, because you can't fuck your wolf?"

It felt like a turning point in our friendship. I held up a hand and showed him my finger. "If I had a wooden spoon, I'd ram it up your nose until it scrambled your brains."

I walked away, leaving him spluttering, and headed straight for where Aaden sat around a fire with Lissie, playing a guessing game. My heart ached. My body ached. Worse, there was a piece of me missing with Cormac gone. I'd lost people—Lilivani and various creatures in Underhill. This was more than grief. Something had happened to me with his death, as though part of me had died too.

Losing Kik only added to the deep hurt that dug into me.

"You're good at this," Lissie said. "My Uncle Wolf was good at this game too! Let's keep playing."

"It's time for you to go to sleep, Lissie. We will have a long day tomorrow." Aaden pointed at the sleeping mat at his feet, and she dutifully lay down, burrowing under the soft blankets woven from spider silk. I sat next to Aaden, and Lissie smiled up at me.

"Good night, Silver."

"Good night, Lissie," I reached down to pat her face. Far gentler than I'd been with Kik.

Within minutes she was asleep, her breath deepening and her body relaxing.

"You're good with her," I said.

"She doesn't have an uncle anymore, because I didn't get back to help you," Aaden muttered. "The tree should have taken me.

Or maybe if it had all three of us to draw from, it wouldn't have killed anyone."

"It almost did take you," I touched his mostly healed shoulder closest to me.

"I ... it wasn't drawing from me." He rubbed at his other shoulder. He looked at me, and I found myself staring into eyes that were not wholly his. One green, the color I knew him to have. The other amber. Just like Cormac.

What the—

I reached to touch his face, wonder and hope and fear all touching me simultaneously. "Aaden, your eyes."

He nodded. "The tree, it did something—"

The crack of several branches—no, the snap of *trees* exploding under great pressure had us both on our feet, drawing weapons as we whirled around toward the noise. I held Cormac's blade in my hand.

Stand with me, wolf.

I faced the shadows, sensing with every fiber in my being that we had to get moving.

"Get the kids, we ride hard for the castle," I yelled the words, and miracle of miracles, the soldiers listened to me.

Every child was scooped up, the carts were cut loose, and the soldiers rode from the oncoming threat.

Aaden tried to hand Lissie off to a soldier, but she screamed for him.

"No, no!"

"Go with her," I insisted.

"I'm not leaving you, Silver."

Another crack of the trees and the presence of one I knew all too well had my body stilling. This wasn't the darkness. "It's not a danger, or at least not the way you might think."

"What does that mean?" Aaden blurted.

What did it mean? "My mother is here." I blew out a breath. "Go. It's fine. I promise."

Aaden grabbed my face and kissed me hard and the taste of him was heady, my winter wolf and my gentle soldier wrapped into one body. *How could this be?*

There was no time to think on it. He was gone, riding off into the night with Lissie clinging to him.

I drove Cormac's sword point first into the ground and went to my knees, bowing my head.

"Mother."

Underhill's presence rolled around me, flattening me to my belly. "Saved children, yes. But done?"

I could barely breathe. Her power hammered around me. I didn't understand why, but she was angry. She was *furious*. A storm cloud broke above us, and rain poured out of the sky, buckets and buckets until my face was half buried in mud and water.

I didn't fight her hold on me. Even if I had been at my full strength, I wouldn't have fought it.

"Mother. I—"

"Darkness not done, daughter. Knows your strength, yes. Comes again, yes. Again. Again."

I spluttered around the mud. "What would you have me do?"

"Find Oracle. Be guided in next path."

The Oracle? The one who'd sent fae from the Irish court to drag me to Earth where I'd felt so much pain and fury and uncertainty? And loss. The Oracle who'd sent out three people *alone* to find the future queen of all fae and a bunch of defenseless children. Cormac would be alive without her interference. I had no desire to see the fucking Oracle, and if I did, then it would be to spill the blood of her soul to keep my bargain with Sigella. "If I do not?"

I felt the wavering in her rolling, golden power as she paused, then said, "I... Darkness take world."

She'd just hesitated. Actually *hesitated*.

She always told me the exact truth, and exactly as much as I needed to know. I'd never experienced her holding something back. Ever. Yet that's what her hesitation felt like.

What in two realms could make *Underhill* uncertain?

"What aren't you telling me?" I asked.

Her face firmed. "Go now. In next breath. Tell none."

Which meant not even Aaden? Or Orry?

"None, daughter. Alone you face darkness if you will survive the darkness."

"No Aaden or Orry, I get it," I told her. *How the fuck was I meant to get through this by myself?*

Her power pounded at me. "No, daughter. Alone. Even within."

For a beat, I couldn't fathom what mother meant.

I gasped, "Sigella."

"Find Oracle, yes. Release prisoner, yes. Alone, face darkness. Defeat darkness." Her power ebbed, as did her voice which then filled with something akin to pain. But it couldn't be. Underhill was meant to be impartial always.

"Survive, daughter," she whispered.

IVY TOUCHED & BRONZE BLADE

Don't miss the next installment!

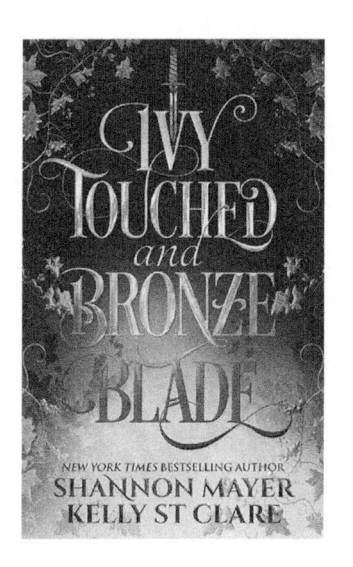

FIND SHANNON AND KELLY

www.shannonmayer.com

www.kellystclare.com

**KNOW MORE THAN THE ORACLE HERSELF
BY SIGNING UP FOR RELEASE DAY REMINDERS**

Printed in Great Britain
by Amazon